The City of Nis

P.J. Fenton

Acknowledgements

The author would like to acknowledge the works of Dante Alighieri, particularly his masterpiece, *The Divine Comedy*, for the inspiration that it played in the writing of this story.

Dedication

This book is dedicated to my nephew, Seth, and niece, Madison.

Table of Contents

Part 1: A World of Darkness Burned by Light

Chapter 1

It was dark, but it was always dark, and that was good, because the world was created in darkness. The land, temperate, neither hot nor cold, and comfortable to the touch was warmed from deep underground. Plants grew vibrantly in the land and the water; the rivers and oceans, fresh, clean, and filled with life. Each plant and animal of the world emitting the Glow—the cool illumination—and dotting the land and sea like shimmering crystals scattered across a single plain.

Then there were the people of the dark world. They were tall, with pure white skin and hair. Pointed ears stuck out far behind their heads. Their eyes looked like they were made of two differing shades of silver, each one shining brightly as they gazed upon both their world and each other. Two horns, one gold and one silver, curved around either side of their heads, forming a coronet, and culminating in a spiral horn on their foreheads. Yet the most incredible thing about them wasn't so much their appearance, but the way they saw each other, and the world around them.

They didn't simply look at the world with their eyes, but with all their senses. Their sense of smell and taste allowed them to recognize scents released not only by each other, but by all of the different plants and animals during their various emotional states. Their sense of sound let them recognize different patterns in each other's voices, revealing emotions underlying every spoken word. Their sense of touch, constantly active, could feel the natural energy everyone and everything radiated. Combined with their sense of sight; the two senses—touch and sight—created unique colors for the different energies, providing external images of emotions and sensations in the world around them. The five senses, in perfect balance with each other, combined with learning and intuition, created a special image, and through that image they perceived the world through a process they called *Knowing*.

The Tribe—the name they called themselves—lived in peace for uncountable ages. Thanks to the ability to *Know*, its members learned much of what their senses, and the world could teach them. They learned which plants and creatures could provide the Tribe nourishment, how much they could take from the land and water without overtaxing it, and how much more to repay in order to maintain the balance in the world.

It was an idyllic age, watched over by a council of nine members, each member revered for his or her wisdom. The Tribe flourished, building beautiful villages and cities for themselves, adding to the world's splendor. However, all ages, even the most idyllic ones, eventually come to an end by one means or another.

The coming of the Light began like any other. Everyone was acting normally. Parents cared for their children, children played with other children, young adults found love, and all who were able—including the council members—worked to make sure they all had enough food to eat, and their world remained as it always had. Then, suddenly they saw it. A great Glow appeared, more intense than anything ever witnessed before. It took the form of a hot orb in the sky, painting the air with strange colors and smells, and destroying the unity of the Tribe's five senses.

The witnesses to the enormous Glow didn't know what to do at first. It seemed to be everywhere, flooding their eyes, causing them to see, at best, only the external surface of their world and each other. Before, the members knew each other by *Knowing* the image formed by their combined senses. Now, as the new Glow filled the world, overloading their sense of sight, the members of the

Tribe perceived both very different and disturbing images.

"Nata, Nata, what is going on?" one member screamed to another. "You are there, and yet you're not. There is another you placed on top of you. I don't recognize this other you. What's happening to us and our world?"

The Tribe's overloaded sense of sight caused its members to see new images created purely by sight superimposed over the ones created by the rest of their senses. But the overload of the Tribe's senses was only the beginning. As the odd Glow continued to radiate its illumination, it *burned* the people of the Tribe.

First, it felt like the skin was simply being warmed. But the warmth rapidly grew from a familiar sensation, to a painful one. The scent of blood filled the air as the odd Glow caused skin to itch, burn, and eventually crack open. Some members of the Tribe attempted to bury themselves in sand, trying to shield themselves from the effects, but to no use. The odd Glow penetrated the sand, literally cooking them where they were buried. Others took shelter in their homes, but it only slowed the effects, providing minor relief at best. The plants and animals suffered the same effects too. Trees and grass wilted, bursting into flames. Everything was burning, but the worst was yet to come.

The strange Glow, now visible for half of the time it took for the Tribe to go from the middle meal time to the small sleep time, produced something new. A strange fiery wheel—the first of many—descended from the strange Glow to the surface of the world. Out of that first wheel he appeared, burning the ground as he walked, leaving footprints of smoldering grass and sand in his path. The Tribe *Knew* at once the figure could have been the personification of pride, envy, and the lust for killing and death. The figure radiated all of those emotions, projecting a horrible red energy, and a ravenous acrid stench, that every member of the Tribe could feel, smell, and taste despite the unbalancing of their senses. They *Knew* the figure was a hunter. But unlike a proper hunter, who respected what he hunted, never taking more than he needed, this being lived for killing. He was a beast, hungry for blood, craving death, and fought for a killing blow. Opening his mouth, he spoke in a loud booming voice that seemed to shake the mountains.

"In the name of my Lord and Master, I, the Light Bringer, have brought the Light to this new world. Come my good and noble brothers in arms. We, the Beings of Light, will strike down these dark and evil monsters that infest this barren land so that we may cultivate it, and make it our own."

3

If the coming of this strange Glow, now known as Light, caused confusion among the members of the Tribe before, then the Light Bringer's declaration created complete pandemonium.

Without warning, without mercy, legions of beings similar to the Light Bringer stormed across the Tribe's land almost instantly and from everywhere. Wherever the legions attacked, not a single life was spared; women, children, the sick, and the elderly were all cut down by legions attacking "in the name of their Lord and Master." The Beings of Light's armor, alive with its own glowing and rotating eyes, generated intense forms of Light. If a Tribe member tried attacking a Being of Light, one of the eyes would focus onto him, and an intense Light would radiate from the eye, striking him, and boring through him like a melo—a small burrowing animal common throughout the ground. The counterattack left the Tribe member either crippled or dead at the Being of Light's feet. The few members who tried reasoning with the Beings of Light, shouting, "Please stop! Why are you doing this? What have we done to you to bring you down upon us like this," found themselves killed by the Beings of Light.

All the Tribe could do was run, saving as many as they could, and hide. It was a genocidal and cultural slaughter. The legions from the Light sought not only to exterminate the Tribe, but also to destroy anything created, or touched by them. The Beings of Light's weapons left entire cities and villages in ruins. Fields and forests that had been tended for generations were burned to the ground and trampled, without even a sapling remaining. The Beings of Light were so thorough in their destruction, that whenever a legion was finished, only ashes remained. The invaders burned the corpses like waste, denying them proper burials. The Beings of Light were determined to wipe the world clean of the Tribe, and any influence they ever had on it.

So intense was the devastation that very land shook under the stress of the Beings of Light's assaults. The greatest areas of devastation were in the center of the continent, most of the central land was reduced to a great desert; also, a large part of the continent's northern peninsula sank into the ocean leaving nothing but a chain of islands, and a few small pieces of land connected to it. It took fourteen sleeping periods for the Beings of Light to complete their conquest of the Tribe's world. However, even though all signs of the Tribe were obliterated from the land, not all the members of the Tribe shared the same fate.

During this time of slaughter, which later became known as "The Coming," a small group survived by using cloths, building materials, pieces of broken buildings, and anything else they could find to shield themselves from the Light. The fittest carrying the injured members, including the Council, deep underground where the Beings of Light could not find them. This lone group of survivors, a small number of what the Tribe once was, found the underground refreshing after being burned by the Light, though that did little to comfort them emotionally. Many of the survivors were orphans, their families killed in "The Coming." Some survivors were permanently blinded by the Light that exploded into their world, the ability to *Know* through all of their senses nearly lost. The council members themselves were no exception. They had also lost family, friends, and loved ones to the vicious invasion. For the first time in the Tribe's history, the council members, who were each referred to by the particular virtue that they most embodied, found themselves at odds over what to do next.

P.J. Fenton

Chapter 2

"We should destroy them! Go back hard, fast, killing as many of these Beings of Light as possible. We must claim revenge for our fallen people!" The Seat of Patience's voice, usually calm and controlled, echoed through the tent where the Council was meeting. Slamming his fist down on the salvaged table, he cracked it, threatening to break it apart completely.

It was the first time the Council had convened since "The Coming." Using cloths donated by the survivors, and some poles used as walking sticks, the Council created a small tent where they could talk in private. A pile of salvaged material rested in one corner, and in the center of the tent was an old table the survivors used for shelter as they fled.

Five long sleep periods had passed since the survivors escaped the Beings of Light. After which, the survivors reached a large cavern deep underground. Stone spikes hung from the roof of the cavern, while similar spikes poked up from the cavern floor. The cavern was warm, and some of the survivors who could still feel through their sense of touch *Knew* that there was powerful natural warmth beneath them; a soothing warmth like the caves themselves. Those who could still see also noticed a warm orange energy radiating throughout the cavern, joining with the comforting sensation that they felt.

All the survivors bore marks from "The Coming." They were burned, scarred, broken, and were eagerly gathering outside the tent, awaiting the decision about what they should do. This disaster, unlike any that had ever struck the Tribe before, affected everyone. Two witnesses, customarily chosen at random, watched as the meeting progressed, and were struck with fear and awe at how the council members seated around the table seemed changed after "The Coming," especially after hearing the Seat of Patience cry out for an immediate counterattack.

The Seat of Patience never displayed anger or wrath before. He was a man of calm demeanor—never too happy or too sad. Instead, he seemed to walk the line between them, and was almost as temperate as the Seat of Temperance. Yet he wasn't the only one to make a drastic shift in personality.

"I agree with Seat Patience," the Seat of Humility barked haughtily. "Ours is an old people; with a long, rich, and proud history. For all that to end silently because of strange invaders daring to call *us* dark and evil monsters, especially after their own behavior, is an unforgivable insult that must be met in turn."

The Seat of Humility, never one to let pride get to him before—in fact, he had often warned others about the dangers of pride—witnessed the joy in the Beings of Light's faces as they called the Tribe "monsters" during "The Coming." The Beings of Light relished in the slaughter of the Seat of Humility's fellow Tribesmen; as if they were on some good, noble, and proud mission for their master. Facing that level of destruction, feeling instinctually the depression, shame, anger, and sorrow in the survivors, and *Knowing* the pride the Beings of Light took in the Tribe's destruction, awakened his own pride in his people for surviving, and for what they had endured. Now that pride was growing quickly.

"Not only that, but it's our land. We have lived here for untold generations. Now these Beings of Light thinks they can just take it from us. Who do they think they are? The world doesn't belong to them. It belongs to us and no one else," the Seat of Charity bellowed, agreeing with the Seat of Humility.

The Seat of Charity, who would have given everything from her home, to the cape off her back to someone in need of it, had also developed a sense of pride and ownership over what was stolen from them. But more importantly, she gained a strong sense of greed and longing for what she had lost. She spent her life giving everything she could and more to others. Now, after witnessing the destruction brought on by the Beings of Light, *Knowing* their greed—their *desire*—for death, conquest, and the Tribe's home, she wanted what was stolen from her returned, and she wanted it with vengeance.

"Respected Seats Patience, Humility, and Charity, while I, Seat Chastity, share your desire to make a quick return and take our rightful revenge, the three of you seem to be neglecting one critical fact."

"And what might that be?" The Seat of Patience threw a challenging glare to the Seat of Chastity with his question. "What critical fact did the other two Seats and I neglect?"

The Seat of Chastity stood up and began slinking back and forth between the other members of the council, partially draping herself over each of them as she walked by, a forward action she had never taken before.

"The reason," she replied, her tone immediately gaining the attention of the other Seats, and the two witnesses. "The reason is quite simple; there are not enough of us to mount a successful attack on them. That Light burns us the moment it touches us. If we want to go back, there needs to be a lot more of us, and that means we need to start *reproducing* and *repopulating* our people. And we need to do it fast if we want any chance to fight or survive in the future."

The other Seats and witnesses couldn't help but notice the way she said *reproducing* and *repopulating*. She seemed eager to begin both processes. Before "The Coming," she always preached about restraining bodily temptations, holding oneself back until the proper time. Now, after "The Coming," with so many of their people lying dead at the hands of the Beings of Light, she was not only supporting but endorsing the idea of freeing their inhibitions if it meant more people. And she was not alone.

"I agree with Seat Chastity." The other Seats turned, looking at the Seat of Temperance, leaning forward with his arms on the table, and licking his lips hungrily as he watched the Seat of Chastity until she sat back down. "We need people to fight a war, people we don't have, so we have to start producing them, even if it will take time."

If the witnesses were awestruck before, now they were totally speechless. Not only the Seat of Chastity, but also the Seat of Temperance—a man known for his incredible self-restraint—desired war and giving themselves over to vice in order to rebuild the Tribe's population. Over half of the Council wanted war with the Beings of Light, a war the witnesses knew many of the survivors might actually approve of. There were only four members of the Council left to speak. By the Council's rules, first established when the Tribe's civilization was formed, each member took turns presenting an opinion of the situation, the Seat of Hope presenting last. After each member spoke, if a unanimous decision wasn't reached, the Council continued arguing until one was. Once a decision was reached, the Tribe would follow that decision without question, trusting the members of the Council because they *Knew* they exemplified the best of the virtues they represented, and the interest of the Tribe.

"Time is also something that can work for us," the Seat of Diligence yawned. The witnesses were curious about his reaction. The Seat of Diligence was normally a hard worker, the witnesses expected him to be walking around the tent making plans and talking informally with the other Council members to help generate ideas, especially since he never stopped working to get as many people underground as he could during "The Coming." Now, he was lazily lying on his back—possibly even asleep at some points—while the rest of the Council sat upright at the table. "The Coming" draining him of all the diligence he once had.

"For all those Beings of Light know," the Seat of Diligence continued, "we are all dead and dust. And as we rebuild our people, they will become lazy in their victory, leaving themselves wide open for us when we are ready. Also, if we are to start making babies like Seat Chastity wants, our people are going to have to stop and rest just to do it. Charging back up there now would be pointless. We need to wait, bide our time, let those Beings become complacent, and when they least suspect it, *that* is when we will bring them down for good."

"And after the destruction they rained down upon us, it will feel so good to see them brought down in kind." The Seat of Kindness laughed, bringing a comforting yet malicious laughter to the previous six council members, who together imagined a future where the Beings of Light would be destroyed—if not by their own hands, then by their descendants—and their land reclaimed. The two witnesses were beside themselves over how much the Council was changing, and how much they liked this *new* Council. The witnesses also pictured a future where they, or their children, would live on the surface again, and the Beings of Light were driven back to where they came from—they liked it. However, the laughter was cut short by one loud declaration.

"I oppose it! All of it!"

The Seats turned, looking with surprise at the one who spoke. Standing up was the Seat of Courage, known for being the finest fighter in the entire Tribe, and more recently the greatest hero of "The Coming." Over the course of her life she had single-handedly protected members of the Tribe during harsh storms, went without food longer than anyone so others could eat, and during "The Coming" faced the Beings of Light repeatedly in order to save more members of the Tribe than anyone else. She was the best at *Knowing* others—better than any who had ever lived in the Tribe—and had suffered the most because of "The Coming." The injuries she received at the hands of the Beings of Light while rescuing others ended her life as a fighter. Wounds and scars peppered her arms and legs, crippling her until she could barely lift a small load. The Light burning her skin to the point where she had almost lost her sense of touch. It had also left her completely blind. Her eyes, once two shades of silver, now burned into black spots. Finally, she had been orphaned, her entire family slaughtered at the hands of the Beings of Light. If anyone should have wanted revenge against them, it would have been her.

"What is this…this…betrayal?" The Seat of Patience shouted, having heard enough objections. "You've lost more than any of us, and you are saying that we shouldn't fight back? Has 'The Coming' turned you, the Seat of Courage, into a scared, cowardly girl?"

"Something has changed, but it's not in me, it's in all of you," the Seat of Courage charged. The attention of everyone, the Council, the witnesses, all caught up in her words as all eyes and ears turned toward the Seat of Courage. This would be the moment when the Tribe's decision about revenge would change, or remain fixed.

"'The Coming' was indeed the greatest disaster the Tribe has ever faced, but is this the way we should be reacting to it? Our people still live, and we know that these caves don't end here. They run everywhere under the mountains, places where the Beings of Light will never find us. We should take this chance, find a new home, and rebuild away from the Beings of Light and their influence.

11

We *need* to keep away from them. I can tell how much both 'The Coming,' and the Beings of Light's ways, have changed you just by listening to the seven of you. If I could still *Know* like I used to, I'd be forced to look away from you because of how warped you would appear to me." The Seat of Courage couldn't see it, but she could tell her remarks were bringing most of the other Council members dangerously close to attacking her.

"You, Seat Patience, were always so calm with your decisions, no matter what they were. Now, after suffering at the hands of the Beings of Light, I can hear the hatred and wrath spewing from your words. You want to charge headlong into a war with them regardless of the outcome. I can smell the putrid anger scent boiling off of you, and feel the wrathful energy pulsing from you like a heartbeat even with my disabled sense of touch."

"And do you think we don't have a right to be angry?" the Seat of Patience bellowed.

"Not to the point where it changes who you are, what you stand for, and for whom you serve," the Seat of Courage replied in a defiant retort. "Seat Humility, you've always been so humble, never letting what others said or did offend you, but now you have this ocean of pride, pride running off of you like water over a dam, pride that's been wounded and demanding immediate retribution—pride that reflects the Light Bringer's own pride. Seat Charity, you've always shared with everyone. Now, after having everything taken from you by invaders, your words ring with a greed neither of us has ever known. I can smell the fungal scent of avarice on you, and feel your desire to take back everything you have lost, despite the risks.

"Seat Chastity, think about how you were talking, walking, practically offering yourself to the other Council members. I believe the words you used were 'reproducing and repopulating our people fast,' am I right? Do you really want to disregard all morality and take drastic reproductive measures?" The Seat of Chastity didn't reply. "You didn't attempt to hide the lust in your voice. Seat Temperance, you have always held yourself back from overindulgence. Now, I can hear the gluttony in your voice, and smell the rotting stench of hunger in the air around you. It's so thick it seems like you want to devour anything and anyone in sight."

"I'd watch your words, Seat Courage. If I'm as gluttonous as you say, maybe I'll start by devouring you," the Seat of Temperance threatened.

The threat however didn't detour the Seat of Courage; as she continued her attack on the other council members.

"Then there's you, Seat Diligence. You would actually use someone's laziness and sloth against them, proposing our own people follow a similar path instead of one where they work for a better future. I feel no energy coming from you at all now. Instead, you feel dead and content. You don't even seem to want to work anymore, have you really spent *everything* you have to offer our people, and now just want to rest somewhere lazily for the rest of your life.

"Lastly, there's you, Seat Kindness. You've always been the gentlest of us. Caring and comforting others at all times, especially when disaster struck. But in one sentence, I can hear how much envious pleasure you would take in someone's downfall. I never would have expected that from you. 'The Coming' has done more than physically harm our bodies, families, homes, and land. You are letting it, letting the Beings of Light, eat away at your very spirits, turning you into something grotesque, and that must not happen. We are still the Council, and the Tribe needs us now more than ever."

"Seat Courage, that will be enough." The Seat of Patience, finally loosing whatever patience he still had, rose alongside the other scorned Council members.

"I agree with Seat Courage!"

All the Seats and witnesses stopped and looked to who had spoken; it was the final member of the Council, the Seat of Hope, long known for being the spiritual center of the Council since hope was the one thing every member of the Tribe acknowledged as the best quality a person could have. Throughout the meeting, the Seat of Hope silently listened—as was his role—until the other Seats finished presenting their arguments. Now declaring his position, he stood defiantly with the Seat of Courage.

"You agree with her?" the first seven Seats said in unison.

"My ability to *Know* others may have been damaged, but what little ability I have left tells me to agree with Seat Courage. I decided to stay silent until now because of my position, and because I hoped I was mistaken, that this tragedy hadn't truly changed you as much as I thought it has. I hoped that the words of Seat Courage would bring you back to your senses, but it seems I was wrong. If I hadn't spoken up just now, you were going to attack Seat Courage and kill her."

The witnesses, scared and trembling, backed up against the tent flap. Never in the Council's history had it been divided to the point where one member would make an attempt to kill another. However, the Tribe had also never faced a situation like this before. The Tribe always relied on the ability to *Know*, it was how the members of the Council were chosen. Damaging that ability caused its members to change in more ways than they cared to admit.

"How could you possibly say that?" the Seat of Kindness asked. "All Seat Patience said was, 'That will be enough.'"

"Don't lie to me," the Seat of Hope responded. "I can hear the falsehood in your words. Not only that, but I can smell and feel both the anger scent and murderous intent radiating from you. I could also feel your approaching joy at seeing Seat Courage killed. That's how great it was. It was almost like seeing the Light Bringer again."

"I wouldn't say too much more," the Seat of Courage injected. The Seat of Hope, turning his attention from the Council to his fellow dissenter could feel the resolve radiating from her. "I was expecting this, and I can accept my fate, but hope is the one thing we can't lose. You can't be struck down with me."

"Neither of us is going to be stuck down, Seat Courage." The Seat of Hope turned back toward the rest of the Council. The Seat of Courage couldn't see, but she still felt the same blue energy of resolve the Seat of Hope always had. Even impaired, she *Knew* he was ready for whatever followed.

"Listen to me. If anything should happen to myself or Seat Courage, you will have to kill our witnesses to keep them from reporting what happened. But even if you manage to cover up our murders, news will get out. You should know, I have told other survivors that I might not walk out of this meeting alive. If any of us die suddenly, the people of the Tribe will know how far the Council has fallen, that it has turned its back on its duties, and by extension its people. I implore you to please turn away from this path. It will only lead to ruin for all of us if you make our people follow it, and I for one will not take part in it. I will continue to speak out against it until the day I die."

The Seat of Hope steeled himself. He knew that what he said was the truth, and for speaking the truth he would probably be killed. But the sound that followed was not the one he expected. It wasn't the sound of both him and the

Seat of Courage being killed, nor was it the Council changing their idea. Instead, it was simple yet maniacal laughter. The laughter of one who saw a pointless effort directed at him, sure that it would work, and now couldn't help but laugh at its failure.

"So, you honestly believe that the people don't want revenge after all that has happened to them?" the Seat of Patience asked.

The Seat of Hope nodded.

"Well, I think I speak for the rest of us when I say that the Tribe doesn't need hope anymore. The hope that you represent, that they can move past what happened to them and create a new home in a foreign land, is nothing more than a fleeting illusion that our people don't need. What they need and want is vengeance."

"So then, our lives will be forfeit to your desires?" the Seat of Courage asked.

"Oh no. I think we can all admit that the sudden deaths of two members of the Council would be more than enough to cause the Tribe to doubt us, especially if Seat Hope has set something into play. So, I offer you this solution. By your own words, you both seem to hold our people to such high hopes and standards. You believe that they don't want vengeance—or to return to their home—but instead want to live like rodents, hiding underground, while they are walked upon by beings that consider themselves superior to us. So, we will let the survivors choose their fate. We will present both of our propositions to them, and the side that has the fewer supporters—whether it is us or the two of you—will be exiled from the Tribe along with anyone who supported them. They can do whatever they want afterwards."

"I agree with your terms," the Seat of Hope boldly pronounced.

"As do I," said the Seat of Courage.

"Very well. We will meet before the people in one hour." The Seat of Patience walked over to the corner of the tent, rummaged through the miscellaneous supplies, and took a salvaged hourglass from the pile, putting it on the table. The sands in the glass began running down, counting down the time until the divided Council would present its positions. "Meeting adjourned. Witnesses, please tell the survivors we will address them shortly."

"Yes, sir," a witness answered, picking himself up off the ground in shock

15

over the shift in the Council. Walking out to tell the Tribe about the meeting in an hour, the witnesses silently wondered to themselves if they should be afraid of this change, or overjoyed. While neither admitted it, they felt both.

Afterwards, the first seven Council members left the tent, the Seats of Courage and Hope remaining alone with the hourglass, and their thoughts.

"You realize we are taking a huge gamble," the Seat of Courage said to the Seat of Hope.

"My friend, we are still alive, which is already far more than I hoped for. I'm sure some will listen, and even if we are banished and have to take those with us away from here, there will be hope for the future," the Seat of Hope answered, still believing in his people.

"Let's just hope enough will listen," the Seat of Courage replied. For all her bravery, she was not so optimistic.

Chapter 3

As the Council members agreed, they presented both of their propositions to the survivors in front of their meeting tent. The Seat of Humility, acting as the spokesperson for the first seven members of the Council, presenting first.

"Look at our arms, our legs, and our bodies. They have all been scarred, racked with pain as a result of the Beings of Light criminal actions." The Seat of Humility spit with contempt, showing off his own injuries to the survivors, who murmured in agreement as they felt the pain of their own injuries across their bodies. "But this pain will not go unanswered. We, 'The Seven,' present you our vision of the future. While those murderous Beings of Light enjoy their victory on the surface, we will be waiting, and preparing. We have a plan—a great plan—one that every member of the Tribe must devote themselves to because, in time, it will give us our just deserved revenge on the Beings of Light."

The members of the Tribe began cheering enthusiastically at the prospect of revenge, the pain in their bodies momentarily forgotten. Not a single member of the Tribe had escaped "The Coming" without sustaining an injury that left them crippled in one way or another. The Seat of Humility, raising his hands to the survivors—who quieted immediately—continued to speak.

"Always remember the pain we felt at the hands of the Beings of Light," the Seat of Humility preached. "Every burn, lost parent, child, and loved one murdered at the hands of those joyful killers, reveling not only in the destruction of our people, but in our land as well, burning under the Light Bringer's feet.

"We are a people that never turn away from a challenge. We will work toward the plan to return to the surface and retake it, driving the Beings of Light back to wherever they came from. That is our goal. Do not delude yourselves with false hopes of creating a home in these caverns. We are a people meant to live on the surface, and that is where we will live, and when we return, we will reclaim the surface and achieve the vengeance we deserve. Abandon all you hope for and believe in. It is an illusion, keeping us from our goal, one that every member of the Tribe should work for." The Seat of Humility cast a sneer toward the Seat of Hope—who stood amidst the Tribe's cheering—after his last comment. The Seat of Hope realized the Seat of Humility's closing remarks were a personal shot directed to him. Yet the Seat of Hope refused to let the comment, or the Tribe's cheering, faze him. Taking his place, with the Seat of Courage at his side, the Seat of Hope and Courage gave their proposition in front of The Seven, and the collected members of the Tribe. Most of the Tribe was still cheering for the Seat of Humility's proposal, but the Seat of Hope knew his people and *Knew* that not all of them wanted revenge.

"Members of the Tribe," the Seat of Hope began, addressing the survivors. "During 'The Coming,' the Beings of Light called us 'dark and evil monsters,' while calling themselves 'good and noble.' In these tragic times, we cannot give in to our anger and hatred, if we do, we only prove the Beings of Light correct, allowing them a second and far more valuable victory over us. We need to show the Beings of Light, and more importantly ourselves, that they are wrong about us. We need to show them that darkness doesn't always equate to evil, just as light doesn't always bring good. This is our chance to build a new world for ourselves in the tunnels below ground, away from the Beings of Light, their influence, and the scars of 'The Coming.'" The Seat of Hope scanned the audience and noticed a woman, heavy with child, in the crowd.

"You there," the Seat of Hope said, indicating the pregnant woman. "Please join me for a moment."

The pregnant woman slowly made her way to the front of the crowd where the Seats of Hope and Courage were standing. Her entire visible body was scarred from "The Coming" except for her belly, which she wrapped her arms around, fearing for the life she carried. As she approached, the Seat of Hope could feel the silver energy of life, and the second heartbeat within her, both strong and healthy. Taking her hand with a smile, the Seat of Hope continued his address.

"This woman's child will not have experienced 'The Coming.' When this child is born, he or she will not bear a single physical, mental, or emotional scar anywhere across his or her body." The Seat of Hope's voice rose as he thought of the prospect of new life and new beginnings. "Future generations of the Tribe will be born without the scars of 'The Coming.' After surviving it, can we really leave our children nothing but a legacy of vengeance and hatred toward beings they have never seen?"

The Seat of Hope's question hushed the crowd as the Tribe considered his words.

"We have survived 'The Coming.' And since we have survived, it is our responsibility to those who didn't to make sure the Tribe has a future, and not to pass on the scars of 'The Coming' to the next generation. It may be easy to desire and give in to revenge, but we all know the right course of action is often harder. The opportunity is here to create a new world for our children, one where they can rebuild our culture, make a fresh start, benefiting all of our people. It's more difficult, but far better than choosing to pursue one generation's vendetta.

"We must never abandon our hope for the future," the Seat of Hope concluded. "We all hope for better lives. We hope for the best for our children. And we also hope for the best from our home and land, wherever it may be."

The Seat of Hope's speech—while passionate—was ultimately futile, as the Seat of Courage feared. At the end of the gathering, it was the argument of The Seven who won the peoples' hearts overwhelmingly. The majority of the Tribe's survivors, burned and injured, craved revenge over new beginnings as much as The Seven did. While the Seat of Hope's speech did force a few members of the Tribe stop and think, they mostly thought the Seat of Hope must be crazy to accept living in exile underground. Laughing in the faces of the Seats of Hope and Courage after the Seat of Hope was done with his speech; both of them stepping back without a word of complaint or challenge to either The Seven or the crowd, happy to have said what they believed in, and prepared to let the Tribe make its own decisions.

Thankfully, not all desired revenge as strongly as the majority of the Tribe. Spiritualist monks, outcasts, wanderers, vagrants who lived on the outskirts of society—like the monks—who drifted from place to place, decided to take their chances with the Seats of Hope and Courage; especially after seeing what the Beings of Light could do. Children, all orphans from "The Coming," also followed the Seats of Courage and Hope. Having realized that it was by a miracle they managed to escape the Beings of Light, and survive *this* long, they didn't want to waste their lives now chasing revenge. The Seats of Hope and Courage could sense the energy coming off every one of them as they joined them. *Knowing* they genuinely believed in the Seat of Hope's vision, wanting a better life for themselves and their children. Their energy tingled animatedly, their excitement building up to face a new challenge with all of the youthful enthusiasm they could give, without the harshness of the people desiring vengeance.

Out of all the survivors, eight out of every ten members joined The Seven's group, who called themselves the "Greater Tribe." The remainder joined, "The Remnant of the Tribe," the remnant of the people deciding to follow the Seats of Courage and Hope—the remnant of the original Council—into exile, going deeper into the caves.

"Humph," scoffed the former Seat of Kindness, watching The Remnant leave. "We are well rid of them."

"Now that the weak remnants of our once-strong Tribe have left us, it is time to begin—for our future, for revenge, for the success of the Plan!" the former Seat of Humility shouted in a loud and prideful voice, standing before the roaring Greater Tribe.

The cheering from the Greater Tribe was so loud it echoed throughout the caves, all the way to where The Remnant was traveling. The sound, so depressing, that The Remnant's members—who until then had been very stoic throughout their departure—broke down, crying for the Greater Tribe that they left behind.

"Do not lose hope my friends and people," the Seat of Hope encouraged, addressing The Remnant and sounding as confident as he ever had been. "Our lost tribe members may have surrendered themselves to their negative desires, but that doesn't mean it will last forever. Time changes all things, and in time our lost ones, or their descendants, will find a way back to us."

"The Seat of Hope is correct," the Seat of Courage added, boosting the morale of the people. "Before 'The Coming,' I remember what the Seats of Temperance and Patience were like. If there is one lesson I learned from the two of them, it is that all things come with the passage of time, the good and the bad. However, with patience, no matter how long it will take, things change, and they will be better."

Amidst the cheers echoing from the Greater Tribe, the Seats of Courage and Hope's words were just what The Remnant needed to continue its journey through the caves. After traveling for four times the length of the "The Coming," The Remnant found a cavern. Those who could still hear could tell by the echo that it was a large cavern, with a natural river flowing through a crack in one of the cavern's walls. The river curved through the cavern, entering a lake in its center, and then snaking out of the lake, down another tunnel. Some, who still had an accurate sense of touch, discovered the lake supported life. Dipping their hands into the water, it pulsed with energy and movement from the aquatic animals swimming within it. The branching caves also yielded moss that was found to be edible, because it didn't contain the foul tang of poisons or toxins when placed on the tongue.

"This cavern, with its caves, river, and lake will be our new home," the Seat of Courage proclaimed to the tired people of The Remnant, who welcomed the news with shouts of joy and gratitude. "However, even though we have found this place, we cannot forget the past and what has happened to us recently. I propose that we build our new homes with the capability to move with us in case we need to move again."

"Do you mean we should build and live in tents?" an old man asked.

"And what do you mean by 'in case we need to move again?'" a younger boy asked.

"To answer the first question, yes," the Seat of Courage replied. "I think we should build a series of tents that can be picked up and moved easily with us should the need arise. We only have a limited amount of supplies, and a good number of our people are injured. Building easy shelters will help us conserve our resources. As for the young boy's question, I was referring to possible cave-ins or another, more frightening possibility—if the Beings of Light found this place and bring a Second Coming down on us."

The idea that the Beings of Light could find them again made most of the members of The Remnant shiver.

"And if not them, and I sincerely hope I am wrong, who is to say that the Greater Tribe may, in time, see us as an obstacle to their vengeance that needs to be removed. Or worse, no differently than the Beings of Light. If we have to leave again, I think *this* time we should be able to take our homes with us."

"Do you really think that the people from the Greater Tribe would attack us?" one of the people asked, amidst the murmurs and whispers spreading among other members of The Remnant.

"I honestly don't know," the Seat of Courage answered. The prospect of being attacked by her own people was, for her, a situation far more frightening than a Second Coming. Yet with all that had happened since "The Coming," she couldn't shake the fear that the Greater Tribe would attempt to wipe out The Remnant—either to expand their territory, or as practice for attacking the Beings of Light.

"The Seat of Courage is right." The people gathering in front of the Seat of Courage shifted their attention to the new voice. It was the Seat of Hope, coming back from where he'd been examining the cavern. "Before I took this Seat, I worked closely with the previous Seat of Hope and her twin brother, the previous Seat of Diligence. Their favorite saying was, 'Hope for the best, but prepare for the worst,' and that is exactly what we must do now. Our people will face trying times from internal and external forces, and as much as we want to believe that some things can't or won't happen, we mustn't ignore the possibility that they could. If we did, we would only end up inviting them to happen. So, from here on out, we must be prepared for anything and everything that might come our way."

"On that note," the Seat of Courage continued, "please listen. All of you, we have a lot of work to do to create our new home." The Seat of Courage set to work organizing teams to collect food, build shelters, and watch for visitors. After everyone was situated in their jobs, the Seat of Courage felt someone tapping her on her shoulder; it was the Seat of Hope.

"Can I talk to you for a moment in private?" the Seat of Hope asked. The Seat of Courage acknowledging him with a silent nod. She could guess what the conversation was going to be about as they walked to an unoccupied corner of the cavern.

"There are two problems that we have to deal with specifically," the Seat of Hope said.

"Let me guess," the Seat of Courage responded. "Who is going to lead the people once you and I are gone, and what is to be done about the Greater Tribe?"

"Exactly." The Seat of Hope's senses were not completely destroyed; he still had some of his ability to *Know* through the image his senses created. To be able to see how the people were changing around them, how they themselves were changing, and how to react properly to that change was something that they were going to need more than ever.

"You have done a wonderful job getting our people here, so wonderful, in fact, that they would probably want you to lead them alone."

"We both know that can't happen," the Seat of Courage adamantly declared. "I've been blinded by 'The Coming,' and my other senses are almost gone. It's only because of my instincts, and the help of others, that I've managed to get this far. There needs to be a Council, and we need to have successors."

"So, we're both in agreement. We need to find and train the next Seats of Courage and Hope before we're gone."

"Not just successors for our Seats," the Seat of Courage said. "All the other Seats must be filled again. When we die, the Council must be restored to nine members. That restoration is a job that only the two of us can do."

"You know, that new Council will probably be the youngest one to ever be formed, considering whom we have here among us," the Seat of Hope mused, quickly examining the people among The Remnant. The bulk of them were made up of extremely young adults and children about to enter adulthood. Council members were usually far into their later years when they were chosen, that was about to change. "Then again, age never was a requirement to join the Council. We'll just have to hope that they'll keep to the old traditions when choosing their successors."

The Seat of Courage smiled at the thought for a moment, but the Seat of Hope quickly returned the conversation to its serious tone. He knew there was another issue that needed discussing.

"So, what can we do about the Greater Tribe?" he asked.

"As of right now, nothing, our primary concern has to be our people." The Seat of Courage closed her blackened eyes in thought, considering their future. "But once we are more secure, then we will send an emissary to the Greater Tribe to see how they have progressed. Do you agree with that?"

"I do," the Seat of Hope agreed. "It may also be a good idea to have a few scouts watch the path our emissary takes, so trouble doesn't follow him or her back to us. But who knows? With a little luck, our emissary might even bring back members of the Greater Tribe who want to give up The Seven's foolish plan for vengeance and join us."

***

Over the next couple of years, the Seats of Courage and Hope worked to build their new society in the cavern and caves away from the Greater Tribe. Using salvaged cloths and coverings, as well as other materials they carried with them, The Remnant constructed a city of tents on both sides of the river flowing through the cavern. The first tents were mostly made of animal hides and cloth, but as time went on, members of The Remnant learned how to weave their own hair into a cloth, eventually making it the primary building material when the original cloth and coverings started to age. A single large tent for community gatherings and Council meetings, pyramid shaped, as tall as two adults standing on top of each other, supported by a single pole running down its center, with tight ropes holding up its sides, stood near the middle of the city. Each family had its own tent that mimicked the communal tent. As the city grew, The Remnant began cutting and shaving the rocks around them to make more poles for their homes. Naming their new city Rem, after themselves, the city could be packed up and be ready to move in less than an hour just as the Seat of Courage wanted. The Remnant's great efficiency was thanks to the training of the Seat of Courage, who made sure every citizen of Rem knew what to do in case of an evacuation. The Seat of Hope, one of the few members of The Remnant who could still *Know* the world, worked to restore the way that people of The Remnant learned to *Know* it. Working especially close to the newly born members of the Remnant, who didn't bear the scars of "The Coming," teaching them the spiritual practices of his own masters, so that they wouldn't be

24

forgotten. All the while, both Seats searched out, and eventually trained, nine members of The Remnant—distinguishing themselves by the virtue of their own character, to become the successors to the Seats of the Council. After twenty years had passed since The Remnant split from the Greater Tribe, the Seats of Courage and Hope—now *Knowing* Rem was stable, and that they were both nearing the end of their lives—decided that it was time to send an emissary to the Greater Tribe. But what that emissary would find, would alter life underground for generations.

P.J. Fenton

Chapter 4

When the emissary, a strong young woman named Rill, arrived in the cavern home of the Greater Tribe, her first instinct was to walk up and greet them. She was one of the most active members of The Remnant, and wanted to take the initiative with the Greater Tribe. But she remembered how the Seat of Hope always said, "Hope for the best, but prepare for the worst." Staying near the tunnel entrance, she leaned up against the cavern wall, hoping she would be invited into their company. She waited an hour before finding a few large rock spears sticking out of the cavern floor near the tunnel. Climbing up one of them, and using a far-seeing scope—a series of glass lenses wrapped in a cloth tube, she scouted the Greater Tribe.

They also built a city, Rill thought to herself, seeing the Greater Tribe's city in the cavern. *But this city is nothing like Rem.*

Through her scope, she saw the city's name, Nis, written on its gates. The words *"Abandon all you hope for and believe in. It is an illusion, keeping us from our goal, one that every member of the Tribe should work for"* were etched just below the name. Unlike Rem, were life and hope breathed throughout its tents, Nis was a horrifying city built from rock and earth gouged from the cavern, and encircled by a large stone wall with only one gate allowing entrance. Rill climbed further up the stone spear so she could see over that wall.

It was ghastly. The sounds, smells, and energy she felt were almost overwhelming. She could hear the echoes of men and women coupling indiscriminately from inside buildings, stinking of sweat and emitting the rosy energy of lust. As well as the wails of children, born in terrible fashion, coming into existence without the comfort or care of others, and left on the cavern floor. Watching as their silver life energy rose if they lived, or disappear if they died. The only law in Nis seemed to be survival of the fittest. Competitions pitted fighters against each other, and she could hear the sounds of stones and tools smashing against flesh and bone, and smell the acrid tang of fresh blood spilling into the air and onto the cavern floor.

Everyone appeared horribly disfigured, twisted, rotted, emitting mossy green decay and crimson anger energies that encircled everyone from the elders to the youngest children.

These children are our relatives? she thought from her vantage point, not daring to speak and risk her voice echoing back to Nis. *How could children become so grotesque when we were a unified people just over a generation ago?*

Wait, what's that? A sudden surge of new energy began making its way through the cavern, drawing her attention away from the decadence of Nis. As it grew stronger, she heard the sound of marching feet, more feet than Rill thought existed. The sound also sent the Greater Tribe into a frenzy of crazed activity, its members gathering makeshift spears, tools, large rocks, and preparing to defend themselves from whatever was coming, casting the scents of anticipation and bloodlust throughout the air.

The Beings of Light have found us, Rill thought, a surge of panic rising up in her. Swinging her scope in the noise's direction, a tunnel at the opposite end of the cavern, Rill searched for its source. *Is it the Second Coming?*

However, as the source of the sound and energy—a marching force— entered the Greater Tribe's cavern, becoming visible as they approached the city, Rill's realized they couldn't be the Beings of Light.

This force doesn't radiate Light like the Beings of Light are supposed to,

Rill observed. *They also don't look as monstrous as the elders described. These can't be Beings of Light. But that's both good and bad. If the approaching army isn't the Beings of Light, then a Second Coming is unlikely. But then, who are they, and what do they want?* Rill didn't even want to think of an answer.

The army marched up to the gates of Nis, all of its members wearing some kind of shroud or veil. Rill couldn't hear anything from the army except their footsteps; they kept completely quiet, and she couldn't feel any energy clearly from them either through her sense of touch.

Something is wrong with the natural flow of their bodies' energy, something has been severed. *The areas where the energy is gone... it looks cut off, like what happens when someone loses a limb, but different somehow.*

As the gates opened to the army, she saw seven old individuals leave the city to confront the army.

The other members from the old Council, she wondered to herself.

Listening to their footsteps echo through the cavern, seeing their crimson energy of anger radiating out toward the army, Rill could hear the shouts and cries from the Greater Tribe behind them inside Nis. The Greater Tribe craved combat and wanted to attack the army. But a glance from one Council member silenced the whole city.

When they met the army, one of the seven Council members, the member who silenced the Greater Tribe, stepped forward to confront them. The sound of his footsteps was heavier than the others. He generated so much prideful teal energy it looked like it could lift him off the ground on a wave, carrying him like a commanding leader above all the others. He projected all that energy defiantly toward the army, determined not to run, even if he had to fight them all himself.

He is going to get himself killed for the sake of his pride, Rill thought as he approached the army, ready to fight to the death. But instead of fighting, the army silently parted, and a figure emerged from it to meet the Council member. This figure, this...creature, was the most terrifying thing Rill had ever seen. When she looked at it, she *Knew* nothing.

So cold..., she thought, her body and mind losing feeling by the second. While it did have a physical body, when Rill tried to *Know* it, there was just the outline of a person, and within that outline, nothing. Just a gaping void of nothingness that felt like it was drawing her further and further in the longer she looked at it. Suddenly, her body lurched as her grip loosened, slipping partway down the stone spear, and bringing her back to her senses. Her mind sharp again, she straightened herself and continued to watch through her scope, trembling and frightened by the effect this creature had on her.

The creature approached the Council member who stood out among the seven. It seemed like it was sizing him up, as well as the city of Nis. Then, it started laughing.

It must realize it could destroy the city if it wanted to, Rill thought. The Council member spoke next.

"I am The Pride!" he said to the creature. "We are the proud Greater Tribe! We will not be chased and slaughtered again by another new tribe of beings. Leave now or *die!"*

"My friends," the creature spoke in a cold and smooth voice, "you do not need to fear me or my troops. Tell me, do you know of the Master of the Beings of Light?" The question brought forth howls of anger and cries for revenge. Starting at the gate, and eventually echoing throughout the entire city.

"I would take that as a yes," It said.

"The Beings of Light stole our world from us," The Pride said. "They destroyed our homes, nearly wiped us out, and forced us to live here. But we have survived their slaughter, hid from their forces, and in time we will have our vengeance. We are The Seven, leaders of the city of Nis, creators of The Plan that will give of our people the revenge they deserve."

"And you are the leader of *The Seven*, I assume?" It asked him.

"Yes, I am The Pride, chief of The Seven," The Pride answered. The other members of The Seven introduced themselves as well.

"I am The Lust."

"I am The Gluttony."

"I am The Greed."

"I am The Sloth."

"I am The Wrath."

"I am The Envy, and who are you?"

So, this is what has become of the Council, Rill thought to herself in deep despair. *I remember how The Seats of Courage and Hope said they were falling into the vices that opposed their virtues, but now they have fallen so far that they*

30

have died to their old selves and become those vices.

"I am called Tanas," the creature said. "If you let my people and me stay with you, we can give you something that you might find very interesting."

"And what could you give us that could be so valuable?" The Greed asked.

"Information on the Beings of Light for a start, force of arms, and the most important thing of all, a way to strike back at the Beings of Light, if you are interested." Tanas spoke to them plainly enough, but there was a subtle way to its speech that was as appealing as it was addictive.

Its words are snaking their way into The Seven's minds, Rill thought as she listened to the exchange echo through the cavern. *Charming them to continue listening, but holding back just enough to make them want more.*

"Keep talking," The Pride said.

"My forces are equal to about a third of what the armies of the Beings of Light once were; before I attacked both them, and the Master of the Beings of Light, Ash Addiel, himself." Tanas boasted, proud of what he had done.

"Impossible!" The Wrath cried out. "The Light burns all but the Beings of Light."

"There is much that you don't know about Light, as well as the world that you have left behind. The world does not only contain Light, but another force called Shadow. We are the Legions of Shadow, and it is through Shadow that we attacked the Beings of Light—attacked their bodies, minds, their very souls. It is also how I assaulted Ash Addiel himself. I can give you this ability." Tanas beckoned to one of its soldiers. It pulled a garment off the soldier. The covering was hazy like mist, but moved off the soldier and into Tanas's hands like it was gliding over water.

"This is a Veil of Shadows. We can recreate them easily with the tools we are carrying, and we will share them with you, so you can work toward your revenge."

"Wait!" The Envy cried. "If these shadows are so powerful, then why didn't you defeat Ash Addiel? And why do you need our help now?"

Why, indeed? Rill did not trust Tanas; whatever it wanted, it wasn't to help the Greater Tribe.

"He and his forces were too strong for us," Tanas said. "We need to weaken him so that the next attempt we make will succeed. You also have a reason to strike at him, so why not work together to destroy him?" The Seven conferred for a moment to decide what to do. When they emerged from their meeting, anyone would have *Known* by their expressions, and the feelings radiating from them, that they had all but accepted Tanas's offer. But they still wanted more.

"You make a good offer," The Gluttony said. "Frankly, I am hungry to accept. But how do we know these Veils of Shadows works?"

Rill couldn't tell, but she was certain Tanas was smiling happily.

The Seven are all but hooked, she thought. *The proof, if Tanas provides it, will be the finishing touch.*

"An understandable request," Tanas said. "Would one of you care to try this Veil of Shadows yourself?"

"Certainly!" The Envy said, approaching Tanas. After he robed himself in it, fitting his hands and feet into the coverings sewn into it, The Envy found a glowing stone stitched into a pocket in the Veil located on top of his hand. Tanas explained to The Envy that he would have to touch the glowing stone—doing that would take him to the surface.

"While veiled," Tanas said to The Envy, "the surface will appear in a 'Reversed State' from how you understood it before you left. You will appear in the shadow of someone you can influence on the surface, remain undetectable to everyone, and return when you wish by pressing the stone again."

The Envy pressed the stone, and vanished to shocked gasps from the people of Nis.

Is what Tanas said true? Rill thought to herself from her hiding place on the stone spear. She waited, not daring to make a sound. *Will he go to the surface and return?* An hour later The Envy reappeared before the city, looking overjoyed.

"It works! It's just like Tanas said it would be! Ha, ha, I actually made two brothers fight each other until one killed the other." The Envy continued laughing while a surge of noise began ringing up from the walls around Nis. The Greater Tribe was cheering, they were celebrating the return of a new hero.

"Tell us!" cried one.

"How did you do it?" asked another.

"Was it hard?" someone begged.

"An explanation would be useful," The Pride said to The Envy, who was quickly becoming the real envy of everyone present.

"Very well," The Envy said. Quickly using cracks in the stone—secret handholds—he climbed on top of Nis's wall so that everyone could hear him better.

"This is what happened. When I arrived back on the surface, the first thing that I noticed was that the color of everything had been reversed. The 'Reversed State' you said I would be in once the Veil had taken me to the surface."

"Yes," Tanas agreed. "Please continue with your story."

"It was true; the Light could not harm me." That single statement brought forth a huge cheer from the crowds within Nis, but quickly quieted as soon as The Envy began speaking again. "I found myself standing behind a Being of Light, inside what must have been his shadow, and managed to get a really good look at them without their armor. They are a bit shorter than us, with no horn, only slightly pointed ears, and weird garments all over themselves instead of the armor they were wearing. At first, I tried to reach out and strangle the Being of Light, but found I couldn't touch him."

Despite the fact that The Envy claimed to have been able to get two brothers to kill each other, once the crowd heard that The Envy couldn't touch them, they started grumbling about the whole idea of the Veil of Shadows. Many of them wanted to kill the Beings of Light with their own hands.

"There is a reason why The Envy couldn't touch them," Tanas interrupted. "It's because the Veil's powers. That way it prevents Light from penetrating and harming its wearer. But even without the ability to touch the Beings of Light, there are ways to influence them, correct?"

"Yes," The Envy said, smiling toward Tanas. "The Being whose shadow I was within was speaking to another Being who he called his younger brother. The younger one was talking about how his proposal got chosen over his elder brother's proposal. I knew the elder brother was getting annoyed, so I said, 'Just punch his mouth shut,' and that is exactly what he did."

"The Veil of Shadows," Tanas explained, "allows its user to send their voice into the ears and mind of whomever they are standing behind. However, the victim only hears what they think is a whisper in their mind. When that whisper matches what the victim is feeling, the victim is tempted to do whatever the whisper says."

"That is exactly what I did," The Envy said with a laugh. "After the younger brother was knocked on the ground, I quickly walked over to him and instantly found myself in *his* shadow."

"The shadow walking ability." Tanas further explained. "It's an ability that allows you to use the Veil of Shadows to move on the surface. Instead of crossing through the light, you jump to the nearest shadow next to you."

"From there, I tempted the younger brother to strike back. Soon I was shadow walking between both brothers, tempting them further on and on, until the older brother eventually killed the younger one. It was so easy, and funny, the best thing of all was that none of the other Beings of Light did anything to try and stop them. They just watched the spectacle until it was all over!"

"That settles it. You, and your forces, may join us," The Pride said. "And to seal our agreement, we will rename ourselves the Tribe of Shadows, signifying the unification of the Greater Tribe with the Legions of Shadow. In time, the Master of the Beings of Light and the rest of the Beings of Light will fall!"

This is bad. Rill realized, watching the creature and its Legions enter Nis, embracing the Greater Tribe like they were family. *This Tanas doesn't mean good news for anyone. The Seven should never have invited it into Nis. It won't leave now. I'm sure it's just going to get stronger and more dangerous until The Seven, the people of Nis, the Remnant, and even the Beings of Light will be in danger of it.*

Rill panicked, realizing the scent and energy of fear must be rolling off her now in increasing waves. So, as the people of Nis were celebrating their newfound alliance and kinship with Tanas and his Legions of Shadow, she slid down from the stone spear, and began running back to Rem before anyone *Knew* she was there.

Whatever this Tanas is, it's worse than the Beings of Light. Whatever freedom the people of Nis had, it's gone. The people of Nis will fall into its void of nothingness until they are worshiping it. If it was telling the truth, about fighting against the Beings of Light, that proves it's dangerous. It's forces could have easily defeated the people of Nis. The fact that they didn't means they want them alive for one reason or another. Rill remembered another lesson the Seat of Hope taught her, that "true evil cannot enter one's home unless it's been invited in."

Perhaps that is why this Tanas made The Seven invite it and its forces into Nis when it could have easily invaded. It wanted them to invite it in so they couldn't resist it later.

Tanas couldn't have come from anywhere on the surface. It had to have come from a similar place as the Beings of Light. Throughout Rill's life, she had never been so badly shaken after trying to *Know* something as she was from trying to *Know* Tanas.

We have to stay vigilant, she thought, pushing herself harder. *With Tanas in Nis, the best Rem can hope for are periods of peace that last for as long as possible. Otherwise, I fear we might all be departing for the Spirit Land—the Glowing Land of our Forebears—sooner than any of us think.*

Future emissaries will need to be told about everything I witnessed so they will be ready for Tanas and the Tribe of Shadows. Rill shuddered at the new name the Greater Tribe gave themselves. *They need to be prepared for what they are going to face. I don't know what Tanas and his Legions will have done to Nis by then, but it won't be good. The next time an emissary is sent, I think it will be changed in ways no one can imagine.*

***

Back in Rem, the Seats of Courage and Hope listened intently to Rill's report. Their hearts wept with sadness and pity for the children of Nis, realizing they can only initially learn what is taught to them by their elders. But even worse, they *Knew* the fear Rill felt about Tanas and what it represented. When the Seats of Courage and Hope were alone in the communal tent, they spoke privately about Rill's report.

"What do you think, Seat Hope?" the Seat of Courage asked, the nervousness ringing in her voice.

"I agree with Rill," the Seat of Hope replied. "Tanas is dangerous, and it will become stronger and more dangerous until it is a threat to everyone both here and on the surface. Rill said it best, we have to stay vigilant and let the next emissary know what he or she will be facing."

"I'll prepare another evacuation drill," the Seat of Courage said, anticipating actions that Tanas might make against Rem. "We can't fight Tanas, and we can't abandon the Greater Tribe, especially now after they have become the Tribe of Shadows. We need to try and keep talking to them and be ready in case we have to leave."

The next year passed. The Seats of Courage and Hope told the story of Nis and Tanas to their successors, the next Council, and continued to teach and prepare The Remnant for the future. However, the Seats of Courage and Hope didn't live to see the next emissary leave for Nis, both of them dying two years after Rill's journey. The entire Remnant witnessed their funeral, burying them deep in their moss fields. Their bodies, rotting away, would become nourishment for the plants that would later feed The Remnant.

In the following years, the new Council would continue to send emissaries to Nis. As they reported back about what they witnessed, it became clear why Tanas hadn't taken the city by force. Since Tanas's entry, there would be a steady increase in the birth of children of mixed heritage between the Legions of Shadow and the Greater Tribe. In fact, there were no reports of children born purely from the Legions of Shadow, and none claiming to be a child of Tanas. The Council soon realized the Legions of Shadow couldn't reproduce with itself. They needed the Greater Tribe to create offspring.

Tanas also grew in strength. First taking on the role of a teacher and guide, it taught the Tribe of Shadows everything it knew about maintaining a civilization and aided in the refining of critical aspects of The Plan—becoming just as important a figure as The Seven were. As the original Seven began to pass on, their positions, at Tanas's recommendation, were filled by children born of the Legions of Shadow and the Greater Tribe. Tanas would later become so instrumental in the establishment of Nis, and its ways, that the new Seven who replaced the first Seven proclaimed "Lord Tanas" their ruler. Lord Tanas was first treated as a man, then a king, and finally, when it became apparent that he didn't seem to age, as a deity to the Tribe of Shadows.

Time went on. As Rill thought when she fled Nis, Lord Tanas and the Tribe of Shadows eventually became a threat to The Remnant. Coming to the cavern where The Remnant had established their home, the Tribe of Shadows sought to expand their ever-growing city and wipe out The Remnant at Tanas's command. However, thanks to the foresight of the old Seats of Courage and Hope, The Remnant was prepared. When the Tribe of Shadows reached the Remnant's cavern, the Remnant had already packed the city of Rem up, moving it, and themselves, deeper into the underworld to protect their way of life.

The City of Nis

Time continued to pass. Years became decades, which became centuries, and then millennia. The Remnant continued sending emissaries to the city of Nis, and moving deeper into the underworld when the need arose. The stories passed on to become history, becoming legends in their retelling. Elsewhere, while both The Remnant and the Tribe of Shadows survived underground, the surface also changed over time—in ways no one could have expected.

P.J. Fenton

Part 2: The Child of Light Descending into Darkness

Chapter 5

"Worm, are you in there?" Reye knocked at the door again, harder this time. She hated being ignored. "It's Reye Jasper, wake up, dig yourself out of your books, and open this door. I need someone to talk to."

"I wasn't asleep," a voice responded from behind it. "I just have my hands full." The door clicked and slowly cracked open, filling Reye's face with the smell of musty books and old papers. Through the crack, she could see a body with a large pile of books for a torso and a head waiting for her on the other side.

"So, are you coming in?" the figure asked, stepping away, and letting Reye into the room.

"Let me help with those." Reye took half of the books out of the occupant's hands so she could get a better look at her friend. "Look at you, you're covered in dust and your skin looks paler than ever. What have you been doing?"

"Research," Worm answered, smiling creepily through his drawn features. Dark circles etched around his blue-grey eyes made him look like he had been reading nonstop. "So, if you can close the door and follow me to my desk, I can get back to it and you can start talking to me."

Like Reye, Worm was a student at Spectral Academy in the Platinum Throne, a neutral and independent island city-state housing the greatest academic facilities and the largest science repository in the world, and his room was one of the largest in the dorms. But with everything he kept in it, "library" more accurately described it. Shelves lined the walls, each one filled with books and copies of documents, both young and old, from the various religions of the Seven Dominions of Prism. History books about great wars of the past, papers by conspiracy theorists, and various other items also lay scattered in piles throughout the room.

As Reye walked in, she watched the floor to make sure she didn't trip over anything. The room's only lighting was dim and flickering, and the cluttered space made her feel confined. She was a natural athlete, and originally from a farm in the Orange Dominion, a fact made partially apparent by her athletic build, her red-orange hair, and tan skin—characteristics of people from both the Orange and Red Dominions, and liked action and being mobile. Worm's room forced its occupants to move slowly. Worm himself, on the other hand, fit the room's mood perfectly; his worn-out looks, musty smells, grey attire, and silent movements completely complemented the surroundings and often made others wonder who he could be. Placing her pile of books on Worm's desk, Reye noticed a topic written on an open notebook page.

"How beliefs of extremists and sects from the Yellow Dominion that died out in the Great Rainbow War still influenced today's culture through works of fiction," Reye said, reading the title aloud. "Is this what you're working on?"

"It is," Worm replied, his eyes narrowing slightly as he looked at the topic, almost like he had experience with it, a sign Reye knew could mean a lecture on conspiracy theories. It was rare, but he sometimes acted like he knew far more than he would let on about. It was the only thing he ever did that bugged her.

"It's important to think about these beliefs and practices to see how they are still reflected today. The results I've found so far would surprise you. Causa latet, vis est notissima, the cause is hidden, but the rest is well known," Worm quoted in Platin, a dying Hy-mun language that used to be spoken by the religious leaders across the Seven Dominions, but could now only be found in scattered parts of the world. It was a language he was surprisingly fluent in, which helped with his research since a number of his older books were only written in Platin.

"Do you think you could do me a favor and read me the marked section in that book so I can take notes?" Worm pointed to a black book with a picture of a seven-colored snake biting its own tail outlining a white circle on the cover—a translated and revised copy of the Tome of the Ouroboros. "You sounded anxious when you were banging on the door and reading helps calm me down. Maybe it will do the same for you, and I think you need to be calm for whatever it is you want to talk to me about."

"Glad to help, Mr. Obvious," Reye replied sarcastically. But Worm was right, she was anxious, anyone could have told her that; still, it always irked her when someone stated the obvious to her. Yet she also knew she needed to relax, willing to try anything, she opened the Tome to the marked section and started to read.

"*In the beginning, there was nothing but chaos, wicked and turbulent, existing without beginning or end, holding the World in the darkest of prisons. However, from that dark prison, light sprung forth. The Light was called Ash Addiel, the Great Master of Light, and from his light were born the Nag-el, the first people of the light. Together, the Great Master and the Nag-el drove away the chaos and the darkness, establishing the first home of the people of the light. The glory of Ash Addiel and the Nag-el eventually reaching a point where the Great Master finally said: 'We must go and bring our Light to a new world.'*

"*The Great Master entrusted this mission to his closest friend, a true friend, to whom he gave the title 'Light Bringer.'*

"*Light Bringer searched and found a world shrouded in darkness and chaos, a world in need of the glory of the light. Light Bringer brought his people to that world, making it ready for the coming of the Great Master, bringing light to the darkness and shaping order from the chaos he found. Upon his arrival, the Great Master looked upon this new world and its potential and was pleased. But as his light touched this new world, a strange thing happened. A new race of beings was born from where his radiance seeped into the ground, a mixture of the earth and the light. Ash Addiel called them the Hy-muns, the second people of the light. Deciding that since the Hy-muns were born not just from his light alone, but also from the earth below him, Ash Addiel gave the Hy-muns stewardship over the new land. However, Light Bringer saw the actions of the*

Great Master as a betrayal of the Nag-el.

"'*Why should this new race be given control of the land* we *found and* we *made ready?' Light Bringer said to his followers. 'Ash Addiel has forsaken us for these Hy-muns.'*

"*So, Light Bringer gathered a sum of the Nag-el, forces he himself had led to the new world, and began a vicious war against Ash Addiel and the Nag-el loyal to the Great Master, a war lasting seven years, each battle more vicious than the last. When the war finally ended, the Great Master stood victorious. For his treason, Light Bringer's 'light,' the very soul of a Nag-el, was stripped from him, leaving him neither living nor dead. Light Bringer, along with his followers, was then banished to a dark prison, to watch as his followers slowly died around him, eventually leaving him alone in the dark for all time. Eight sentinels took watch across the land to make sure that Light Bringer would never return. Should he try, the sentinels would ensure that he suffer a fate even worse than what he had already been condemned to.*

"*Life went on, but the betrayal and long war created wounds that would not heal. The Hy-muns continually found themselves in conflict with each other. The war had given the Hy-muns a taste of violence, a sensation many found themselves drawn to, and when any of the Hy-muns tried to turn to the Great Master for relief, they found him engaged in his own troubles with the Nag-el; the war leaving heated divisions among the Nag-el as well.*

"*Finally, the Great Master Ash Addiel and the Nag-el left the new world, until a time when the war's damage had properly healed itself. As the Great Master was leaving, he christened the new world Prism. From then on, a great orb of light existed in the sky which the Hy-muns all pointed to and said, 'There is the Great Master, Ash Addiel, watching over us all.'*

"*And when the great orb set, the sky filled with lights and the people cried, 'There are the Nag-el, servants of the Great Master.'*

"*And so, the people continued to live, under the Great Master in the light of day and under the Nag-el in the shadow of night.*

"Seriously, Worm," Reye said exhaustedly, closing the Tome of the Ouroboros, rubbing her strained eyes, and placing the book back on his desk. "I don't know how you are able to read through this, and all this other junk you've got scattered around here, and still manage to get anything done. Let alone live comfortably, buried under all these books and dust."

With all of the heavy reading scattered around, Reye could easily remember the reason her friend had picked up the nickname "Worm." It was because he was such a bookworm. He didn't mind, though; in fact, he liked the name so much that it was the only one he ever used. Reye didn't think anyone even knew what his real name was. Aside from Worm, the only other name she ever heard him called was "Mr. Wood" once by a teacher. It was a name he fiercely avoided afterwards whenever possible. Worm was from an island in the Indigo Dominion. It was the northernmost and most isolated of all the Dominions on the Cherubi Continent—Prism's only continent—located west of the Platinum Throne. It was also the smallest Dominion, consisting of a peninsula extending from where the mountains of the Violet Dominion dropped down to meet the Seraph Sea—where the Tanzanite Ziggurat was located—and an archipelago of various islands extending from the Dominion's shore out into the ocean. Some radical geologists believe that the dominion was once part of an even larger landmass, one that sank into the sea, but nothing had ever been confirmed. Worm was one of an extremely small number of students at Spectral Academy from the Indigo Dominion. All of whom, like Worm, possessing extremely fair skin, and the only one she knew personally.

"It's a talent I thank the Great Master for gifting me with," Worm said, looking up from his writing and flashing her a brief toothy grin. His fair skin, made fairer by the complete lack of daylight, glowed slightly in the flames of the candles flickering on his desk and throughout the room, only increasing his ghostly appearance. All of his candles burned within glass containers, so his books and papers stayed safe from the flames. For some reason Reye decided not to ask about—she never liked prying into other people's past—he always kept his windows and shades closed, blocking out the sunlight and working by candlelight rather than artificial light. Reye, tossing her head playfully aside at Worm's smile, letting her orange-red hair whip across her face, sat down and took a deep breath. She was ready to talk.

"Listen, Worm, there's a couple of things I came to talk to you about." Reye's tone was serious, but her voice trembled a little as she spoke. "It's about the mining project."

"Did you get onto the team?" Worm immediately stopped, dropped his pen, and turned away from his desk to face her. Normally whenever Reye talked to him while he was occupied, he would listen and speak plainly enough, but his eyes and focus were always on what he was doing. His work ethic could have made most of the farm hands she knew back home jealous. It took something big to get his attention, and she knew this qualified. He looked directly at her. His stares made most people uncomfortable, since the dark circles around his eyes, combined with his fair skin, made most think they were looking into the eyes of a living skull instead of a live Hy-mun. But for her, looking into those eyes, all she could see and feel were honesty and concern. That was why, despite others believing that he was weird and creepy, she liked him—he was honestly interested in the happiness of those he considered his friends.

"I don't know yet," Reye said, fidgeting in her chair. "The names are going to be announced in an hour. I'm nervous, Worm."

"That's understandable," Worm replied, trying to sound supportive. The two of them were in completely different areas of study, Reye a student of geology and volcanoes, and Worm a student of theology. They met when she had taken a class on symbology as an elective and became good friends. Reye learned that Worm was not only good company, but also a good listener, he also had a certain way with words, and wouldn't tell her something if he didn't feel it was true.

"I know I'm a straight-A student," Reye said, playing with her hands as she talked, cracking out each knuckle nervously. "I have the best marks when it comes to handling explosives, and I'm one of the best athletes in school. But what if that isn't enough? I know that the captains of both the martial arts and the marathon teams I'm on have applied, and academically they're just as good as me. What if that gives them an edge?"

Worm knew how important this project was to Reye, and he also knew what it felt like to lose something that important. For Reye, getting accepted into this project would be a massive step toward making her dream of becoming a terranaut—a dream she had devoted herself to since long before she even came to Spectral Academy—come true. Terranauts piloted terraships underground and through the lava streams beneath Prism, performing similar tasks that were going to be accomplished on the mining project, but with a far greater level of danger. He privately hoped she would never have to experience the pain of having her effort be for nothing. When he experienced that pain, it had been hard for him to pick himself up afterwards.

"You've been working as hard as you can to be accepted. At this point you can only wait until you know whether you were better than the other candidates who applied. Just hope for the best."

"And prepare for the worst, right, Worm?" Reye said, finishing off one of Worm's favorite sayings—one of the few he spoke in common language. Another thing she liked about him was his dependability. Reye knew she could walk into his room, spill out her problems, and expect him to come up with some saying for it. It was that dependability that made her want to talk to him in the first place.

Most of Reye's nerves about the final selection came from not having anyone to talk to who wasn't also involved. Yet Reye knew she could talk to Worm without seeing her own stress reflected back at her. Worm never took part in any projects outside of class, he was the dependable one who was always accessible, and the one person that could constantly be counted on to talk with. Especially since he could listen to others, keep himself calm in the face of whatever was thrown at him, and not go crazy. But she wasn't finished just yet.

"Anyway, there was something else I wanted to ask you."

"And what might that be?" Worm asked.

"A number of us are going out for a group dinner at AB's. Sort of a celebration for any of us that make the program, or a way to drown out our sorrows if we don't make it, and I wanted to know if you would like to join us." Reye didn't even need to try and guess his answer. After knowing him for a year, one of the things that she had learned about him was that AB's was his favorite restaurant, and unless he was extremely busy, he would never turn down an invitation.

"When?" Worm asked excitedly, getting up and going to the refrigerator in his room.

"We are meeting there at 18:30 tonight," Reye answered.

"I'll be there," Worm replied, taking out a drink and sipping it.

"Okay then, I'll see you at 18:30. Just try to get some of the dust and smell off you first," Reye finished, turning around and making her way to the door, leaving Worm puzzled and sniffing himself, wondering what "smell" she could be talking about.

Once outside and in the hallway, walking down the stairs, Reye felt much less confined and let her thoughts drift back to the mining project. Talking with Worm had helped settle some of her nerves, but not all of them. Glad to be moving again through fresh-smelling air and in light that wasn't provided by candles, she quickly glanced at her watch, noticing that it was now ten minutes to 16:00.

Wow, she thought to herself, surprised by how much time she let slip by. Reye never did have a good sense of time—a problem her brother constantly nagged her about, it was one of the reasons she became a marathon runner. She found she could easily focus on a task like running long distances since the time didn't mean as much, provided she finished the race first.

The application form said the names of the selected students would be announced at about 16:00 today, Reye thought. Over one thousand students had applied for the project, but only one hundred would be accepted. The odds alone were one out of ten, assuming that everyone would be given a fair chance. But one thing she definitely counted on was that no one would be given a fair chance. Anyone could apply, but after that, what mattered became a combination of achievements in academics, physical performances, additional activities, standing in character… and any contacts applicants had with anyone else. Reye tried being optimistic, having earned a large number of academic and athletic awards over her life, and being an active participant around school. Yet she felt fairly certain that the one hundred chosen would not only be the ones that had everything she did, but also possessed a large number of family connections—something she didn't have. Reye left her home on the farm and entered Spectral Academy through the Dominion Advancement Program; a program that sought to restore the Seven Dominions to their pre-Rainbow War status by bringing able-minded applicants to the Platinum Throne who were ready to learn about technology, and were also physically prepared for the curriculum.

However, coming from a small community farm, the only people Reye knew were the ones in the town she grew up in, not the kind of people—the industrialists, politicians, and company heads—that cared about what happened to her at Spectral Academy. Despite how much she applied herself to athletics— skills she was especially adept at, thanks to years of farm work giving her extremely strong muscles—or academics, she knew she didn't know anyone else outside of the school to whom she could become a potential windfall after graduation.

The number of people with a fair chance is probably going to be far fewer than one hundred, Reye thought to herself, opening the marble doors of the dorm building and walking out into the sunlight.

No matter how many times she saw it, the city of the Platinum Throne still took her breath away with its sheer majesty. In the distance, she could see an airship lifting off from one of the airfields, its gondola carrying passengers and reflecting the light from the Platinum Throne's buildings. The same light that was making her eyes squint as they readjusted to their surroundings. The entire island was easily larger than the bases of all Seven Ziggurats put together. The Seven Ziggurats were the capitals of the Seven Dominions. Each Dominion—or nation—was named after one of seven rays of light in the visible spectrum—Red, Orange, Yellow, Green, Blue, Indigo, and Violet—and each Ziggurat was a pyramidal structure built out of a gemstone signifying its Dominion, dating back to before recorded Hy-mun history. However, unlike the Seven Ziggurats, almost all of the buildings on the island of the Platinum Throne, their insides and outsides, were made of a rare metal called platinum, hence the city-state's name. Diamonds embedded in the buildings' walls reflected and refracted the light in all of its different rays in an ever-changing kaleidoscope of color.

The Hy-mun people believed the Platinum Throne was where they first rose from the earth after Ash Addiel came to Prism with the Nag-el, building the city before his and the Nag-el's departure into the heavens to become the sun and stars. Because of this, the Platinum Throne was declared a place of peace for all time. That declaration saved it from being touched during the Great Rainbow War, in which most of the world's science was lost—almost returning it to a preindustrial age—leaving the only scientific devices and knowledge in the Platinum Throne and the Indigo Dominion, which had remained a neutral state throughout most of the conflict, to help restore the world after the war. The process, however, proved to be very slow, because of the time needed to train people in the use of technology, the harsh demands other Dominions made for it, and also the Indigo Dominion's fear of other nations following the war, leading it to isolate itself and keep its own technology and resources mostly within its own boarders. Having been born and raised in the time following the war's conclusion forty years ago, Reye often wondered what the world had been like before the war.

The Orange Dominion used to create fantastic airships, Reye thought to herself, watching the airship lift into the sky. *We might have been a family of engineers instead of farmers. We might have designed that.* On some of her runs through the forests back home, she had seen the ruins of old airship factories. Her daydreaming ended abruptly as a loud *PING* sounded across the academy, signifying that an announcement was about to be broadcasted over the speakers.

"Attention, students, this is Professor Bridget Heart of the Volcanology Department, calling all students who applied for positions in the Red Dominion's Demp Cavern Mining Project. Please report to Zirconium Auditorium for the announcement of the selected candidates."

Snapping like lightning, Reye started to run. Her nervous feelings returned, but only until she remembered her conversation with Worm.

"Hope for the best and prepare for the worse," she said to herself, running across Spectral Academy toward Zirconium Auditorium, feeling nothing but hope and excitement.

Chapter 6

From the outside, Zirconium Auditorium looked like an overturned bowl made entirely of solid diamond; the inside was another matter entirely. White marble walls and pillars supported the roof as the floor turned downward, an inverse of the ceiling, arranged with thousands of seats on all sides descending toward a central stage at the bottom. The auditorium, already filling when Reye entered, vibrated with sound as students talked excitedly to each other. She was trying to find a place to sit among the mass of students when she heard a familiar voice call her name.

"Reye, over here!"

Reye knew who it was even before she saw his head of red-orange hair sticking out among a group of dark-haired students. The hair was the same color as hers, but not as long, cut short to the shoulder, and the face—so much like her own, but more masculine—was one that she had known from birth; it was her twin brother Raymond. Raymond waved her down to an open seat he had casually laid his gym bag on top of. Reye slowly made her way down the aisle to where he was sitting.

"I made it here a little while ago, so I thought I'd make certain I got a seat for you as close to the front as possible," Raymond said, clearing the bag away, allowing Reye to take a seat next to him. "I know how terrible you are when it comes to time, and how much you like to be in the center of the action. Remember orientation? You were—"

"Thanks Raymond," Reye said, cutting him off and making herself comfortable. She didn't need any brotherly reminders about how terrible she was with time. "I don't need another reminder about our first day at Spectral Academy, and the big orientation dinner for the new arrivals from the Dominion Advancement Program we almost missed because I lost track of time trying to see every part of the campus possible."

"It took all my convincing just to get you to the dining hall, and all my foresight to plan how long it would take for the two of us to get there, to make certain we weren't locked out," Raymond joked.

"Why do you always know what it is that I like?"

"Because I've followed you into every school, sport, fight, and craziness you've gotten yourself into since we were born," Raymond answered, with a teasing sigh.

"Don't lie to me and say you didn't want to do it also," Reye said accusingly.

"Live no regrets," Raymond responded, adding a wry smile. Reye knew she made her point.

Despite the playful banter, Reye was thankful Raymond managed to get these seats. While anyone on the main stage could be heard clearly throughout the auditorium, she wanted to be near it. Her brother wasn't kidding when he said she liked to be "in the center of the action." From the time they were little, she was always the first to jump into the middle of any happening on or off the farm, a habit responsible for getting her into trouble on more than one occasion. Whenever the kids of the other farm hands would play and dare each other into crazy stunts and challenges, Reye always seemed to appear on the scene—with Raymond right behind her—to volunteer for whatever was going on. Together, the two of them ran over the hill by their farm to the Amber-Leaf forest and back retrieving flags, held underwater breathing challenges, and proved they could hot wire and drive farm equipment. However, while her brother might have been a troublemaker too, he always knew where to draw the line—often bailing Reye out of trouble, making sure she never went too far, and stopping her whenever she tried something really crazy. But the thrill shared between them, the excitement of either beating the clock, or getting out of a difficult situation, just made the bond between them stronger. Now that the two of them were again "in the center of the action," right where she liked to be, all that was left was for the action to begin. Thankfully, they didn't have to wait long.

A large *boom* suddenly echoed throughout the auditorium, followed by approaching footsteps as the outside doors closed, and the remaining students quickly took their seats. A middle-aged woman began descending down the central aisle, a woman Reye, with a surge of excitement quickly building in her, immediately recognized from pictures as Professor Bridget Heart.

Professor Heart looked to be in her fifties or sixties, but despite her age she still conveyed a formidable appearance, walking straight down the aisle, a large bag slung over her shoulder, oblivious to the noise from the other students. Half her hair had gone grey, leaving the other half a bright red. Her eyes were deep brown, as brown as the earth she used to travel through when she was a terranaut, and still etched with the memories of every mission she had been on.

Reye had never had a class with Professor Heart before, but she had heard the stories about her. Originally from the Red Dominion, a nation known for its deep canyons and large number of active volcanoes, Professor Heart had been one of the best terranauts alive until she developed a mental and physical disability that forced her to use a cumbersome suit filled with breathable fluids if she wanted to travel underground and into the magma flows. Since terranauts needed to be able to move fast, she retired from the service and made Spectral Academy her new home. Since her arrival, she helped train more specialists on volcanoes than anyone else who had ever come to Spectral Academy, and was also rumored to have a wicked sense of humor. Placing herself in the podium at the center of the stage, Professor Heart began addressing the students.

"Good afternoon everyone," Professor Heart welcomed, her voice—alive and full of passion—reaching clear to the back of the auditorium. "First of all, congratulations to everyone who was accepted. And to everyone who wasn't, don't let it get you down. One rejection isn't the end, and there will be many more projects in the future. You will have another chance to make your job connections for after you graduate, and get the stories you'll want to have to brag about to your boyfriends and girlfriends." Professor Heart's last comment brought a ripple of laughter throughout the auditorium.

How many of these students signed up just to get *a story to boast about?* Reye wondered. She knew Professor Heart meant the last comment as a joke, but unfortunately, the students looking for an impressing story were probably the ones present with the backing and connections needed to be chosen for the project. The laughter ended as Professor Heart placed her bag on the podium, the sound of it hitting the marble surface echoing everywhere.

"We on the Platinum Throne realize the need for additional resources to bring the Dominions back to the technological and economic state they were in before the Great Rainbow War, and both the Platinum Throne and Spectral Academy are honored to not only provide some of the technology used during the project, but also able bodies and minds of students to assist in this restoration. If you are accepted, you will be expected to conduct yourselves in a way that does credit to your Dominion and school." She pulled out a sheet of paper from her bag.

"I'll be reading these names alphabetically by last name," Professor Heart said. Each student—Reye included—now hanging onto her words. "After I am done, I ask the accepted students to remain here in the auditorium for a few minutes so I can explain in greater detail where you will be going, and hand out some material for you to go over at your leisure. Now, let us begin."

Every student in the auditorium held their breath as Professor Heart began to read. Reye listened as the names passed by, recognizing Ann Branley, one of her friends who would be joining them later at AB's. As the list went on, Reye noticed more and more students getting out of their chairs and leaving the auditorium, a look of complete defeat in their faces.

Students who weren't accepted, Reye thought with a shiver, realizing she could easily become one of them as Professor Heart began reading the "J" section of the accepted list.

This is it, Reye realized, listening intently for her name, when Professor Heart said something that made her eyes open wide with both surprise and delight.

"Jasper, Raymond," Professor Heart said.

Yes! Turning to look at her brother, she could see that his eyes had opened wider that she ever thought they could. The smile on his face—wider than she had ever seen it before—looked like it was trying to meet on the other side of his head.

"Live no regrets," Reye said, quickly repeating Raymond's three-word motto that he developed during a lifetime of following her around on every crazy dare and stunt she attempted.

Raymond loved the thrills and excitement he shared with his sister, repeating his slogan to himself daily to remind himself to live a complete, and extreme, life. Unfortunately, Reye didn't have much more time to congratulate her brother further, because the next name Professor Heart spoke made all time around her stop, and all the other people around her fade away, leaving her, her brother, and Professor Heart all alone in the gleaming auditorium.

"Jasper, Reye."

Reye nearly passed out in her seat. She didn't know what to say. She didn't know what to think. All she could do was just sit and stare at Professor Heart on the podium, who continued reading names she couldn't even hear anymore. The Great Master Ash Addiel himself could have come down from the sky and stepped right in front of her, and she still wouldn't have noticed him. In fact, she might have kept sitting there if a hand hadn't touched her shoulder and a voice said her name.

"Reye," the voice called.

Reye turned around and saw her brother staring back at her. His smile was even bigger now, and he was talking rapidly, only no words seemed to be coming out of his mouth. His green eyes, the same green as the hill overlooking her family farm, were alive with excitement. The same excitement she could see in her own face, reflected in those eyes, an excitement linking them on what she knew was going to be something spectacular. Then she remembered.

We made it into the mining project, she thought, moving her mouth slowly to whisper some words.

"Raymond... I... we..." Up until that moment, Reye truly didn't believe that she would be accepted into the Demp Cavern Mining Project. But now, that belief had been completely uprooted and thrown into a volcanic fire. She had been accepted, she was going to the mining project, and her brother would also be coming with her.

It's just like the day when I received my acceptance letter, Reye remembered. She always wanted far more out of life than just what the farm could offer her, feeling that staying there, while easier, was not as challenging and exciting a life that the world could potentially offer her. Eventually leading her to dream of becoming a terranaut, applying to the Dominion Advancement Program, and finally her acceptance into Spectral Academy. Now she was experiencing that feeling again, the pure joy that could only come from receiving a sign that her life was going exactly in the direction she wanted it to—despite the odds. Just then Reye felt her brother poke her in the shoulder, bringing her back down to earth.

"Pay attention," Raymond said with a grin on his face, recognizing his sister's look as the same one she had that day. "You are going to want to hear what Professor Heart is going to say next."

Reye's attention immediately returned to Professor Heart, who took a deep breath, returned the list of accepted participants into her bag, and prepared to address the remaining students.

"That concludes the list of accepted students," she said. "Congratulations on being selected for the mining project. Now, please shift your attention above me."

Professor Heart pressed a button on the podium; projectors at the base of the stage came to life, casting an image of a large cavernous area across and around Zirconium Auditorium.

"This is an aerial shot of where you are going, the Demp Caverns in the Rise Palace of the Red Dominion." Professor Heart's map detailed a mountainous region of the Red Dominion with a cave entrance marked "Demp Caverns." There were also numerous shaded regions—some shaded black, others red—leading from the entrance to points marked "Mining Location" above a list of what was being mined there. The black areas were previously explored regions, while the red areas, including the point marked "Project Site," were the unexplored regions. Reye was getting excited just looking at the map.

"According to sonar pictures, there is an even larger series of caverns below the ones we know about, caverns that could contain soil and mineral deposits needed for agriculture and construction, as well as mining territories in the form of gold deposits and other precious metals used for creating electronics and building tools."

"When do we leave?" Reye shouted, gaining a round of cheers from the other students in the auditorium.

"Now don't get too excited," Professor Heart chuckled. "Although I can understand why you would be. There are some final details we have to attend to."

Professor Heart took a large stack of folders out of her bag and gestured to the doors at the far end of the auditorium. A slightly middle-aged man descended the center aisle, took the folders from Professor Heart, and began passing them out. Reye and Raymond, two of the first students to receive a folder, quickly opened them up as Professor Heart began speaking again.

"The folders my secretary, Mr. Light Ryder, are handing out contain the following information. First is a waiver that you can read at your leisure, but you must sign and return it to me by 12:00 tomorrow."

"A waiver?" Reye whispered to Raymond inquisitively.

"These forms are just standard procedure to say that you're participating in this mining project of your own free will," Professor Heart explained. "Also, if any harm befalls you as a result of your own actions, the actions of others, or some industrial accident, then neither Spectral Academy, the Deep Earth Mining Corporation, nor the Red Dominion can be held responsible."

"In other words," Raymond whispered back to Reye, "we're doing this because we want to, and if we get killed, it's no one's fault but our own."

"However, you don't have to worry about getting hurt. All of the serious operations are going to be completed before you even get on-site. But 'the powers that be' like to have their protection in case of lawsuits. Or in the event of a public relations disaster, like if a bunch of Academy students did something stupid and ended up getting killed in a mining accident." Professor Heart's famous sense of humor displaying itself in a smirk on her face; her comment earning some mild laughter from the crowd.

"The rest of the paperwork includes a complete list of all the students accepted into the project. It would be a good idea to try and get to know them now, because you are going to be spending a lot of time with them later. Believe me, things get cramped pretty fast when you're underground and that tends to make people edgy. I was often close with the people I worked with, and trust me, when you are underground, those people can mean the world to you."

I don't know how many of these *people I'll be able to get close to,* Reye mused, taking a quick glance around the auditorium. She could easily tell that most of the accepted students around her—just like she suspected—came from well-connected families. They carried an air of superiority in the way they sat and mingled with each other that immediately made Reye want to find better company as soon as possible.

At least I have Raymond. No matter what might happen, I know he is one person I can count on.

"There is also a list of what items you will need to bring—passport and birth certificate, the number of clothes, emergency supplies and contacts—and a summary of your travel plans that I will go over right now."

Professor Heart pressed another button on the podium and the images above the students' heads changed to several different pictures, including an airship and a bus.

"You start here at Spectral Academy and travel via tram to Light Point Airfield. From there, you will take an airship to the city of Aka in the Rise Palace near the caverns. Then you will take a bus the rest of the way to the mining site. Once you arrive, you'll be paired with a technician who is experienced in whichever field of expertise matches your own. You will then assist that technician for the duration of your time on the project."

Reye's smile was growing more and more by the second. She wanted to sign her wavier and get packing right away.

"As you can see, it's all laid out in black and white," Professor Heart concluded. "Once you've signed the waivers and returned them to me, you'll receive your tickets. After that, all you need to do is show up at the appointed place and time indicated on the travel plans with your tickets, luggage, necessary traveling papers, and it's off to the Demp Caverns. Any questions?"

"Are we really not going to see any serious work?" Raymond asked quickly. "That sort of takes the fun out of it."

Raymond knew and understood why all of the dangerous work would be completed before any of them even arrived at the site, but he still felt it would be boring if he couldn't be a part of it, or at least witness it. He was a challenger and explorer at heart, and any chance to explore a region that was unknown to him and challenge himself in a new way, physically or mentally, was more than enough reason for him to get excited. He wanted this to be an experience he could fully enjoy.

"I admit it does take some of the fun out of it," Professor Heart agreed, sighing. "But you have to learn to crawl before you can walk, so you just have to take what is available right now. You will all leave to join the project two weeks from today. That will give you time to pack and get your affairs in order. Now, are there any other questions?"

No one answered.

"Then that concludes the briefing. If anyone wants to sign their waivers and hand them to me now, they are free to do so."

Reye began scouring her pockets, looking for a pen, so she could write her name on the waiver and get her tickets.

You really would be dead without me, Raymond thought, sighing nonchalantly, pulling his gym bag onto his lap, opening up a side pouch, and taking out a pen that he handed to his sister. Reye quickly took the pen, ready to sign her waiver. Right as she touched it to the paper, her eyes caught a figure walking past them toward Professor Heart with a waiver in hand. He was taller than most of the students Reye knew, with sun-bleached blond hair and blue eyes, dressed completely in white, and walked with a stoic look and attitude that didn't seem to be phased by being admitted into the project.

"So, Sol is going to be coming on the project." A wry smile and thoughtful look crossing Reye's face as she recognized the student from the Yellow Dominion. "This will make the project interesting." Realizing that Sol—who was mostly a loner—was going to be in a position where he would have to actively work with other students.

Reye and Raymond both knew Sol through Spectral Academy's Martial Arts Club. He was a driven student, always putting his mind toward accomplishing whatever goal he set for himself. He attended Spectral Academy to study water purification techniques, skills he could use in his home, the Yellow Dominion, a nation covered mostly by deserts of yellow sand, with the main Hy-mun settlement located in the Grand Oasis, where the Topaz Ziggurat stood like a pillar of solid sunlight.

However, during the twenty-five years prior to the start of the Great Rainbow War, the Yellow Dominion became the home to a large number of fanatical and fundamental religious movements. The movements started from the discovery of non-Hy-mun remains and artifacts, artifacts that not only dated back to the proverbial era of myth, but also provided evidence that the creation stories of the Hy-mun, the Great Master's arrival, and Light Bringer's Seven Year Rebellion may have been factual events. The greatest find was a text believed to have been written by Ash Addiel himself, instructing his followers to "live simply." Since the text was discovered in the Yellow Dominion, its people considered themselves the model for "living simply," because they had limited technology to begin with. The fevered pitch of the movements' beliefs in this doctrine led to a forceful removal of anything that was seen as a heretical challenge to the Great Master's power, especially technology. Eventually starting the Great Rainbow War fifty years ago, costing Hy-mun civilization almost all of its technology. That war ended ten years later, and with it the fanatical and fundamentalist groups. However, many still regarded the Hy-muns from the Yellow Dominion with contempt because they had started the war.

It was because of the Yellow Dominion's history that Sol often had to deal with jeering and other forms of resentment from the students, even though the academy was supposed to be a place where all were welcome. He often kept quiet about what would go on around him, always maintaining his stoic, calm attitude and keeping to himself. Just like now, as he handed in his waiver, received his tickets from Professor Heart, and walked away with only a "thank you" coming out of his mouth.

Whenever Reye questioned him about the bullying, all he would say was, "The energy I need to deal with this I can better use for my work."

Chapter 7

"So, why didn't you tell me that Sol was selected for the project?" Reye asked Raymond, quickly signing her name on her own waiver and standing up with her brother to turn it in.

"I did Reye," Raymond answered, a touch of annoyance creeping into his voice. He knew exactly where this conversation was heading. "You were off in your own world again after you heard you were selected and weren't listening when I told you."

"I don't believe you," Reye said. "It just happened. How could I have not heard you say Sol was selected? That would be like telling me—"

Reye suddenly bumped into someone, cutting her off midsentence. Turning around to see who she ran into, her eyes lit up.

"Stella!"

Staggering backwards, dusting herself off, and blushing after bumping into someone, was Reye's dorm room neighbor, Stella Sky. A vibrant farming student from the mountainous regions of the Violet Dominion, she was about the same height as Reye but with fairer skin, blue eyes, blond hair, and possessed a natural magnetism in her voice that made people notice her. Stella often tried sitting in the back of classrooms to avoid unwanted attention; unfortunately, all it took was one word from her to immediately gain it from everyone, her voice carried that much presence. Stella regained her footing and looked up, her own excitement quickly replacing her embarrassment as a large smile stretched across her face.

"Reye!" Stella exclaimed, brightening with the same brilliance of a clearing sky. "I should have known you would be sitting at the front of the auditorium. Sorry I ran into you, I was going over these papers again. I'm guessing you are pretty excited right now?"

"That's right, Stella! Raymond and I both got…" Reye paused, and then suddenly twisted her head around to Raymond.

"You had better not have known that Stella was also accepted and *forgot* to tell me, *dear brother*," Reye accused Raymond, accenting the words "forgot" and "dear brother." She suspected she was the victim of one of his practical jokes.

"I *didn't* forget," Raymond denied, sighing. "I told you Stella was accepted just before I told you about Sol." The conversation was going exactly where he knew it would, and he didn't like it. Besides being very enthusiastic, running off into trouble with very little prodding, Reye also had a tendency to hear only what she wanted to hear, remembering things in a way she wanted to remember them—especially when she was excited. Raymond often ended up chastising Reye for that habit whenever it got her into big trouble. Once, prior to leaving for Spectral Academy, the two of them were given permission to use some of the farm tractors, and Reye got so excited about it she never listened to the warnings, went too fast, and almost got herself and her brother killed, and the tractors destroyed. Reye tried to laughingly pass it off, since no one got hurt and nothing was damaged, but Raymond chewed her out fiercely.

"What does it matter? We're in!" Stella exclaimed. "We are all going to the project in the Red Dominion. You couldn't ask for better luck. I mean, the odds of all three of us being selected for the project, I don't even want to calculate them, and yet we beat them, and we are going together."

Stella was just as giddy as Reye to find out her best friend would be joining the team. Stella and Reye had been friends and teammates from the moment they first met. No matter what the challenge, the two of them had always strived to be on the same team. Now they would be working together on the best project either of them could ask for. But as quickly as they had started to congratulate each other, another voice called to them from the stage.

"Unless you would rather stand around celebrating, which I completely understand, given how much being on this project must mean to you, please come on up and hand me your signed waivers. Then the three of you will be completely registered for this project and you can celebrate all you want."

Reye looked behind Stella to see Professor Heart sitting at her desk on the stage. She was smiling at the display going on between Stella, Reye, and Raymond, and watching numerous other displays of emotion from other accepted project members across Zirconium Auditorium. Reye suspected that Professor Heart might also have seen some of her own past excitement reflected in the other students' faces. From what students had told Reye about the way she taught, the passion she put into her lessons, and the far-off look she sometimes had in her eyes, a look Reye clearly saw as she approached her desk alongside Stella and Raymond, Reye could tell Professor Heart hadn't lost her love for volcanoes, or for being a terranaut.

Professor Heart would probably go back underground again in an instant if given the chance, opportunity, or reason—even if she did need to wear the special suit, Reye guessed.

"I still can't believe this is really happening," Stella whispered, the three of them placing their signed waivers in front of Professor Heart. Stella's comment made Reye steal one more glance at her own waiver, now alongside Raymond's and Stella's. Reye wanted one last look to know that this was really happening to her.

"You, Raymond, and I all got into the project," Stella whispered again to Reye, "It's almost too good to be true."

After seeing that each of the forms had their names signed and printed on them, Professor Heart gave each of them an envelope from her bag with their names typed on it.

"These envelopes contain all the tickets you will need to get from Spectral Academy to the Demp Caverns and back again," Professor Heart said, a wistful grin creeping across her face as all three of them took the envelopes, putting on even bigger smiles than the ones they were wearing.

"There is also a more detailed copy of the itinerary we just covered. I hope all of you have good fortunes and a safe journey. That just leaves *one more thing* before you go." Professor Heart's face turned deathly serious as she said "one more thing."

"And what is that?" Reye asked, suddenly worried that there might be a chance she could be disqualified from the project. A similar look of dread crossing both Stella and Raymond's faces. Stella's mouth shuddered open, as she looked to Reye and Raymond for support; Raymond's mouth began turning from a smile into a deep frown, as he dreaded whatever request Professor Heart was going to make.

Is there some requirement that all participants needed to fulfill? A test, something else that can cause me to be dropped from the project? Reye thought. The change in Professor Heart's mood made Reye feel like this "one more thing" could be what separated her from the people that were chosen.

"Congratulations again on the three of you for being accepted into the mining project," Professor Heart replied with a cheery tone and a big grin stretching from one side of her face to the other, amused at making the three of them sweat.

Laughing in spite of themselves, Reye, Raymond, and Stella walked out of Zirconium Auditorium and into the late afternoon.

The sun was beginning to set and the first stars had started to show in the night sky as Reye, Raymond, and Stella walked back across campus to their dorms. All across Spectral Academy, the light beautifully reflected and refracted multiple shades of red, orange, and yellow, painting the landscape in a variety of rainbows and different colors that complemented the blues and violets in the night sky and the reds and yellows of the setting sun.

"I never get tired of this sight," Reye said, walking down the path toward the dorms.

"Me neither," Stella agreed, the light dancing off her face and hair giving her the impression of being part of the Platinum Throne's ever-changing kaleidoscope of color. "Every time I'm out here, it feels like I'm being robed in light." Not too long ago, during the Day of the Rainbow Light, the Platinum Throne's effect looked so intense on Stella, who had decided to dress in white that day, that she practically vanished into the swirling colors until her voice alerted Reye as to where she was.

According to legend, Ash Addiel, after leaving Prism, cast his light down from the heavens and struck the Platinum Throne, which divided the light into seven rays, each a different color. The people divided and followed whatever ray they wanted, and the light led them to the Seven Ziggurats, Reye thought, remembering the story Worm told her during their symbology class, a story that may have been inspired by the Day of the Rainbow Light, when the sun rose in direct alignment with the Platinum Throne and the Cherubi Continent. When that happened, the sunlight divided into its seven distinct colors and projected one of those rays across to the continent to each of the Ziggurats, which would then shine its particular color of light over its Dominion. Reye knew there was more to the legend, but she couldn't remember it all.

Great, I'm turning into another Worm. Reye laughed, realizing she was seriously thinking about an ancient legend.

"What's so funny?" Stella asked.

"Nothing much," Reye said, trying to hide her own embarrassment. "I just realized for a second I was starting to think like Worm."

"Oh," Stella replied, slumping her shoulders.

Big mistake, Reye thought, remembering how at the mention of Worm's name, Stella would wrap her arms around herself, almost shrinking in stature. Sometimes she even pulled her hair slightly around her face, watching her surroundings, almost afraid she would be seen by someone.

Stella was originally from the Violet Dominion. Before the Great Rainbow War, it had been the greatest seat of religious power in the world, and the religious leaders of the time always held their council there. Hy-muns believed it to be the most ideal place among all seven of the Dominions to pray and call to the Great Master because of its location high in the mountains, meaning it was the closest any Hy-mun could get to the sun, the physical form of Ash Addiel. Given this background, Stella had been raised to be very religious, but also sociable toward everyone she met, an attitude she demonstrated to everyone in Spectral Academy, being easily one of the friendliest people on campus. When Reye first introduced her to Worm, she didn't think there would be any friction between them. Yet, for some reason, there immediately was.

"Why do you always get so nervous every time I mention Worm?" Reye asked, constantly confused by Stella's repeat reactions to Worm's name. "He seems as harmless as it gets, just a dusty bookworm who is more at home in a library or classroom than a sports arena. He's also into religion like you. I always thought you might have found some common ground there."

"There is just something *odd* about him," Stella said, accenting the word "odd," as if telling Reye that should be reason enough. "He just makes me want to keep him at a distance." Stella knew that Reye and Worm were friends, but getting close to Worm made her extremely uncomfortable. Stella was perhaps one of the few people on the Platinum Throne who knew some of Worm's past, and what she *did* know was potentially dangerous, so dangerous she couldn't tell anyone—not even her best friend.

"On another note," Reye began, trying to take her mind off Worm. "How do you feel about Sol going on the project?" Reye's lips curling into a mischievous smile.

"I… ah…" Stella faltered, instantly coming out of her Worm-induced shell and blushing vibrantly.

"So, are you planning to tell him how you feel on this trip, or are you going to let another opportunity pass you by?"

"Well…" Stella tried, but couldn't speak, her face turning as red as the Ruby Ziggurat. Stella knew, that Reye knew, she liked Sol despite the grief that people gave him for being from the Yellow Dominion. In fact, she liked him a lot. She had tried to tell him how she felt before, but embarrassment and nervous hesitation stopped her every time. Sol, on the other hand, completely ignored Stella. Reye knew if she didn't keep encouraging Stella to open up and tell Sol how she felt, nothing would ever happen.

"*Well*, is that a yes?" Reye asked, slyly starting her question the same way Stella had begun her previous sentence before choking up. "Or is the sun and star dance going to continue between you?" Reye laughed at her own pun on Stella and Sol's names.

"That's not a fair question to ask!" Stella snapped, forcing herself right into Reye face. Reye, in shock, almost stepped backwards, falling to the ground from Stella's sudden outburst. "And yes, the dance will end, eventually."

"Heh, heh, sorry about that," Reye apologized. "You're right, I shouldn't have asked that. But you seemed to be a little depressed when I mentioned he who shouldn't be named, so I figured I had to do something to bring you back to life." Stella crossed her arms again, more out of aggravation this time than the mention of Worm. Meanwhile Raymond, who had been watching intensely as the girls exchanged comments like blows in a martial arts match, decided to remind them he was there, too.

"I swear, I'll never understand women," Raymond said in a mock exhausted tone, as if listening to two of them were enough to tire him out.

"Hey, if men did understand women…" Reye began.

"Women wouldn't get to have so much fun teasing them," Raymond and Stella answered at the same time. Reye had said that same line to Raymond so many times after he tried to inject himself into a "girl's conversation" that whenever Raymond started to say it, Reye could finish the line for him. Stella had also heard it enough times since she had known the two of them that she could finish it just as well as Reye, a habit that always made her smile, because she felt closer to her friend through it.

"So, Stella, at 18:30 a group of us are going to meet at AB's for a congratulatory dinner. Do you want to come?" Reye asked.

"I don't think so. I'd like to start packing and getting myself ready for the trip."

"Okay," Reye sighed, not surprised by Stella's answer. One of Stella's biggest traits was that she always prepared herself ahead of everyone else. If a teacher gave their class an assignment due in two weeks, she would have it done in one. However, Reye also figured Stella didn't want to come because she guessed Worm might be there. Stella had already faced more awkward encounters at AB's because of Worm's presence than she would like to remember.

"Well then ladies," Raymond said, reaching the dorm building, "this is where we part for the time being. Stella, Reye, I'll see you later tonight at AB's."

"Bye Raymond," Reye and Stella said in unison, watching Raymond run off to his dormitory. As they walked toward their own dorm rooms, Reye's mind drifted to the mining project. Even now, after calming down and having finalized her position on the project, Reye was still excited.

"To think Stella, if you consider the time difference, the mining project is already underway, and I do mean under. Just imagine what we are going to see under there. This is going to be a project to remember."

P.J. Fenton

Chapter 8

Deep underground, crews of Hy-muns were hard at work. After drilling into a sealed cavern and assembling an elevator, miners worked to construct a base camp, assembling prefabricated trailers and buildings to serve as the miners' dormitories, communication facilities, laboratories, and every other function they needed. Yet deep in the shadows, away from the noise and lights of the construction, two pairs of red eyes glowed in the darkness, watching intensely.

"Do you see it, Gab-re? Hy-muns, more Hy-muns than ever before, coming into our territory, and it looks like it's only the beginning."

"What's worse, Mi-che, is that they are near both the Great Tunnel and the Keyblast point."

"You need to return to Nis, Gab-re. Lord Tanas must hear this news at once. This could be the start of a Second Coming. I'll tell Ra-phe to alert the guards at the other observation points."

Gab-re nodded and began running back through the dark maze of caves and tunnels. For uncountable generations, Gab-re's people—the Tribe of Shadows—secretly fought the Hy-muns, the final enemy, the last remaining foe keeping them from regaining a world long stolen from them by the Beings of Light. Gab-re knew the stories, when the Beings of Light came, led by the Light Bringer, they almost destroyed his people, forcing the few survivors deep into the caves below the surface, while the Beings of Light reshaped the land to suit their own needs.

After being chased underground, a splinter group—The Remnant—was expelled from the Tribe and moved deeper into the underworld of the caves. They were a constant plague for the Tribe of Shadows, spying on them every few years, living off the Tribe of Shadows' scraps, and trying to talk "sense" into them: giving up the fight for the surface, and scurrying away into the caves like rodents. This led the Tribe of Shadows to refer to members of The Remnant as Rodents. Later, under Lord Tanas's leadership, with The Seven Vices as his aids, the Tribe of Shadows began striking back against the Beings of Light. Attacking them through their shadows, tempting them to turn on each other, and their master, Ash Addiel. The Tribe of Shadows finally forced them to leave the surface in what would later be called the First Great Attempt. Unfortunately, they left behind a reminder of their presence, the Hy-muns, creatures created by the Beings of Light that protected their tools and prevented the Tribe of Shadows from returning and retaking the surface.

Yet the Tribe of Shadows wouldn't be detoured. Using the same methods that were successful against the Beings of Light, the Second Great Attempt started a war among the Hy-muns, destroying most of the tools they called "technology," but failed to destroy them completely. Now a Third Great Attempt, one that had actually started in the days of the Beings of Light, was nearing completion.

The Hy-muns will hide in caverns, Gab-re thought to himself, tingling at the prospect, *while the Tribe of the Shadows retakes its rightful place on the surface.*

Just thinking about it made him push himself harder as he approached the Tribe of Shadows' home, the city of Nis. If the Hy-muns stopped this plan and discovered them, it could mean the dreaded "Second Coming" every member of the Tribe of Shadows learned to fear would eventually happen, unless the surface was retaken.

In the generations following "The Coming," the city of Nis had been built, expanded, and rebuilt. Approaching the city, Gab-re met its primary defense, huge jagged slabs of volcanic rock that his ancestors had collected and placed around the city, constructing a protective ring. The magma flows, running between those rocks, gave them an illuminating tint that made them look like a ring of solidified fire. Making his way through the Ring of Fire-Stone, Gab-re saw a large crowd of Rodents being led under guard in the same direction. He heard of times when Rodents were caught either spying, or approaching the city willingly, but this was by far the largest group he had ever seen.

The two massive stone slabs forming the gates opened slightly so the Rodents could be herded inside. The gates used to be kept in place and moved with simple round stones, pulleys, and ropes; now they used Hy-mun technology procured over the Tribe of Shadows' struggle against them during the Second Great Attempt. Two large metal beams, with a saw-toothed edge on them, were connected to the gate, and they opened the gate when one beam was pulled along the matching saw-toothed beam by a mechanical device. Entering the gate, Gab-re read the inscription on the archway above it.

"Abandon all hopes that you believe in. They are an illusion, keeping us from our goal, one that every member of the Tribe should work for."

The First Seven Vices spoke those words uncountable generations ago, Gab-re mused, remembering the origin of those words. *Back when the Tribe of Shadows first devoted themselves to The Plan and expelled The Remnant from its company. Since that day, every member of the Tribe of Shadows adhered to those words as the basis for all of their actions until they died.*

"Open the Jac-ob Way!" Gab-re announced to the guard at the city's gates, snapping out of his reminiscing. "I have urgent news for Lord Tanas in Yam-Preen."

The Jac-ob Way was the central passage leading directly into the heart of Nis—Yam-Preen. Located besides the main gate, where the surface of the outer wall dipped inward, the entrance to the Jac-ob Way rested behind a barred door with a downward leading staircase. Compared to the colossal main gate, the entrance to the Jac-ob Way looked small and unassuming, but that narrow door led directly to Lord Tanas.

"The Jac-ob Way is unusable at the moment, orders straight from Pride Aster. With the large capture of Rodents just now, we are increasing security; we want to make sure that no one gets into the Way from here. You can enter in the

Fifth Circle."

Gab-re silently cursed his luck and the Remnant Rodents. Any other time, a message for Lord Tanas would have granted him passage. Now there was no other choice but to take the longer route through the outer circles of Nis. Traveling through Nis was never easy. In order to make it difficult for an invading force, the city was built like a maze. Entrances between circles were constructed at random points, so going from one circle to another meant having to run completely around the entire city. Gathering up his stamina, Gab-re began running through the winding passages of Nis.

A city of ten circles leading inward, Nis's outermost circle, Maestri, served as its primary defense fort and prison. With watch towers, multiple cell blocks, and training areas, Maestri lived up to its reputation—the circle for those who broke the laws of Nis. Looking up, Gab-re could see lines of metal wires creating a web across the top of the city, wires appropriated from Hy-mun vaults during the Second Great Attempt, that carried messages throughout the city and prevented invaders from climbing over the walls. Traveling through Maestri, Gab-re could hear the Rodents pleading as loud as they could while his fellow Tribe of Shadow members herded them into the cells like animals.

"Stop the Third Great Attempt!" one cried.

"The Third Great Attempt's completion will doom us all!" another said.

"Please! In the name of our ancient kinship, we *Know* it will mean the end of us all!" a third one begged, receiving a rod across his face for mentioning the Tribe of Shadows' relationship to The Remnant by Maestri's head jailor, Don-ati, who ordered the pleading Rodents' skills to be put to more *productive uses* once they were all under lock and key. The locks and bars—once made of stone, but now made from reinforced metals—served as the only other evidence of Hy-mun technology in the circle.

Leaving Maestri, Gab-re didn't dwell on the Rodents as the odor of roasting meat hit him like a wave. Entering Gluttony Mesh-Re always made him hungry. This circle was one of Gab-re's three favorites. Whenever he entered the circle, his nose filled with the smells and odors of the food and meals prepared and served there. As Gab-re moved through the circle's many streets, other members of the Tribe of Shadows moved around him in a joyful dance going about their duties. Some were preparing and seasoning meat so it would taste just right, others drained blood to use for cooking or drink ingredients, hoisting carcasses upside down and splitting them open so the blood would drain into vats beneath. Yet everyone had a smile on their face. All of the jobs that members of the Tribe of Shadows did were considered important to both Nis and the execution of The Plan. However, Gab-re always had a soft spot for those who worked here. The Tribe couldn't function without food, and it wasn't just any food either, it was created from those who died for The Plan. As in other parts of Nis, the walls and buildings of this circle bore rows and rows of names of every member of the Tribe of Shadows who died, along with how they died, and what they had given to The Plan.

"Gab-re, is that you?" a voice called. Gab-re turned and saw his old friend Ju-Nian, one of the head chefs of Gluttony Mesh-Re.

"I'm afraid I can't talk right now, Ju-Nian. I have to get to Yam-Preen. There is urgent news I have to deliver to Lord Tanas, and with the Jac-ob Way closed right now, I can't stall for too long."

"Take this then," Ju-Nian said, passing Gab-re a large tankard. His face, usually a happy one, turning serious. "You'll need it for the rest of your run."

Gab-re gratefully took the tankard and gulped down its contents, an energy soup. He could taste the soup's meat washing over his tongue, refreshing him, and feel it warming and filling his body as energy pulsed from him as it raced down his throat and into his stomach.

"Thanks, Ju-Nian," Gab-re said, passing back the empty tankard and running again with even more speed through the mixing odors of Gluttony Mesh-Re. But the smells of the Second Circle soon gave way to an even more intense sensory stimulation. Turning a corner, he passed through the gate leading into the next circle. The smell of sweat and blood, combining with the heated rosy pink energy of decadence from warriors like himself, pounded against him like the force of multiple heartbeats. It almost made him want to take a short stop from his mission so he could enjoy himself in another of his favorite circles, the Third Circle—Lust Atrophied.

From the time of Nis's construction, the Tribe of Shadows realized it needed more members to combat the Beings of Light. This led to a large-scale breeding program, receiving a needed boost from the Legions of Shadow who arrived with Lord Tanas—who also helped restructure and reorganize the process. In the

71

following generations, the Tribe of Shadows would also include the occasional Remnant Rodent, if one could be caught, to diversify the blood and increase the number of children if a generation was low on females. Sometimes the breeders even added Hy-mun women in an attempt to create a child that could stand Light. But the pure-blooded members of the Tribe of Shadows saw those children, at best, as second-class citizens, and none of the children of Hy-mun women could ever stand Light.

Lust Atrophied was its own self-contained kingdom. All of the women in Nis lived there to provide future generations for the Tribe of Shadows. Running through the circle, Gab-re could smell the fumes from the moss mixtures burning in lava as they filtered through the breeding rooms—a process that never needed refinement. During the city's construction, the Tribe of Shadows discovered mosses that, when burned, produced a gas that both relaxed and stimulated men and women. It was encouraged that every male, whenever he was not engaged with the execution of The Plan or the operation of Nis, spend as much time in Lust Atrophied as possible. Gab-re often found his most pleasurable memories were made in this circle. After running halfway around Lust Atrophied, Gab-re finally reached the entrance to his least favorite circle, Envy Opal-Lo.

Envy Opal-Lo was the teaching circle. In this circle, members of the Tribe of Shadows learned their history, how to tempt, the dangers the Hy-muns presented—including a Second Coming—and the justice in their cause. Gab-re hated this circle because he considered himself a creature of action, not a scholar; although he did enjoy learning how to use the Veil of Shadows and other Hy-mun technology. Envy Opal-Lo, home to Nis's vaults, contained much of the technology the Tribe of Shadows appropriated from the Hy-muns over the generations, especially during the Second Great Attempt. During the Attempt, Hy-muns started burying technology out of fear it would be destroyed, allowing the Tribe of Shadows to claim it, learn how it worked, and eventually use it throughout the city—and against the Hy-muns. The Third Great Attempt, however, would take more than technology and skills learned in Envy Opal-Lo, it would take physical action as well, the kind that echoed around him as he left Envy Opal-Lo and entered his favorite circle, Wrath Eras.

Even if Gab-re had used the Jac-ob Way, he would have heard the din from Wrath Eras. Filled with coliseums and training arenas lit by the glow of the magma, the circle was where creatures of action like Gab-re trained and pitted themselves against one another to become the strongest warriors for both Lord Tanas and Nis, preparing themselves for when the Tribe of Shadows returned to the surface to take it back from the Hy-muns. Making his way through the pathways of Wrath Eras, he noted more names written on its walls, countless members of the Tribe of Shadows who died here, either in training or in actual coliseum battles. Continuing on, he heard the final screams of someone dying, followed by the thunderous roar of the crowds threatening to shake the whole cavern ceiling and bring it down on their heads. A cheer rising up from some place in Wrath Eras signaled only two things, the arrival of a stronger warrior for the Tribe of Shadows, and the birth of a new martyr.

The Tribe of Shadows devoted everything to The Plan, so when one of them died fighting in the coliseums, or during a task for Lord Tanas, he was hailed as a martyr and became a final offering to The Plan. Their bodies were taken back to the Second Circle, where they were prepared and served as food for the strongest warriors in Nis. Gab-re himself fought hard in the coliseum to the roar of the crowd, creating a great number of martyrs whose flesh and blood he later enjoyed alongside other warriors. Coming to the end of Wrath Eras, he turned down a side path to a gate at the end of an alley with stairs leading downward. At the bottom of the stairs he came to a small stone building—barely large enough for five of the Tribe of Shadows warriors—with a gatekeeper on duty standing just inside the metal door and visible through the barred window. Gab-re had arrived at one of Wrath Eras's entrances to the Jac-ob Way.

"I have urgent news for Lord Tanas. I need to get to Yam-Preen and I have been running since Maestri, so open the Jac-ob Way now!" Gab-re shouted to the gatekeeper, extremely frustrated at having to run through five circles. Hearing Lord Tanas's name alone made the gatekeeper obey, quickly. Turning away from the door, and opening a panel on the side of the wall, he revealed a series of switches that he threw to unlock the interior gate in the gatehouse and deactivate the Jac-ob Way's traps. Afterwards, he took a key from his belt and unlocked the gatehouse's front door. Gab-re shoved his way past the gatekeeper and into the gatehouse, almost bumping into the call box mounted on the wall. The gatekeeper, picking himself up, then opened the interior gate, a door rising up from the floor on a slant, like a Hy-mun cellar door. Once opened, Gab-re quickly ran down a series of martyr-inscribed stairs leading to the Jac-ob Way, a simple tunnel lit by two streams of magma funneled down either side of it— where the floor of the tunnel met the curved ceiling—that went either back under the previous circles to the main gate in Maestri, or the rest of the way under Wrath Eras toward the center of Nis. Gab-re was soon on his way and under the next circle, Greed U-Sez.

Greed U-Sez was one Nis's three ruling circles, where decisions were made affecting both The Plan and Nis. Normally, when traveling through the Sixth Circle, Gab-re would have to stop at multiple checkpoints to give information about who he was, whom he was going to see, and why before he could continue. Appropriated Hy-mun technology had sped up the procedure, but it still took a long time. The Sixth Circle of Greed U-Sez conducted all of the main functions occurring within Nis, from the fates of prisoners in Maestri to the scheduling of the gladiatorial fights. However, thanks to the Jac-ob Way, Gab-re could bypass the checkpoints and move on unobstructed. Following the Jac-ob Way, he continued on beneath the Sixth Circle, and eventually underneath the Seventh Circle, Sloth Cur-Nos.

Sloth Cur-Nos was the city's planning circle, where members from the Sixth, Eighth, and Ninth circles gathered to plan strategies without rest. The final details of the Three Great Attempts were planned there before being carried out. Sloth Cur-Nos also contained one distinctive feature, the Great Staircase, an immense flight of steps one had to scale to enter the next circle. The Great Staircase, combined with Gab-re's growing fatigue, was another reason he was thankful he could take the easier route through the Jac-ob Way. Having made it this far, he knew he was only a short distance away from Yam-Preen. Picking up his pace, he continued on down the Jac-ob Way, passing underneath the second of the three ruling circles, the Eighth Circle, Pride Aster.

While Sloth Cur-Nos was where plans were made for what happened outside the city, The Seven ruled on them before carrying them out in Pride Aster. If anything happened outside of Nis, but still below the surface, then it was under the jurisdiction of Pride Aster. This included fortifications and developments around Maestri, the ever-present problem from The Remnant, and current construction of the Great Tunnel—vital to the completion of the Third Great Attempt. As Gab-re approached one of the only two gates located inside the Jac-ob Way, a solid wall taking up almost the entire tunnel, with a single door in it that was protected by an armed guard, he knew that he was almost there.

"Halt!" cried the gatekeeper, his mace whipping out before him as Gab-re approached. "Name, mission, destination, mark?"

"Gab-re Nuance Nor. I am delivering an important message to Lord Tanas in Yam-Preen. Here is my mark." Gab-re pulled at a piece of clothing to show a griffin surrounded by three tears branded onto his chest. It signified him as a full member of the Tribe of Shadows, and gave him unrestricted access to all points in Nis, including the Jac-ob Way.

"Proceed." The gatekeeper said, opening the gate and allowing Gab-re beneath the next circle.

The circle past this gate was no ordinary circle. It was the Ninth Circle of Nis, Circle Emporium, home to The Seven Vices, where they held secret council with Lord Tanas on matters concerning the surface. It was in Circle Emporium that Lord Tanas and The Seven Vices first conceived the Three Great Attempts.

From this point on, Gab-re knew he was entering sacred territory. Circle Emporium was the first section to be built when Nis started expanding, serving the functions of all the others that would follow. The builders constructed it around the original city of Nis—renamed Yam-Preen—in order to protect it, also starting the practice of calling each new section of Nis a "circle."

Journeying this far into Nis was not something that Gab-re, nor any member of the Tribe of Shadows, did very often. He lived in the barracks of the Fifth Circle of Wrath Eras; it was the most his work had merited. Being permitted to live in Circle Emporium, so close to Lord Tanas and The Seven Vices, was an extremely rare privilege only a select few enjoyed after a lifetime of service. However, he knew that soon there would be an even better place waiting for him, the surface. Having seen the cities and buildings built by the Hy-muns after using the Veil of Shadows to travel there, he had a number of places chosen for where he would want to live. The thought made him run even faster to the second gate within the Jac-ob Way, the one separating Circle Emporium from Yam-Preen.

"Halt!" cried the second gatekeeper.

After answering the same questions again, Gab-re passed through the second gate and up the stairs to his destination, Yam-Preen, the home of Lord Tanas.

P.J. Fenton

Chapter 9

After Circle Emporium was built, and the Tribe of Shadows began expanding outward, Yam-Preen—the original city of Nis—fell into ruin and disrepair. Despite petitions to restore Yam-Preen, Lord Tanas declared if Yam-Preen wanted to fall into ruin, the Tribe of Shadows should let it. It would serve as a constant symbolic reminder of the ruin the Beings of Light brought down on their world, and a physical timekeeper showing how long the Tribe of Shadows remained in exile. Almost all of Yam-Preen now stood in an advanced state of decay and rot. All around Gab-re, buildings as old as the Tribe of Shadows itself wasted away.

Once they were solid, Gab-re thought to himself, running through Yam-Preen. Buildings originally built from pieces of black stone now appeared granular, made of dust and sand, as the veins of decaying brown and sickly yellow rotting energy continued to eat through them. *A child could easily demolish any one of these bare-handed, and the wreckage wouldn't even hurt the child as it collapsed.*

Yet looking around at his surroundings, Gab-re felt a great sense of pride. Despite everything that the Beings of Light had done to his people: stealing their world, making it uninhabitable by bringing Light to it, killing their kin, forcing them underground, and creating another race that continued living off their land, the Tribe of Shadows had endured, survived, and fought. Now the time was finally within reach when they would remove the Light from their world and retake it.

As long as the Hy-muns don't get in the way, Gab-re thought privately. *I had better hurry to Decca-Ju Tower, and fast.* Taking a deep breath, he made his last sprint to his destination.

Built like a step pyramid, Decca-Ju Tower had triangular sides resembling stairs climbing from the square base of the tower to its apex. The main entrance, on the second tier of the tower, was a solid stone door at the top of a normal stairway. Decca-Ju Tower had been the private home of Lord Tanas ever since it was constructed, soon after he arrived in Nis. It was also the one structure among all of the rot and decay of Yam-Preen that seemed immune to the effects of age. The obsidian-black walls, which should have aged to dust, looked as fresh as the day they were cut, gleaming in the illumination of the four great rivers of magma below that slowly snaked and oozed their ways out of the corners of the tower, before breaking into the various streams filtering throughout Nis. The illumination from this magma creating a glow throughout the city said to be similar to the Glow experienced on the surface before "The Coming." Except the old Glow was supposed to have been a myriad of different colors instead of only a few colors; also cool, not scorching hot like the magma glow.

The doorman silently greeted Gab-re, leading him into the main foyer of the tower, a long hallway adorned with griffins—the personal standard of Lord Tanas. Giant carvings of the winged creatures with fierce claws outstretched lined the walls, continuing up the stairs to the tower's highest level, to Lord Tanas's chambers. After a loud knock on the door, the word "Enter" echoed from inside. The door opened, and Gab-re found himself face-to-face with Lord Tanas, standing by a window and wrapped in a simple cloth robe with a hood over his head.

What would happen if an enemy reached Lord Tanas? There are so few here, and most are only servants. Gab-re once wondered. However, after standing in the presence of Lord Tanas, he immediately knew the answer. Lord Tanas himself was all the protection he ever needed. Their ruler was at least as old as Nis itself, only he knew how much older. Some said it was his sheer determination to best the Master of the Beings of Light that had allowed him to stay alive, while the members of his original Legion of Shadows grew old and died; others said it was a curse placed upon him. No matter how he managed it, one thing was certain; he was still by far the mightiest being in all of Nis. Being in the same room as Lord Tanas, gazing upon him, surrounded by griffin statues that bowed to his feet as he walked across the chamber, Gab-re struggled for words. Lord Tanas's sheer presence felt so immense, so deep, and—despite the heat from the magma—so cold that by just standing before Lord Tanas, he felt like he was falling into him, freezing solid, quickly approaching the point where he would simply shatter.

"Speak," Lord Tanas commanded. His voice was calm and level, yet it carried an authority that demanded response.

"Yes, my Lord!" That one word from Lord Tanas was all the motivation Gab-re needed to pull himself out of his trance. "I have a report from Observation Point 6. A team of Hy-mun intruders have invaded our territory and are setting up a base dangerously close to the Keyblast point where we will trigger the Third Great Attempt. Initial observations show a definite possibility that more Hy-muns will be joining them. It is unknown at this time whether or not the Hy-muns are aware of our plans. Mi-che is still observing them while Ra-phe is alerting other observation points in case more Hy-mun intruders arrive at those locations."

Lord Tanas walked to the window where he had been standing, looking out over the rotting Yam-Preen and beyond it to the rest of Nis. Gab-re heard he often did this when he was with someone and needed to think about something. He also heard Lord Tanas could take anywhere from a few minutes to enough time to make a person nearly die of thirst before he came to a decision. Thankfully, Lord Tanas didn't take that long. He went to his desk and took some paper out of a drawer. After writing on it and engraving it with his seal, he handed it back to Gab-re.

"Take this to Pride Aster," Lord Tanas commanded. "This is a requisition order. War Control will provide you with the best warriors from Wrath Eras.

Take them and attack these intruders, and if more come, attack them as well. Take no prisoners, unless you find them useful to us in one way or another."

"So be it, Lord Tanas." With those words, Gab-re left Lord Tanas's chambers and made his way out of Decca-Ju Tower.

After Gab-re was a fair distance away, Lord Tanas looked out of his window again.

This is very bad, he said silently to himself. *I have spent more generations among these... these... savages than I would have wanted, thanks to that cursed Ash Addiel's punishment. Invaders arrive, and that fool Gab-re needs to run all the way here for me to tell him what to do. My original legions wouldn't have needed me to speak to know what to do. It's amazing that any of these creatures survived being exterminated during "The Coming." Still, they have proven useful over the ages. My legions certainly found their women enjoyable, and after seeing what I could do, the savages were certainly quick to follow me like vermin to the sound of a flute.*

Lord Tanas chuckled to himself, gazing out over Nis, a city built mostly at his direction by a people who had come to love, fear, and worship him.

This plan will not be stopped. I have been working on it ever since the betrayal that led me and my legions to being locked down in this hole to rot. Once it is done, I will finally be free of this pit and these savages for good. Lord Tanas started laughing out loud as he thought about some of the Hy-mun stories that grew up around their activities.

"I hope those Hy-muns believe in legends, because they are about to have a very bad run-in with some cave snatchers."

Chapter 10

"I can't believe you actually think Cave Snatchers exist, Worm."

The Pre-Mining Project Party was going on at AB's. Reye, Raymond, and Worm were eating dinner alongside their friends, Edward Heller and Ann Branley—the only other person from their group selected for the mining project. They started dinner with talk about some of the dangers early miners and spelunkers encountered when Worm brought up an old legend about creatures called Cave Snatchers, which Edward—the king of rational thought—quickly dismissed.

"Doubt me all you want, Edward. Reports go back to the earliest spelunking journals involving the Prison Caverns in the Yellow Dominion. They all talk about seeing unknown beings, moving in the darkness, shying from light, that are responsible for snatching people and disappearing with them into the darkness."

"He's right, you know," Raymond agreed, swallowing a forkful of food. "I've read those reports about creatures in the Prison Caverns. Personally, I would love to get in there and try to meet them."

"Raymond, your opinion on the matter doesn't count," Edward countered, with a disregarding sneer. "You would jump into a volcano if you thought there was an island in there populated by a race of mysterious beings."

"Well, maybe not 'jump' in, just so long as I can 'live no regrets,'" Raymond admitted, slightly embarrassed, before remembering his dinner and shoveling more food into his mouth. He knew full well that Edward was right. He would go to the ends of Prism if he could discover something new, driven by his own personal desire to make the most out of his life and to see his name remembered.

"Anyway Worm," Edward continued. "The Prison Caverns are the oldest and deepest caves on the continent. Deep caverns mean people get lost and never come out. The strangeness comes from their sense of self degrading with time and solitude, which is also documented. Why they shy from light? It's because their eyes become so used to darkness they can't stand the light anymore, and when people follow them, they get lost too."

"So, you do agree with me that there are Cave Snatchers?" Worm said, feeling hopeful.

"No, I think people can get lost in those caves and go crazy if they're not careful, not that there are strange creatures native to the dark that go around snatching miners and spelunkers." Edward was getting irritated at Worm now. "It's ridiculous that someone of your age Worm, would *still* believe in legends and stories like Cave Snatchers. Those stories are used to scare children at night, not to be taken as literal truth.

"There is just no logical way a race of 'creatures' could have lived undetected beneath the surface of the world without anyone finding some trace of them. On the other hand, everything I've just stated is perfectly logical, and psychologically proven. For example, staying underground for long periods of time results in delusions and bouts of paranoia." Edward spread his hands in conclusion, preparing to make his final point. "One of the first things I've learned in my pure logic and psychology classes is that everything can be explained scientifically, rationally, and logically. Developing a mature mind means dismissing superstitions for reality. Why you Worm, a constant believer in ghost stories and legends, can't seem to do that is beyond me."

"In other words, as far as you're concerned, nihil ultra," Worm replied. Edward looked at him blankly.

"Nothing beyond," Worm translated. "Meaning 'nothing beyond' your range of thinking could possibly exist."

"Worm!" Reye interrupted, hoping to change the topic. She knew an argument with Edward on rational explanations could easily go back and forth all night. "Don't the Prison Caverns have some kind of religious significance?"

Worm turned to Reye and smiled, recognizing immediately what she was doing.

"Yes, the Prison Caverns do have religious significance attached to them. They are actually connected with Cave Snatchers lore, would you like to discuss *that*, Edward?" Worm turned his head directly to Edward while making his last point about Cave Snatchers.

Reye, cursing herself silently, realized she had forgotten that Cave Snatcher lore was tied with the religious significance of the Yellow Dominion's Prison Caverns, and while Worm might back off if he had an excuse, he didn't give an inch in an argument when he got into one. Worm's last comment brought both him and Edward back into the debate. It wasn't long after that they were arguing again, this time about griffins and unicorns.

On the other hand, with Worm locked in debate after debate with Edward, it took his mind off not being selected for the mining project, something that he had been trying to explain logically to himself all day. Reye secretly thought Worm had that in mind when he started the dispute; it was the kind of nice thing he would do. Raymond, meanwhile, was still working on his own plate of food after being shut out of Worm and Edward's argument.

Raymond never could hold a conversation with Edward for very long, Reye thought to herself, watching her brother eat, and Worm and Edward argue. *The fact that my brother is not only an adventurer, but the second biggest adrenaline junkie I know after myself, doesn't help him much in an argument with Edward. All he has to do is bring up any one of the extreme challenges that Raymond's done since coming to Spectral Academy—like skydiving from an airship—to make his point. As far as Edward's concerned, anybody who likes thrill seeking is acting irrationally and illogically.*

"I believe we were talking, Reye?" Ann asked, frowning even deeper than usual, and annoyed at being put off while Reye tried to handle someone else's situation.

Ann Branley was one of the most pessimistic people Reye had ever met. When they all first arrived at AB's and Reye congratulated Ann on being accepted into the project, it was one of the few times she had ever seen Ann smile. Ann believed that if you are always expecting something to go wrong, you'll be less disappointed, and more prepared, for when it did. A student of physics, especially entropy theories—the idea that the world is becoming increasingly chaotic—only made her pessimism worse. But Ann was also a brilliant student of volcanology, having studied volcanoes even longer than Reye, and was thrilled to be using that knowledge. Originally from the Red Dominion, she had the same red hair and brown eyes as Professor Heart, and the same complexion. She also came from the Rise Palace, the state where the Demp Caverns and the mining project was located. Because of that, she had lots of information on the Demp Caverns, including maps and books to review with Reye during dinner, so getting put off by her only made her more annoyed—even if she was expecting it.

"Sorry, Ann, what were we talking about again?" Reye apologized, with a slight chuckle.

"You really need to pay more attention when people are talking to you," Raymond added from behind her shoulder after swallowing his food. He knew how easily Reye could get distracted and not listen to others. Reye, on the other hand, just grumbled under her breath at Raymond's remark.

"What was that?" Raymond asked.

"Thank you for your advice, Raymond," Reye responded politely, but mentally added, *I hate it when you do that.*

"Yes, thank you Raymond," Ann continued, glad that at least one person in this group would listen to her when she talked. "Reye does need to pay better attention when people are talking to her. Otherwise she might miss something important one day." Ann and Raymond both shared a brief laugh while Reye blankly looked at Ann, waiting for her to continue, to show she could "pay better attention when people are talking."

"Anyway," Ann said, her normal gloomy attitude returning, "back to this new fault system." She pointed to the composite map taken from airborne balloons showing the Red, Orange, Yellow, and Green Dominions.

"Oh yeah," Reye said, leaning forward excitedly.

"These early signs show a new fault system that could run from the Red Dominion to the Orange, Yellow, and Green Dominions, beneath Tri-Dominion City, and into the Violet Dominion." Ann ran her finger across the supposedly affected areas of the map, studying the fault system and pulling out new maps detailing each new region as she explained them. "You realize what this means?"

"An increase in seismic activity throughout all of the affected regions," Reye said, as if answering a question in class.

"And a possible increase in magma flow under all of the affected areas. That could lead to the appearance of new volcanoes, *on land.*"

"Now, that I have to disagree with," Edward said, joining the discussion. "Volcanoes only appear in the ocean, and I should know. There is no scientific reason to believe that volcanoes will *ever* form on land. The land is far too stable and all volcanic pressure is vented through the Red Dominion, as well as the faults and tunnels terranauts dig into the sea. That's been documented and proven ages ago, even Worm will agree with me on that."

Edward, with his tan skin, blue eyes, and black hair, was from the Blue Dominion, a dominion made up of a large island in the Great Lagoon Sea and a few small peninsulas attached to the continent. Both the Great Lagoon Sea and the oceans north and west of Worm's native Indigo Dominion were spotted with various active, dormant, and extinct volcanoes that erupted out of the water. Those volcanoes—created, like Edward said, from releasing volcanic pressure—formed their own little islands, and were often the subject of study, and attempts at forming new settlements by citizens of both nations. Throughout recorded history, Hy-muns had only witnessed volcanoes forming out in the ocean, bursting from the surface of the water before taking a cylindrical form—similar to a chimney on a house roof.

"I agree that volcanoes have only appeared in the oceans," Worm replied. "The one that formed near my home Palace still produces the best ash storms I have ever seen. The sight is second only to a winter snowstorm."

"Ha!" Edward shouted triumphantly, feeling he brought Worm over to his *rational* side.

"But that doesn't mean that they can't form on land as well," Worm continued. "The volcanoes of the Red Dominion are proof of that. Unless, of course, you strictly believe they were created by the Nag-el as forges for their devices, like it says in the religious texts."

Edward just grumbled, turning his face away, and returned to his dinner.

"Thank you, Worm," Ann gracefully responded. She never expected support, but was glad to have it whenever it came. "Now, like I was saying, with this possibility of new magma flows and the chance of volcanoes appearing on land, it means potentially more projects being offered, and more training missions with terranauts!" Ann, like Reye, was also studying to become a terranaut.

"So, what's the bad news?" Reye asked casually. She knew that with Ann, there had to be bad news.

"Like I said before Edward butted in, it means more earthquakes happening across the affected regions, and the absolute worst—volcanoes appearing on land. Imagine, for a second, what would happen if a volcano popped up in the Yellow Dominion and cut the Great Line River in half. The Dominion's chief water transportation route and habitable zone would be destroyed. Then there's the Green Dominion. If a volcano erupted there, the lava would incinerate the agricultural plains practically overnight." Ann's expression was grim; she was clearly worried about the possibilities. She had been theorizing what would happen if even one volcano erupted on land with Professor Heart, and what she came up with scared her.

"You're being a doom talker, Ann," Edward complained, recognizing that she was going into her chaos mode, when she would start making theories based on nothing but chance and conditions, factors that Edward refused to deal with. "This is supposed to be a dinner party. You keep up like this and you're going to go into that theory you've been working on about how a volcano can destroy the world."

"It can happen Edward," Ann replied, looking straight into his eyes, her face deathly serious. "If the conditions are right—"

"Ann," Reye interrupted, also recognizing her chaos mode, "give it a rest and eat your food." Reye had heard Ann's volcano-related destruction theories before, and was just as tired of them as everyone else.

"She's right," Raymond added, joining the conversation. "Dessert is going to be here soon, so why don't we forget all the doom talk and focus on the sweets instead?"

Ann slumped in her seat; she hated getting cut off just for the sake of food, but she expected it.

"Nobody thinks about these things until it's too late," she murmured. But with dessert soon to be added to their table, even Ann found it easy to get off the subjects of the project, and volcanic danger, and focus on the party.

After dinner, the group split up, heading back to their dorms, or out to have fun of their own kind. Worm went back to his own dorm after collecting some material from Ann.

"So, you're sure you don't mind holding this stuff for me, Worm?"

"Don't worry about it, Ann. With all the books I've got, a few more bags won't be so much more to look at. Besides, I could always use a change of pace to my reading, provided I find it interesting."

"Well, see you later," Raymond cried, walking off in the movie theater's direction.

Worm waved good-bye to everyone and left, along with Edward and Ann, who said they were going to stop by the library on the way back to Spectral Academy to look for some books.

Or so they claim, Reye thought privately to herself. Reye often paired people in her mind as a couple if she saw them going anywhere together alone, whether they were a couple or not. Once, while visiting Worm, she found Ann with him looking for religious material she could use for her volcano papers. Reye quickly became flustered left, her imagination getting the best of her, and leaving them wondering what she was so nervous about.

I think I'll also go and see a movie. Maybe I can catch up with Raymond, we always have fun together, Reye thought to herself, imagining the two of them sitting together and making fun of the movie and its characters.

"Raymond, wait up! I'm coming with you."

Raymond turned around and saw his sister racing up behind him.

Why am I not surprised? Raymond thought to himself, wondering why his sister didn't just leave with him in the first place.

"You sure you want to go out tonight, you wouldn't want to rest, pack, or get mentally prepared for the trip?"

"Of course I'm sure. The way I feel now I don't need any rest. I can always pack later, and I'm already mentally prepared for whatever excitement is waiting for me on the project. What's wrong with having some fun now?"

Raymond smiled and shook his head, not just because his sister was being his sister, but because he could guess how she would behave once they had left for the trip. He agreed that it would be better to have their fun now while they still could.

"Okay Reye, let's go, just promise me one thing."

"What's that, Raymond?" Reye asked.

"Don't complain when we don't get to the project as fast as you are expecting to get there."

Reye replied by playfully punching her brother in the arm, walking off into the night.

Chapter 11

"How much longer do you think until we get there, Raymond?" Reye asked from her seat next to him in the wagon. The wagon ride was the last stretch of their trip, and a necessary one since the bus they were going to take broke down before they arrived.

"Not much longer now," Raymond answered, sighing through the big smile on his face, just as excited as she was to be on the project.

On the day of their departure, as all the selected students gathered at the station to take them first to the tram, and then to Light Point Airfield, Reye and Raymond never looked more alike. Every bit of the excitement and joy Reye felt over being a part of the project perfectly mirrored the looks on Raymond's face. She knew her brother felt just as happy as she did about being a part of the project, and more importantly, since they were going together, it made being a part of the project mean so much more to her. No matter what happened, he would be there, and she could count on him to know *exactly* what she was feeling throughout the entire project.

"I'm glad you're here," Reye whispered to Raymond privately as the airship took off from the Platinum Throne for the Rise Palace in the Red Dominion. "There isn't anyone I can think of I would rather have by my side on this project."

"Not even Stella?" Raymond asked, a little surprised that she would choose him over her best friend.

"Not even Stella," Reye admitted, "but don't tell her I said that."

Raymond laughed at the comment, enjoying the excitement as they traveled to Aka, the closest city to the Demp Caverns. After Aka, traveling became less luxurious because of the unexpected change from bus to wagons. The wagons were both slow and uncomfortable. Every slight hole jarred them around on the hard wooden benches.

While just as excited as Reye to be going on this trip, Raymond didn't feel the need to ask, "How much longer," every five minutes like she did from the moment the wagons started to move. He knew it was just his sister's way of venting her excitement on the one person she could count on to take it, but it was quickly becoming annoying to everyone, including the director, who eyed Reye disdainfully.

"You know," Reye said wistfully, "I bet I could run the rest of the way to the site, be there before these wagons, and let everyone know we are on the way. You think the director will let me?"

"Absolutely not," Raymond said, giving Reye a cautious look, warning her not to do anything that could get her into trouble, or worse, sent back to Spectral Academy.

"Come on, Raymond, I can tell the director that I'm going to announce our arrival and to get everything ready for us so we can head down to the camp once we arrive. I'd bet my spot on the mining project that I'm not the only one who wants to get off these wagons and get to the camp."

"Betting your spot's exactly what you would be doing," Raymond said, concerned at what his sister was thinking. "Don't tell me you've already forgotten what almost happened to us the day we left for Spectral Academy?"

"I think I've improved a lot since then," Reye challenged smugly, yet they both knew it still wasn't as long ago as she pretended it to be. When Reye and Raymond first left for Spectral Academy, she was so excited about going, she shot up out of her seat on the bus and ran to the front of it and started fiddling with the door, trying to get out so she could try running to the airship port before turning around and bolting for the back of the bus to try its back door when Raymond stood up in the aisle and caught her. He talked her down afterwards, but the outburst nearly got the two of them expelled and sent home before they even reached the Platinum Throne.

"You're thinking I'm still the same person I was when we left home, aren't you?" Reye asked, flashing her brother an accusing look. "If I was the same person, then I would have already jumped off this wagon and started running."

"And you would probably beat everyone else there," Raymond conceded, knowing firsthand how fast she was. "But once everyone caught up to you, the director would have no problem sending you back to Spectral Academy."

"He would have to catch me first." Reye laughed. "I'm the number two runner on the marathon team for a reason. I have the second fastest pair of legs on the Platinum Throne. Besides, who says I'm the only one who has to jump off the wagon and start running? I *know* you hate this ride as much as I do, and you want to get started on your dreams of becoming an adventurer as much as I want to become a terranaut, so why don't we get a few people together and all of us start running?"

Raymond couldn't lie to himself, he did hate the wagon ride, and the idea of ditching the wagons to run the rest of the way on foot did appeal to him.

"Come on, Raymond, let's do it, all of us together, racing toward our dreams, just like back home when we were working to get into the Dominion Advancement Program so we could go to Spectral Academy. It would be no different, I *know* that the idea must get you excited."

Raymond did smile at the idea of him and Reye jumping off the wagon and racing toward the project site. He still remembered the days from when he and Reye decided to join the Dominion Advancement Program, to when their acceptance letters came in. Every day felt like a constant race toward their dreams, a race where they supported and encouraged each other daily. Not that she needed much encouraging; once she set her mind toward a goal, she always kept running until she reached it. For Raymond, sometimes the best he could do was just keep up with her and make sure she didn't get distracted. Now that they were students in Spectral Academy, and on their way to a mining project, with both of their dreams just the proverbial one step away, all that seemed to be standing before them was one terrible wagon ride.

"What do you say Raymond?" Reye asked, looking at the other students in the wagon. "Which students do you think we should talk to first about running the rest of the way? Live no regrets, right?"

Raymond chuckled at the absurdity of the thought. Despite what someone like Edward might think, he knew the difference between a crazy idea, and a stupid one.

"You're right, I do hate this ride, and I do want to get started toward my own dreams as soon as possible, and have no regrets about it." Throughout the whole trip, he fantasized about life as an adventurer after Spectral Academy. Exploring the unmapped regions of the Seraph Sea, deep caverns and fissures around the continent, and any other unexplored area he could get to.

"However, if you're hoping to encourage *this* crowd to jump out of the wagons and start running, you're wrong." Raymond cast his eyes over the other members of the project, many of whom seemed perfectly content to stay in the wagons, letting themselves be pulled along.

"I just thought it would be a good idea," Reye puffed, crossing her arms, frowning, and trying to get comfortable in the seat again. "You know I want you to get the chance to grab your dreams as soon as possible too. You're my brother, and I want the best for you," she added with a grin.

You have gotten a little better, Raymond thought, matching her smile. He knew Reye wanted to get started on this project, they both did, and he knew that she was thinking about him as well, but he also didn't want either one of them to lose their spots because they let their excitement and enthusiasms get the best of them. *But deep down, I still think you are still the* same person *you were when we first left for Spectral Academy; otherwise you wouldn't need me to be by your side. I don't want you to mess this project up for yourself and regret it before you even arrive.*

"So anyway, how much longer do you think until we get there?" Reye asked, making Raymond throw his head back in humorous exasperation.

Ann wasn't that much different from Reye. Being back in her home Palace again was getting her to shake off her pessimism and get excited, and she was expressing her excitement by pointing out sites and rock formations she recognized.

"Those rock towers that look like salt shakers were formed by ancient solidified volcanic ash from the land-based volcanoes in this dominion. And those formations…"

Even Sol, who for most of the trip hadn't said anything to anyone, just hanging around wearing a hiker's backpack, turned cheerful as they approached the descent site, surprising everyone with special mission badges he made.

"I would like each of you to have one of these," Sol said, gracefully handing a badge to each member of the project. Each badge showed a sun shining over a cave entrance. "They're my gift to everyone on this project, so we can head underground and bring our light to a new world." Reye noticed Stella looking at her badge more affectionately than the other students, stroking the badge tenderly as they arrived at the Demp Caverns Descent Site.

The descent site wasn't much to look at; the camp's main feature was the descent elevator, assembled for bringing the base camp materials down into the cavern after it was scouted. Pitched around the elevator were a number of large circular tents that almost looked like giant white tires lying on the ground. The project director led the students to a waiting room tent pitched next to the elevator and went inside the communication tent to use the radio. Reye and the others took the chance to stretch their legs in the shadow of the elevator's immense framework and its exposed cables, pulleys, and counterweights. Seizing a momentary break, Reye decided to take the opportunity to quickly chat with Stella.

"Sol's given you an opening, Stella."

"An opening for what?" Stella asked, pretending she didn't know what Reye was talking about, even though her face was turning bright red.

"You know what I mean. Sol gave you a badge, so go and say thank you. It's a good way to start talking to him."

"He gave *everyone* a badge, Reye," Stella replied stubbornly, with a look showing she was not going to be moved easily. "It's not like it was just for me."

"Oh, boy, what am I going to do with you, Stella?" Reye felt like she was running into a wall with Stella every time she brought Sol up, a wall she didn't know how to break down. But considering all of them were going to be spending a lot of time together underground, she knew she would have another opportunity.

"Okay! Everyone, gather around!" The director called, coming back into the waiting room tent, summoning the students to join him.

"I just got off the radio with the people down in the camp, and they are ready for us. Everyone move quietly and orderly into the elevator, and we'll bring you down. Once we are at the base, you will be handed over to the powers that be down there, and they'll take charge of you, directing you to your supervisors, and your living quarters. From there, you will be given your duties, and you *school kids* will get a taste of what it really feels like to be part of the working world."

That last comment elicited a few laughs from some of the more "prestigious" students, and Reye could understand why. She didn't doubt the workers realized it too, joking about how most of them didn't look like they ever seriously worked a day in their lives. The prestigious students came to the project dressed in designer work gear, all clean, never been worn, and probably destined for the trash or a trophy case after the project was over. The most stress these students suffered came from choosing what clothes to put on in the morning.

It bugged Reye a little that there were so many of these types of students here, because they took spots from students that *really* wanted to be a part of this project, and probably signed on just so they could have story to tell back at Spectral Academy. However, Reye wasn't about to let anything distract her now. Soon she would take her first real step on the road to becoming a terranaut, an underground dive, a necessary prerequisite for most of the co-op projects she encountered at Spectral Academy, and her first chance to make contacts of her own. As the director gathered everyone into the elevator, she saw the look in her brother's eyes. They were burning with the same adventure's excitement she always saw Raymond get whenever he was about to go somewhere new. As the silver elevator doors closed with a bang, the elevator's motor came to life, and Reye began feeling herself descend underground—imagining her future once the project was done.

First, she thought to herself, *I'll get back and brag to everyone about how great I did, how many friends and contacts I made, and how I finally got Stella and Sol to become a couple. Then I'll sign up for every project I can find, using the contacts I make here for references, and do great on them. Once I've graduated, I'll join the Terranaut Training Team. Before I'm thirty-three, I'll have my first mission piloting a ship through the lava flows of Prism. It all starts here.*

The deeper Reye sank into the ground, the higher her dreams and plans for the future soared into the clouds. Looking around during the descent—through the elevator's transparent windows inside the car—she memorized different rock types and formations so she could tell anyone where one type of volcanic rock ended and another began and what each protrusion and crack meant from a terranaut's perspective. As the elevator slid down its guide rail, Reye identified another rail next to it, the emergency one-man rocket's track, a special elevator that could hold one person and be launched quickly via rocket propulsion to make a trip to the surface in the event of an emergency, or to sound an advance alarm for supplies, medical assistance, and evacuation in case the main elevator broke down.

Reye's train of thought came to an abrupt halt when the elevator hit ground with a shake, compressing the springs beneath it as the doors opened before her. A rush of cold air from the cavern filled the elevator compartment, bringing her imagination to life. Pictures of herself working with technicians around the camp and piloting magma ships flashed through her head. Fighting every urge to run out and start working, she walked with the other students into the giant cavern the miners transformed into the project's base camp. Off to the side she spotted Sol, hanging back a bit and standing alone by the one-man elevator—a metal egg-shaped capsule fixed to a rail with a rocket on one end of it.

However, as the elevator door closed behind her, and the group walked into the base camp, she quickly noticed something was wrong. Nobody met them; the whole area was quiet as a tomb. Reye knew enough from her studies about mining project base camps to know they were hubs of activity. It didn't matter what time it was; there was always something going on, making noise throughout the camp, causing a mess, or creating some kind of disturbance. But this camp was quiet, completely clean—as if it had been professionally washed—with no oil stains from machinery, and no dust or dirt from mine cars, the camp was spotless, and devoid of all activity.

"Hey!" a student yelled to the director. "The guys down here said it was clear, right?"

"Yeah," the director answered, sounding just as puzzled. "It was a new guy over the radio, and he said they were cleaning up a mess, but we could come down. He also said they decided to do something special for the group, so maybe this has something to do with it."

Reye didn't believe the miners would do something as childish as disappear, and then jump out and scream, "SURPRISE!" Miners had a reputation for being more serious than that. In fact, she felt they would probably be so busy down here with work they wouldn't even have time for jokes.

"Reye, what's wrong here?" Stella asked nervously, moving next to her. Raymond quickly joined them.

"Something funny is going on," Raymond muttered.

He's worried, Reye thought, peering into her brother's eyes, and recognizing the look in them. It was the same look he had whenever he felt the two of them were getting in over their heads. What was worse, she felt worried too.

These mining projects were supposed to run like well-oiled machines, even when everyone was asleep. To arrive at the base camp and find it deserted with nothing but silence waiting for them was not right. It made Reye begin to realize how people could become claustrophobic in these caverns. Alone with the surrounding walls, a person could feel as if he or she was buried alive.

"All right, people, listen up!" the director announced, projecting his voice over the crowd, all of whom were beginning to talk nervously about what was going on. "I am going to the radio room to check with whoever called us down here. I want the rest of you—"

The director didn't finish his next sentence. The lights in the base camp suddenly went out, plunging the camp into complete darkness, and sending the students into a panic.

Chapter 12

Reye was alone in the dark; stripped of light, she felt stripped of breath. The sounds of students shouting and running into each other echoed throughout the cavern, creating an awful din of curses and stumbles, only adding to the chaos.

This was the second time Reye ever found herself lost in darkness—the first was when she went into a cave alone on a dare and her lantern broke. Reye decided that, to be safe, she would stay still and not move. Both Reye and her brother studied blind fighting in martial arts to learn how to move and act without sight—a decision based on that cave incident—but this was nothing like their martial arts school. When she trained with a blindfold on, with her eyes closed behind it, she could always see a glow behind her eyelids, telling her the light was still there, and she could still feel the reassuring presence of her brother. Now she was alone, completely removed from all light and sense of who and what was around her.

Dropping to one knee to help keep her balance, Reye placed both her arms across her face to protect it from anything that might be thrown in her direction. Suddenly, a body bumped into her back, and a hand grasped her shoulder. She almost lashed out on instinct until she heard a familiar voice.

"Reye, is that you I'm holding?" It was Stella's voice, but Reye didn't know if it was her hand.

Reye grasped the arm, following it up, she slowly stood up until her hands were feeling the head and face that the arm belonged to. Her own head and face now set against an unknown forehead.

"Can you feel my hands on your face?" Reye whispered, hoping only Stella could hear her if they were as close as she thought they were. "What about my forehead, my breath?"

"Yes," Stella said. "And by the way, lay off on the onion sticks, your breath stinks."

"Thank goodness." Reye laughed, happy to have Stella right in front of her. "Don't let go of my shoulder, Stella. Whatever you do, stay right at my back, don't leave that spot. Raymond, are you still standing?" Reye shouted, placing Stella's hand back on her shoulder and crying into the darkness.

"I'm still standing!" Raymond yelled back. His voice came from behind Reye, sounding as tense as she was, but also relieved to hear his sister's voice again—a feeling Reye mutually shared.

"Ann, are you around anywhere?" Reye called out to her other friend, feeling more secure now that she knew Raymond and Stella were okay, but receiving no reply.

Instead, she heard footsteps—light ones, the kind that someone made if they walked barefooted, or with flimsy boots, instead of the heavy footsteps the students and miners made with their construction boots—followed by a scream. Not the confused scream of someone who fell over in the dark. This was the kind she had heard numerous times on the farm, when an animal was struck with a killing blow, and cried its last breath before dying.

"Someone… something is out there," Stella sputtered, terror making her voice shrill as more screams began echoing throughout the camp, accompanied by the sound of even more footsteps coming *into* the camp *from* the caverns.

"Just stay close, Stella, and do not let go of me!" Reye said, fear creeping into her voice. Sweat dripping down from her forehead as her heart started racing.

No such thing as Cave Snatchers, eh, Edward? Reye thought to herself, remembering Edward and Worm argument at the restaurant. The thought alone would have made her laugh if she wasn't so scared. Her eyes burned as they strained trying to see anything in the darkness. But try as she might, she could see nothing, only hear the ever approaching sounds of killing and death. As far as she could tell, these *were* Cave Snatchers. But unlike the stories, they were *killing*, not snatching, and Reye knew the only reason why she wasn't dead yet was because the other students created a buffer zone between them, a buffer zone that was quickly shrinking with each student cut down.

"Reye, get ready, here they come," Raymond said to her, the light footsteps almost upon them. Reye didn't know how anyone could be "ready" in a situation like this, but she was relieved to have him nearby.

Raymond's always been there with me, especially when things were really bad, Reye thought to herself, wondering how near or far Raymond could be from her based on his voice. Straining her own ears until she could feel them burning, struggling to hear the next footstep over the screams.

Was it getting closer, moving away, what were the attackers doing? The next sound she heard was a grunt from Raymond, his fist hitting something solid, followed by several more impacts as he fended off whatever was attacking him.

Now where will they come from...left! Reye felt something threaten her from her left side, and stepped back to her right with Stella just as something passed by her. Reye punched forward, feeling her fist connect with flesh. A slight moan came from the attacker while Stella stumbled behind her. Reye was glad she could land a hit, but knew it would only be a matter of time before the killing blow struck her, or worse, Raymond or Stella. Whatever these creatures were— Cave Snatchers or something else, they didn't need light. The metallic smell of blood saturating the air was a testament to their effectiveness at killing in total darkness.

Oh, Great Master Ash Addiel, Reye silently prayed to herself, *if you're listening, please give us a miracle, please LET THERE BE LIGHT!*

A whistling sound like a firework echoed in the cavern. But instead of a flowery pattern of light, a bright orb hovered in the air, illuminating the cavern, and giving Reye her first glimpse of both her attackers and the damage they caused.

They were about a head taller than Reye, wearing metal plate armor around the upper parts of their bodies, had diamond-shaped pointed ears, and were lean and muscular. Stopping their assault, the attackers covered their red eyes as they began writhing in pain. Reye watched as their blue skin turned black, the light burning them, as a rotting smell filled the air from cracking and blistering skin. Looking around, Reye saw a large number of these creatures standing amidst a field of bodies.

These creatures must be what happened to the mining crew that was supposed to meet us, Reye suspected.

The creatures tried resuming their assault, though still hindered by the pain. As for the students who were still alive, at first they froze in shock when they saw their attackers, then a flurry of activity broke out. Some of them tried fighting back, but most ran for the elevator. Glancing toward the elevator, Reye couldn't believe what she saw. By the one-man rocket lift—the last place she saw him—was Sol, wearing dark-tinted glasses over his eyes, and a manically wide smile across his face. His backpack sat open on the ground, with some sort of smoking launcher coming out of it.

Sol did this. But how— Reye's thoughts were cut short as Sol, without looking back, climbed into the one-man lift and shot off toward the surface, leaving a number of questions racing through Reye's mind. *Is Sol getting help? Is he leaving us? Is he running away? Is he…?*

CRACK!

"Ah!"

Reye heard the cracking sound of bones breaking, followed by a piercing cry of pain, and the sound of a body hitting the ground next to her. Remembering the people still there, she turned around.

Reye saw a sight that would haunt her for the rest of her life. Raymond, lying on the ground, his leg twisted into a completely unnatural position. Distracted by the sudden appearance of Sol's light orb, he didn't notice one of the creatures rise from the ground and make a swing at his leg with a giant hammer made of stone and metal. Now, towering above him, the creature prepared another—final—hammer strike. Raymond looked up to both Reye and Stella, all of the adventure's excitement gone from his eyes—replaced by fear, worry, and an eerie sense of calm acceptance—and managed to say three words.

"Run, fight, live."

"Light Bringer!" The creature screamed, in a voice that echoed throughout the entire cavern. Bringing his hammer straight down onto Raymond's head, he crushed it like an egg.

Reye felt like the air had been knocked from her lungs as the creature slowly raised its hammer, revealing the remains of Raymond's head splattered over the rocky surface of the cavern. Stella, who throughout the fight had managed to hold onto Reye, collapsed with a thud at Reye's feet, her mouth gapping open in shock at the sight of both the creature, and Raymond's headless corpse. Reye, regaining her breath, and turning her head slightly, seeing Stella unconscious on the ground next to Raymond's body, lost all sense of fear and hesitation, pure rage taking its place.

Raymond, Stella, Reye thought, looking down at the bodies of her brother and her best friend, feeling her eyes bulge in their sockets. *This isn't how it's supposed to happen,* Reye thought to herself, shocked and enraged. *You're not the one who gets himself killed. I'm the one who does something crazy, and you stop me and chew me out—just like the tractor, just like the hill. You don't get to die first, how can you live a life of no regrets if you're going to leave me—your twin sister—alone, especially now!*

The creature who killed Raymond took a step toward her—that step was the trigger. All of the rage, quickly building inside Reye from the moment Raymond was killed, was released.

Reye lost all control of herself. Charging the creature that killed Raymond, she grabbed a sword one of the creatures dropped on the ground after the light appeared, and ran it straight into her brother's killer. The creature might have been taller than Reye, but she ran the sword straight through the center of his chest, the exact place where the Hy-mun heart was located. Blood as red as her own washed over Reye from the wound as the creature dropped dead, uttering a loud cry that quickly attracted the attention of the other creatures, who were also recovering from Sol's light device—now losing its power and fading. Hearing the creature's cry, and witnessing his death at Reye's hands, the other creatures charged. Reye, possessed by fury, was not about to allow herself to be taken down. Holding the sword so tightly her knuckles turned white, she created a circle of death around her brother's dead body and Stella's unconscious form. The creatures approaching her died before they could get close. The more creatures she cut down, the more the rest of them turned their attention to Reye and her deadly dance. Even after the light from Sol's device completely faded, and darkness encompassed all of them again, allowing the creatures to move freely, Reye kept circling around the bodies of Raymond and Stella. She felled every creature who dared to approach her, leaving bodies upon bodies strewn around her, and painting herself red in the creatures' own blood.

Chapter 13

Gab-re had stationed himself in the radio room to monitor communications from the surface and conceal the Tribe of Shadows' presence in the Hy-mun camp. If any of the Hy-muns managed to slip through their grasp, and tried to call for help, he was waiting with his sword drawn for whoever might walk through the door. But it wasn't easy, and he was getting restless, pacing the room, despite the blistering pain he still felt.

All I have to do now, is send a message to the surface about a devastating accident in the camp to prevent other Hy-muns from entering the Tribe of Shadows' territory until the Third Great Attempt is executed. Then I can get out of here and join Mi-che and the others, Gab-re had thought, preparing himself for battle. Originally, he planned to join the attack on the second wave of Hy-muns soon after it started. Unfortunately, certain events changed those plans, forcing him to stay in the radio room to monitor communications, much to his immediate discomfort and displeasure. The first was the appearance of Light in the camp, created by one of the Hy-muns. His skin still burned, black from the places where the Light managed to penetrate the radio room, and stinging with every move he made. The Tribe of Shadows were expecting a bunch of Hy-mun insurgents they could catch unaware, and slaughter at their leisure, not a Hy-mun who would bring a device capable of creating Light. The Tribe of Shadows discovered long ago that only the Light in the sky, and from the Beings of Light's devices, could hurt them. Artificial light created by Hy-mun technology, and light from other sources like magma, was harmless.

I'm certain the device the Hy-mun used originally belonged to the Beings of Light, Gab-re reasoned. *If the Hy-muns are using the Beings of Light's devices— instead of worshiping and studying them in their churches and schools—then the Tribe of Shadows is in even more danger than we originally believed.*

Second, after the Light's appearance, was the escape of the Hy-mun who used the device to create it. Secrecy had always been essential to every operation the Tribe of Shadows conducted. They could not allow their presence to be discovered until the right time, after the Light had been removed from the surface. A Hy-mun escaping put them all at risk, making it even more necessary for Gab-re to listen to the reports coming from the surface.

According to the Hy-muns on the radio, only one group was scheduled to enter the camp, Gab-re thought, remembering the conversation he had with the Hy-mun on the surface just before the attack. *But if this Hy-mun alerts other Hy-muns to our presence in the caverns, it would certainly mean the start of the Second Coming.*

But the third thing to happen, and the strangest of them all, made Gab-re wish he had a chance to *Know* this particular Hy-mun. From the reports, not only was the Hy-mun concealing what he witnessed, but his story *helped* the Tribe of Shadows. He told the other Hy-muns that there was an accident, that he was the only survivor, and not to return.

Gab-re honestly didn't know what to make of this Hy-mun, but it seemed he was attempting to hide the Tribe of Shadows. Gab-re was still mulling over this puzzle when he walked back into the Hy-muns' camp, noticing a large number of warriors gathered around a small area of the battlefield, hollering the martyr cheer.

"Out of my way!" Gab-re screamed, pushing his way through the crowd as the other warriors made way to give him a chance to see what was happening.

"This is a day for surprises," he said to himself, finding the source of the gathering, and realizing why the other warriors were so worked up.

Inside a ring of bodies was a Hy-mun, one that could not only give his warriors a challenging fight, but also the high honor of becoming a martyr. The Hy-mun, if she could still be called that, stood completely warped by rage and fury, fighting out of pure instinct and madness. She emitted a bittersweet aroma of pure hatred. The energy Gab-re felt, as she lashed out at whatever approached her with her sword, chaotically rolled around her. The Hy-mun couldn't see, but somehow knew where they were. If one came too close to her, he died. He noticed two other Hy-mun bodies just inside her perimeter. One was dead and headless; the other, a female, alive and unconscious.

This Hy-mun is already past the point of collapsing from exhaustion, Gab-re mused. *Her body is straining far beyond what it can handle, and fast approaching a final breaking point. The only things keeping her up now are the sheer desires to protect the dead and the unconscious Hy-mun, and to fight.*

Watching the Hy-mun dance from opponent to opponent, Gab-re was awed by her movements. Surprisingly, he also felt an overwhelming sense of regret that this Hy-mun's life should end here.

I've never seen anyone like her, Gab-re thought as she continued to fight. *She can't stop, not here; other Hy-muns we've captured are nothing next to her. She needs to continue serving the Tribe of Shadows in a more fitting arena.*

"Bring ropes, cables, anything; I want this Hy-mun captured *alive!*" Gab-re shouted to his warriors, who looked slightly confused over his decision.

"This Hy-mun fights fiercer then anything I have ever seen," Gab-re explained. "It's too great a waste for the life of one such as this to end here. Rather, it should be finished in the Grand Coliseum of Wrath Eras, after training our finest warriors to defeat the Hy-muns. Lord Tanas has given me the right to capture whomever I want, and I want *that* Hy-mun!"

Some warriors grumbled at Gab-re's orders, wanting to fight the Hy-mun themselves, but his trump card was that his orders originally came from Lord Tanas; no one disobeyed *him.*

Ropes and metal cables were collected from around the camp. Keeping at a distance, the warriors ran at the Hy-mun, tripping, binding, and carrying her off to the side. Gab-re walked into the perimeter she created, looking more closely at the bodies she was guarding. Alongside the headless Hy-mun and unconscious female Hy-mun, Gab-re noticed a third body laying facedown, the only Tribe warrior to make it into her perimeter. Judging by the hammer in his hand, he was the one responsible for the headless body. Turning him over, Gab-re looked at his face.

"So, Mi-che," Gab-re said in a final reverent address, "you were the one who both delivered this boon to us, and became the first martyr at her hands. You are truly blessed. I thank you and promise to take all of what you were into me." Gab-re turned his attention on the unconscious Hy-mun. With every step he took toward her, the captured one thrashed and howled more loudly.

"Quiet that one before she kills herself from overexertion," Gab-re shouted to the guards holding the Hy-mun. Quickly responding, a guard slammed the hilt of his sword into the back of her head, rendering the Hy-mun unconscious.

I'm not surprised that it only took one hit to knock her out, Gab-re thought. *She was barely consciousness to begin with. At least now she'll stay quiet long enough for us to return to Nis. Considering how the she reacted as I approached this other Hy-mun female, I'm guessing this one is also important to my prize.*

"Keep this Hy-mun alive, and bring her back with us in case we need to 'encourage' our pet," Gab-re ordered, examining the second Hy-mun. She was no fighter, yet she did have *other capabilities* that were just as valuable. "Deliver her to Lust Atrophied. She can be useful there."

Both of the Hy-muns, and the few other camp survivors—one girl and a few sobbing boys—were bound up like meat on a stick along with the Tribe of Shadows' dead, and carried through the caves.

Overall, Gab-re was pleased with himself. He had repelled two incursions by Hy-muns, claimed two victories for his people, and kept the Third Great Attempt secret. Marching back to Nis, he couldn't wait to put his captured Hy-mun into the gladiatorial arena. He already knew about an event going on before he left involving two Rodents bound and determined to fight in the Grand Coliseum. A battle with the strongest warriors in Nis on one side, and a Hy-mun with Rodents on another, would definitely be a fight that he would want to see— even fight in if given the chance. He'd just have to wait until his Hy-mun woke up and recovered before it could happen.

But for the match he was envisioning, it would be worth the wait.

Part 3: The Birth of the Horror

Chapter 14

"Eat," the creature said, speaking the Hy-mun language with a central continental accent. "That food was provided by Hy-muns like yourself, and where you are going, you will need the strength. I can see why they wanted you here." The creature said his last comment with a snort of laughter, before leaving the food bowl at Reye's feet and exiting the cells.

Reye's fury died down as the guard left. Eyeing the food, she thought it looked like some kind of unappetizing meat stew. Black, hard chunks of meat floated in a murky brown broth that both looked and smelled like excrement. However, her stomach growling at the sight of the food, combined with her parched throat, reminded her just how hungry and thirsty she was, so she wasn't going to turn down any food—regardless of what it might be. Also, the creature said, "Where you are going," and that told Reye she was eventually going to be taken out of the cell, meaning she needed her strength. Picking up the bowl, she poured the contents into her mouth, the taste almost forcing her to gag it back up. All the while, thinking about what those creatures did and took from her.

The first chance I get; I am going to make them pay dearly.

Before the creature with the bowl arrived, Reye had woken up with a lingering pain in her head and heart. Her last memories, before blacking out, were the attack on the mining camp by the blue creatures, the creatures turning black and withering in pain from Sol's light, the cavern floor strewn with dead Hy-muns, Raymond's own death at the hands of one of the creatures, the last words she heard him speak, "Run, fight," Stella collapsing at her side, and lastly the pain. The pain that her brother was gone, that she would never look into his face again, that he wouldn't be by her side to go on crazy dares anymore, make sure she got to places on time, or stop her from getting too deep into trouble. The pain of knowing he would never be able to live the adventurer's life he wanted, that he wouldn't see her accomplish her dreams; and the screams of pain, echoing across the camp, until a shot of physical pain to the head knocked her out. When Reye finally woke up, she found herself gasping for breath and her throat dry in the hot air of her surroundings.

Pushing herself off a stone floor, Reye found herself in some sort of prison. The walls, floor, and ceiling were carved from stone, but the bars and doors were fashioned from refined metal. Soon after, the iron door screeched open and a blue creature—similar to the ones who attacked the camp and killed Raymond—entered the prison carrying the bowl of disgusting food. Reye ran at the door with mad fury in an effort to reach the creature, only to be stopped suddenly. Examining herself, she found that her arms had been locked in old iron manacles. Each manacle connected to a long rusty chain extending to the wall behind her, where they were fixed on metal loops. The creature only snickered in amusement at the display, before placing the bowl on the ground, pushing it to her with a stick, and telling her to "Eat."

After finishing the disgusting soup, Reye looked around to study more of the prison she suddenly found herself in. Her wrists still hurt from when she had tried to run for the door, causing the chains and wrist manacles binding her to snap taunt. Attempting to pull at the chains again, all she accomplished was causing some rust to fall off the chains to the floor of the cell. At the base of the cell's wall, and in other parts of the room, she noticed a red and orange light glowing dimly through a metal grate. Walking to the grate, she looked down it, surprised by what she saw, and flinching at the heat.

Magma, Reye thought to herself, recognizing the molten earth running through a tube beneath the grate. *That explains the heat and the light.*

Reye continued examining her surroundings. The magma didn't provide as much light as she was used to, but it was enough. Other nearby cells, like her own, were empty. Outside, in one corner of the room, there was a solid iron door that the creatures came through. She guessed it had to lead out of the prison. Above her, Reye heard a roar she first thought was thunder, but soon realized was something else.

Cheering? Reye knew she must be underneath, or at least near, some form of sporting arena.

The blue creature soon came back though the door after the cheering faded, accompanied by five others. Two of the creature, also bound up in ropes, looked completely different from the other creatures. The new creatures—as far as Reye could tell in the magma light—were a pure white color. Their hair was cut haphazardly above the neckline, as if done with a knife. They had longer, pointier ears sticking out behind their heads, and were dressed in cloth and leather garments; unlike the blue creatures, who wore metal plates of armor, like they were preparing for war. Yet the most noticeable thing Reye spotted, was that the white creatures had two different-colored horns, one gold and the other silver, growing out and around their heads, forming a coronet that spiraled together into a single short horn coming out of their foreheads. One of the new white creatures was also female.

Do the blue creatures have females? Reye asked herself, realizing she hadn't seen any women among the blue creatures, either in the prison or during the attack on the camp. But she stopped wondering about it when one of the blue creatures tried putting his hand through the bars of her cell to touch her. Instinctively, Reye hissed at the creature, swiping at his hand—only to be stopped by the chains before she could catch it.

"They were right about this one," the blue creature who put his hand close to Reye said.

"Get too close to this one and she will tear you apart," another creature replied.

"Yeah," agreed the third, "I heard how she left a mountain of martyrs last week when they captured her."

Last week? Reye thought to herself. She knew she had been knocked out. But she didn't think it was possible she could have been unconscious for a week

109

and still be alive. The story about a mountain of martyrs was also puzzling. She remembered her brother telling her to fight, and she knew she fought, but she never thought she had created a "mountain of martyrs."

The two white creatures were placed in a cell across from Reye. After being bound in chains similar to her, the ropes were removed and they were also offered food, which they quickly spilled across the floor, pity and sadness spreading across their faces.

"Ha! Typical Rodent behavior," one of the guards said to the others. "Give them food of their own kind, and they just waste it. It's going to be interesting to see how these two are going to keep fighting in the coliseum."

Coliseum, Reye mused. *Then I am near an arena. I guess these white creatures are used as some kind of entertainment for the blue ones, and from what that first guard said, I'm also going to be made a part of the event. Well, first chance I get, I am out of here.*

"You can say that again," one of the other guards continued, turning to leave. "They have been on a hunger strike since they started. It makes you wonder how much longer they are going to last. I once heard of a Rodent that went six weeks without food before dying of hunger. These two have to be close to that by now."

The white creatures did look starved, their faces ragged and hollow, skin withdrawn to the point where Reye could see traces of their jawbones and skulls through it. The white creature's arms and legs were similarly thinned.

Why are they doing this to themselves? Reye wondered, as the guards left the three of them alone.

"You have been hurt," the male white creature said to her. The white creature spoke with a different accent than the blue creatures; it sounded horse-like, almost as if a horse or a pony learned the Hy-mun language, but still couldn't get rid of the neighing sounds it made. "You are letting it change you for the worse."

"Thank you, Mr. Obvious," Reye responded harshly. She *really* hated it when people stated something apparent to her, and after recent events—the attack on the camp by strange creatures, the loss of her brother and best friend, and blacking out to wake up a week later in a strange prison—the fact that she had been hurt should have been the most obvious thing in the world. Reye didn't

110

need some strange white creature telling her that.

And what did he mean by "change you for the worse?" Reye wondered. Both white creatures looked at her with pitying gazes.

"And stop looking at me like that," Reye barked. "You've only just met me and you act like you know everything about me. You know nothing about me, you talk like I'm dying, and between the three of us, I'm the healthiest one here." Reye stood up, rolled up her sleeves and pants, and exposed her own non-emaciated arms and legs to the creatures to make her point.

"I apologize for my brother," the white female creature said, immediately averting her eyes from Reye to avoid *Knowing* her to the full extent of her senses' abilities. "Our encounters with Hy-muns are extremely limited, so we tend to forget the different ways our people perceive and *Know* things about each other."

"Whatever," Reye puffed, exasperated.

These white creatures are beginning to sound like Worm, but even more Worm-like, and I don't need one of his *lectures down here right now*. Reye enjoyed talking with Worm because of his dependability, honesty, and his attempts at finding the right words for the right situations. However, those rare times when Worm started lecturing—acting like he possessed secret knowledge about the world—always bugged her.

"Let's start again. My name is Dan-te, and this is my elder brother, Ice. We are members of The Remnant of the Tribe."

Remnant of the Tribe, Reye thought to herself as she looked at the two white creatures. *What is a "Remnant of the Tribe," and what is a "Tribe" anyway?* Reye might not have been as religious as Stella or Worm was, but she did know that the Hy-muns were the only race of beings on Prism. They were created by Ash Addiel and the Nag-el, and left in charge of Prism when they left the planet. Whatever this "Remnant of the Tribe" was, she didn't like it. However, the two white creatures, Dan-te and Ice, were the only source of information at her disposal—and she was going to use it.

"My name is Reye. I'm from the Orange Dominion. So, what are the blue creatures that locked us up down here, and for that matter, where is *here?* Also, what did you mean by 'different ways our people perceive and know things?' Can you read minds or something? And why aren't you eating? I know the food tastes bad, I've already tried it. But if I heard right, they plan to stick us in some kind of gladiatorial arena. Wouldn't you need your strength?"

At the mention of food, the two white creatures from The Remnant became noticeably more depressed.

"Let me answer those questions in the order you asked them," Ice said, taking over the conversation again.

"The '*blue creatures*,' as you called them, are our distant kin—the Tribe of Shadows."

"Hard to see the relationship," Reye interrupted sarcastically.

"The two Tribes split long ago, and since then, the greater of the two, the Tribe of Shadows, have incorporated *other blood* into itself."

Incorporated "other blood," *what kind of other blood?* Reye nervously thought. The way Ice said "other blood," combined with the fact that she hadn't seen any other women yet, made Reye shiver over its possible meanings.

"So then…" Reye said, trying to move the conversation away from whatever "other blood" could mean. "Where are we now, besides in a prison?"

"The city of Nis, the Tribe of Shadows' home."

"Huh?" Reye was lost, both figuratively and literally. She heard Ice say they were in their captor's home, which she could understand, but a *city*?

These creatures have a city! Reye stressed, trying to picture it. *How do I get out?*

"You're the kind of person who wants to ask a number of other questions after hearing the answer to one," Ice said, almost reading her mind, and annoying her in the process. "Your mental energy feels confused and annoyed. You're also directing your voice, intentions, and energy toward us; it makes you easy to read. Now, let me answer your questions about Nis.

"First of all, yes, this is a city. Its inhabitants sometimes bring back people like you, captives from raids."

Captives, Reye thought intently. *Then perhaps other members of the project are alive. Stella could be alive; she was only unconscious when I blacked out. Ann could be alive too. She never replied when I called out to her in the camp, but that doesn't mean she's dead. Maybe they are alive and together.* Hope began to spark in Reye as she examined her manacles, looking for any weakness in them while Ice kept talking.

"It was built over the course of many generations around a central point, the old city of Nis—now called Yam-Preen—and has multiple layers called circles built around it to serve different functions. We are in the Fifth Circle, Wrath Eras, the middle layer of the city, which is used for gladiatorial fights and training. To get out of Nis you need to either take the long and winding path through the city or the direct but heavily booby-trapped Jac-ob Way. Also…" Ice paused to steel himself. "If you are thinking that there are other Hy-muns alive here, I don't know, but I wouldn't count on it."

"Why not?" Reye asked.

"Because…" Ice looked nervous about answering Reye's question. Unable to look her in the eye, he looked down, his voice shaking. Reye realized Ice knew he was walking on uncomfortable ground. "The Tribe of Shadows takes very few prisoners, and when they do, prisoners are either made into gladiators—like you—or if they are not too damaged, they may be sent to the Second Circle, Lust Atrophied. From what we have heard from the crowds, Hy-muns have been killed recently. Your meal is proof of that."

"Why would my meal be proof that Hy-muns have died?" Reye wondered.

"Did the guard say your food 'was provided by Hy-muns like yourself?'" Ice asked. "Just like ours was the 'food of their own kind?'"

"Yeah, so what? I know it tasted terrible, but what's the big deal? Hy-muns and your Remnant of the Tribe make the food, right?"

"That's just it," Ice sputtered sorrowfully. "Hy-muns did more than make the food; they *were* the food. Your food was the prepared flesh of dead Hy-muns, just like ours was made similarly from the dead of our own members."

Reye, acting partially on instinct, but mostly on disgust, dropped to the floor, forcing herself to throw up every piece of the stew she had eaten.

That could have been Ann, she realized. *Or Stella!* Reye manically thought, regurgitating food as her mind swarmed with fears.

"And this second circle, Lust Atrophied?" Reye asked, hoarse from vomiting.

"You may or may not have noticed, but there are no women present among the Tribe of Shadows. They're all kept in Lust Atrophied, where they are used by men for breeding."

"Used for breeding!" Reye screamed, flying into a rage that scared Ice and

Dan-te, even though the two of them were in a different cell.

Ice knew Reye's emotional and mental states were damaged before being thrown into her cell by their ability to *Know* her through the image created by their senses. The energy rolling off Reye was erratic and tainted red; the energy that accompanying anger, hurt, loss, and sadness. During the past week, both Ice and Dan-te watched Reye as she laid unconscious on the cell's floor. Sometimes she would start screaming the names Raymond, Stella, and Ann, her voice carrying tones of sadness and loss with each name, and every time she screamed those names, they could feel horrible energy pulsing from her. Energy slowly choking her natural brown energy, the energy of someone close the natural world. Reye also reeked of blood from the Tribe of Shadows; she had been cleaned when they first encountered her, but a lingering smell remained. Ice and Dan-te *Knew* she had killed a lot of them, and by her unstable energy they *Knew* she had killed them in madness. Now, Reye was releasing that same horrible red energy again.

She must be imagining what could be happening to Ann and Stella if they are alive in Lust Atrophied, Dan-te thought to herself, as two guards entered their groups of cells in response to Reye's cries.

"We will have to knock this one out again," a guard said, entering Reye's cell. "This Hy-mun isn't going to be anywhere near as tamable as ones we've dealt with in the past." However, before he could get close, Reye—who had started working on one of the chains during her conversation with Ice and Dan-te—pulled the chain on her right hand so hard it broke. The guard had just enough time to be surprised before Reye punched him to the ground.

"This is going to be fun," the guard laughed, getting back up and forcing his way behind Reye, taking a few punches and lashes from the loose chain in the process, before knocking her out with a blow to the back of her head.

"I see why they want her in the Grand Coliseum," the guard huffed, fixing a new chain in Reye's cell and reattaching her manacled hand. "Before long they will be calling her the Hy-mun Horror. Were the other Hy-muns this enjoyable?"

"Who knows?" The second guard replied, hungrily anticipating his own chance to fight this Hy-mun for real. "If there are any left alive, they're probably being used for training, experimentation, or breeding. Doesn't matter, *this one*, is worth more than all of them."

As the guards left, snickering as they passed by, Ice and Dan-te looked to each other, instantly *Knowing* what the other was thinking.

"When she wakes up again, we are going to have to talk to her," Ice said, watching Reye sleep and radiate the horrible energy. "She would be a great help to our plan to stop the Third Great Attempt."

P.J. Fenton

Chapter 15

Live…

Stella slowly opened her eyes. Each eyelid felt heavy, begging to close again, but her last clear memory, Raymond shouting, "Live," followed by his death at the hands of the blue skinned hammer wielding creature, forced her to keep her eyes open.

Where…am…I, Stella thought groggily. *Yuck, I smell like I haven't bathed in a week. But I don't feel like I've wet or soiled myself, has someone been cleaning up after me?*

Her mind starting to clear, Stella's eyes started to focus on her surroundings.

I'm in a small room, the same size as the single person dorms at Spectral Academy. I'm face down on some kind of mattress—hair is sticking out of it. There are vents scattered across the floor and ceiling, is that how I'm supposed to shower or relieve myself.

Stella quickly dismissed the idea as she became more focused.

No, the vents are producing heat and light, a shifting red and orange light—

like the light from a fire—and that sound above me. Stella turned her gaze upwards. *Some kind of smoke or gas is being pumped into the room.*

The gas, which Stella could now see better, hung throughout the room like clouds blanketing the sky; the red and orange light from the vents illuminating it, giving it the same color, made the entire room glow red and orange.

How long have I been in this room, Stella wondered meekly. *At least, I'm too tired to be afraid.*

Stella did feel tired, and calm—strangely calm.

Could this be from the gas?

Stella's thoughts came to her bit by bit. She could also feel the heat from the room, and her own body heat, the latter raising quickly.

Is this gas making me sick? Stella asked herself, the closest thing she could relate her current feeling to was a time she had been sick, and after a long rest had trouble getting up, but this still seemed different.

Why am I here? If those blue skinned creatures wanted to kill me they would have already done it. So why am I still alive? Suddenly, as if answering her silent question, Stella heard footsteps.

Is someone else stuck in here with me? Stella thought.

Stella tried to move to see who the person was, but found she could just move her head from left and right—and barely at that. Whoever this person was, he or she was approaching from behind her and outside her field of vision.

"He... hello," Stella weakly called out, trying to get the person's attention. However, instead of a response, Stella felt cool hands on her feet and legs.

What?

Sudden shock dragged Stella's mind from its lethargy. Quickly now she began to realize what was happening to her.

Why is this person feeling my legs? Why can he even feel my legs at all? Am I even wearing anything?

Stella's answer soon presented itself, the strange hands continued examining her more and more.

By the Great Master Ash Addiel, I am naked!

By the time the hands reached her upper body, she felt her assailant's form against hers. She quickly realized two things—that person with her was male, and that he was undressed as well.

No! Stella cried in her mind. *This isn't happening, someone please tell me that this isn't happening! Someone* stop *this! Reye, Sol, Great Master Ash Addiel,* where are you?

But it was happening, despite Stella's silent cries; her mind frantic with shock, wishing and praying for someone to stop what the unknown male was doing to her.

Move! Stella begged, her own body refusing to cooperate with her wishes. *Please, before it's too late, please let me move so I can stop this!*

Unfortunately, she quickly knew that it was too late as something large and unknown, painfully ripped into her, swelling, pulsing, until finally erupting inside her.

When it was over, Stella didn't know what to think. Set down on her side, she was finally able take a look at the man who was with her. She thought she couldn't have been any more shocked than she already was, yet this revelation completely undid her.

He's just a boy.

Stella would have recoiled further in shock, but now after everything, all she could do was just stare at him, taking in every inch of the person before him.

He's younger than me. If he were a Hy-mun I would think he had just become a teenager. But he's not a Hy-mun boy, and not one of those blue skinned creatures either. In fact, I don't think I have ever never seen such a more feminine-looking boy before, ash grey skin—but soft looking, a slender built body, and that jet-black horn and coronet coming out of his head. If I took off the horn and coronet, and added some make-up, he could easily pass for a girl.

"Th… that," the boy gasped between breaths. "That was incredible! I had no idea it would feel this good. You were great, sis."

"What?" Stella managed to say, the boy's words further shocking Stella's mind. Not only did she realize what this boy had done to her, but she couldn't believe what she was hearing and seeing. The boy enjoyed what happened, not only that, but he didn't show any realization that he had done something wrong.

"Yeah, they gave me you for my first time since I'm half Rodent and you're a Hy-mun, but I'm glad they did."

Questions and emotions were forming in Stella's mind faster than she could put them into words.

What do you mean it was incredible? How could you? Stella wanted to ask in anger, shock, and disbelief, but she was too shaken and numb to form the words.

"I'm going to ask if they'll reserve you for me. I doubt it will be a problem since no one is probably going to want a Hy-mun, especially now. I got to go, but I'll see you again soon; the name is Met-on."

"Met-on," Stella mumbled, still shocked, repeating the boy's name.

"That's right! You can say my name! I'm so glad you are my sis." Stella was left with more questions unanswered than answered.

Did that really just happen? Stella, unable to accept how this Met-on boy could have behaved like he did, or that he would be back to do it again.

This isn't really happening is it, Stella panicked, trying to find some way to rationalize what had just happened to her. *None of this is really happening, I just blacked out and soon I'll wake up surrounded by Reye, Raymond, and Sol. It's all a* dream!

Stella tried to laugh, but not a sound escaped her lips.

It has to be a dream, what else could it be, soon I'll wake up and be back with everyone and I can start the mining project with Reye. I'm sure she's right next to me, waiting for me to wake up.

Reye unfortunately wasn't next to Stella, but next to Ice and Dan-te, who were explaining to her their plan for stopping the Third Great Attempt.

Chapter 16

"Let me get this straight," Reye huffed, rubbing her head. "You want me to help you get a cloth that's in the Grand Coliseum?"

Reye had been in a perpetual bad mood since her first conversation with Ice and Dan-te ended with her being knocked unconscious by the Tribe of Shadows again. When she finally woke up—more irritable than ever, Ice and Dan-te began explaining their mission to her, a plan to reach the surface and stop the Tribe of Shadows' Third Great Attempt.

"Not a cloth," Dan-te repeated. "It's the Veil of Shadows used by the First Envy generations ago."

"And you need this one, why?"

"We already tried using more recent Veils," Ice explained. "But they only work for members of the Tribe of Shadows; it's something about the *other blood* in their ancestry that keeps us from using them. That's why we need the First Envy's Veil of Shadows. The First Envy was just like us, so his Veil is the only one that should allow us to go to the surface."

I wonder how much "other blood" *like Stella and Ann's might have been spilled in this coliseum,* Reye thought angrily. *Stella, Ann, and who knows how many more Hy-mun, slaughtered liked pigs, and turned into food to be fed to more Hy-mun only to die the same way.* Despite the pain, Reye welcomed those thoughts and held onto them, knowing the anger would driver her harder to escape, and keep her from thinking about what might have happened to Ann or Stella, or who it was she ate in her cell.

"And why can't you just travel to the surface normally?" Reye asked.

"The Light there will kill us," Dan-te said.

"Right," Reye chuckled. "That means you are no different from the Tribe of Shadows. I remember seeing just what light is capable of doing to you when the camp was attacked. Those attackers burned to death thanks to the light Sol produced." Reye's chuckle clearly disturbed both Dan-te and Ice.

"You are not this kind of person, Reye," Ice said, a sorrowful expression on his face. Continuing to watch as Reye generated the horrible red energy, it strangling and blocking her other energies and thoughts.

"Oh, excuse me! How do you know what kind of person I am... oh wait, you do know, don't you?" While Ice might have been trying to help Reye, he could tell she was trying to block off the memory of her brother and friends by relishing in her anger, and in the memories of the Tribe of Shadows' actions. But even without the ability to *Know*, Reye didn't need reminding that both Ice and Dan-te could *Know* things about her, an ability she still didn't like because she didn't understand it. The only thing she wanted to care about was making the Tribe of Shadows suffer. "Anyway, if light can kill you, why try go to the surface?"

"To save us all," Dan-te said, keeping her voice level.

"Right." Reye was still unconvinced about the story they had told her about the Tribe of Shadows' plan to remove light from the world, rise up from the caves, and conquer them.

"We are telling you the truth." Dan-te tried to keep her voice down and their conversation hidden, but it was getting hard. "We *Know* if the Third Great Attempt succeeds, it will mean the deaths of all of our peoples. We can feel it in the ground around us, it is sparking with the energy of fear and destruction, and it just gets worse as the Third Great Attempt nears completion. The ground is scared for its life and the lives of all who live on and in it. The Hy-muns, the Remnant, and the Tribe of Shadows will all die. That is why we have to try to talk to someone on the surface to get help, or at least to warn them."

"'Try' being the word," Reye said smugly. "From what you have said, these Veils make you invisible on the surface and only let you tempt people into doing something. In the end, this is just one big gamble for you."

"Yes, Reye, it is a gamble," Ice replied. "But if we are going to live, it is a gamble we must take."

"I have never been much for gambling unless I know I can win," Reye scoffed. "Just give me someone to fight."

Reye didn't have long to wait for her request to be granted. No sooner did she make her wish, then they heard the sound of the door opening from further in the cells. A team of jailers and handlers approached both of their cells, a small team for Ice and Dan-te, and a large team for Reye—armed with poles equipped with nooses at the end of them.

"Okay," called one of the jailers who seemed to be in charge. "Let's get our Horror and these Rodents up to the Coliseum. There are a lot of eager gladiators waiting for them."

The small team in charge of Ice and Dan-te had little trouble handling them. From the first moment that they were brought into Wrath Eras, the only thing they ever proved difficult at was feeding. The obeyed everything else with nothing more than a sorry expression, and a desire to get into the Grand Coliseum.

The team in charge of Reye, however, didn't find it so easy. They needed to use the poles on each of her arms and legs, noosing them so that they could control her movements like a puppet, while at the same time keeping a safe distance from her. She refused to make anything done to her by any of her captors easy. Reye was certain to let any member of the Tribe of Shadows know if they were to get within an arm's reach of her, they would start losing whatever parts of their bodies she could grab onto. The handler who put the noose around her neck lost a part of his ear because he came too close to her. Once noosed, it took two handlers per pole to make Reye move where they wanted her to move. By comparison, Dan-te and Ice were led effortlessly into the coliseum, while Reye had to be pushed through the gate, which closed behind her, breaking the poles, and freeing her from the nooses. Once free, Reye quickly cast off the nooses and the broken pieces of poles, flinging them across the coliseum.

Built above the Jac-ob Way, the Grand Coliseum lived up to its name. It took up a fifth of the entire size of Wrath Eras, allowed room for the entire city to be in attendance, opened completely to the cavern ceiling so the roar of the crowds could be heard throughout all of Nis, and was reserved for only the finest gladiators and warriors Nis could produce. For a citizen of Nis to walk into this coliseum as a gladiator was one of the highest honors a member of the Tribe of Shadows could receive. Yet for Reye, Ice, and Dan-te, the Grand Coliseum was the stage for them to attempt to capture the Veil of Shadows of the First Envy, and then try to stay alive. As the three walked further into the coliseum, toward a small pile of weapons on the ground, the crowd erupted into a deafening roar that seemed to make the whole cavern shake so hard, Reye wouldn't have been surprised if the whole ceiling came down on their heads. The roars suddenly stopped as a voice began echoing across the coliseum.

"Citizens of Nis," an announcer proclaimed, gaining the attention of Reye, Ice, and Dan-te, who started looking throughout the audience. "See what has come to bless and honor our great city, its people, and the Great Lord Tanas. First, we have a pair of Rodents from The Remnant, who have graced us with many martyrs and strengthened our noble people as we prepare to begin the Third Great Attempt."

The announcement about Dan-te and Ice brought the crowd to an immediate frenzy of cheers and stomps. Hearing the noise, Ice and Dan-te hung their heads, ashamed about their actions, all so they could get a chance at stealing the Veil of Shadows. Reye also noticed the way they were down on themselves, shame etched into their expressions.

"Also," the announcer continued, "before us is the Great Martyr Maker, who by her own hands created a mountain of martyrs to bless us all in Nis. She is the most vicious of her kind to ever set foot in any coliseum in Wrath Eras, the Hy-mun Horror!"

Like before, the crowd erupted into a deafening roar that echoed throughout the cavern, shaking its ceiling. However, unlike Ice and Dan-te, Reye reveled in the praise from the crowd. She knew that they saw each warrior she had killed as a martyr, not as a loss. But right now, all she cared about was that she had killed a large number of them, and they were praising her for killing them.

However, glancing at Dan-te and Ice, Reye noticed the two of them had a problem. They were looking about widely, scanning every inch of the coliseum, but hadn't settled on anything. If fact, they looked panicked.

"What's wrong?" Reye asked.

"It's not here," Dan-te said nervously.

"What's not here?" Reye asked again.

"The Veil of Shadows that we came for," Ice said. "It should be hanging right there." Ice looked to a spot beneath a balcony on a far wall. "But it's gone!"

"And now, citizens of Nis," the announcer's voice began to thunder over the crowd again, "I present your gladiators!"

A fanfare sounded from a horn as two different gates opened from the floor of the coliseum on two of its opposite sides. From those gates, two teams of gladiators marched out onto either side of the trio of Reye, Dan-te, and Ice. They were lightly armored, but the armor they did wear glowed in the dim red light of the coliseum. Each gladiator was armed with a different kind of weapon; some had swords, others carried pikes, nets, axes, spiked ball and chains, and some wore spiked gauntlets, but all were geared to fight. If weapons weren't imposing enough, each gladiator was a tower of hardened blue skin and muscle, every one lethal with or without a weapon. However, as they cleared the gates, only one closed. The gladiator team in front of the open gate set up a line of defense, while the team by the closed gate put up a cross in the center of their group, and on it reverently hung an old black piece of cloth.

"That's it!" Dan-te exclaimed. "That's the Veil of Shadows."

"Citizens of Nis," said the booming voice of the announcer, "as some of you might already *Know*, these Rodents have a reason for being here, and the Hymun Horror has a purpose as well. In order to put our gladiators to the test, we present our Rodents with one of our most sacred objects, the Veil of Shadows worn by the First Envy, the object of the Rodents' desire for a while now."

"So much for keeping your plan a secret," Reye said to Ice. His expression turning sour after the announcement. "I'm guessing that the Tribe of Shadows can *Know* things the same way that you can. But if they can do that, how could they end up like this?"

"*Knowing* and understanding are two very different things," Ice answered bitterly.

"We knew that this could possibly happen," Dan-te added. "We were trying not to be too focused on the Veil. Since the Tribe of Shadows inducted the *other blood* into its ancestry, they don't seem to *Know* things the same way we do, but they still have the ability to a degree. On the other hand..." Dan-te was grinning now. "This works in our favor."

"How?" Reye asked, frustrated that the only thing happening was the gladiators setting up their defenses. She wanted to fight, but guessed from some of the looks she received from the spectators—a greedy look similar to a hunter waiting for his chance to shoot—she realized that if she started early, she would be killed before she had the chance to fight any of them.

"We were after the Veil of Shadows, and now they brought the Veil of Shadows to us. It seems that they are giving us a way out, too." Dan-te was starting to sound hopeful, but Reye was unconvinced. The Veil and the open gate were at opposites positions from of each other. Considering the number of gladiators, it would take all of them just to reach one of the two goals. Then, there was no guarantee the gate would stay open long enough for them to get out with the Veil once they had it. It didn't matter to Reye, though. All she cared about was fighting, escaping, and revenge. Dan-te's and Ice's problems were their concern. If it let her fight the creatures that killed her brother and did who knew what to Stella, then she would go along with any plan that the two of them had.

"Now, citizens of Nis..." the announcer began. "You may have noticed the open gate guarded behind one of the gladiator teams. Well, that's a gate to the Jac-ob Way, leading out of Nis, with all its traps disabled, prepared especially for the Hy-mun Horror!" Reye's eyes became alert, focusing on the gate the gladiators were guarding.

"The gate will remain open for ten minutes. After five, the traps in the Jac-ob Way will reactivate. We know how much the Hy-mun Horror wishes to both fight and leave our city, so we have prepared an opportunity for her to do both. Now, members of the Tribe of Shadows, who will our proud gladiators have the honor of fighting? Will the Rodents and Horror honor all of our gladiators, or will they only fight some before they die? Begin!"

A gong sounded across the entire Grand Coliseum as two teams of gladiators began to rush at Reye, Ice, and Dan-te from the groups guarding the Veil of Shadows and the entrance to the Jac-ob Way, attempting to trap the three of them in a two-pronged attack. Meanwhile, all around them sections of the floor slid away, the heat suddenly intensifying as pools, fountains, and rivers pumped full of magma appeared throughout the coliseum, providing obstacles for the three of them and the gladiators.

"Reye," Dan-te began, turning to tell her to stick with them so they could have a better chance of surviving. Unfortunately, as soon as the gong sounded, Reye took off toward the gladiators guarding the open passage leading to the Jac-ob Way, picking up an ax as she ran toward them, and completely oblivious to the heat of the magma. Seeing and *Knowing* Reye was intent on making for the open gate no matter what, Dan-te and Ice picked up weapons of their own, a pair of metal quarterstaffs and a dagger for Dan-te, and an ax for Ice.

"Ice," Dan-te said franticly, "go with Reye and stay with her no matter what."

"You are not going to take on all of those gladiators by yourself! I *Know* you, so I know what you plan on doing with those staffs, and it is still crazy!" Ice knew his sister was prone to doing stupid things—she did volunteer for this mission—but to take on a whole team of the Tribe of Shadows' best gladiators with nothing but a dagger and two quarterstaffs was crazy even for her.

"Give me a chance and I will reach the Veil. Reye will die if she goes up against them alone."

Ice looked over at Reye. Reye didn't look like she needed help. The way that she was fighting—lashing out with both a berserker's rage, and the horrible red energy pulsing out of her with every swing of her ax—caused her to live up to her reputation as the Hy-mun Horror. Each time she swung her axe either injured or killed an incoming gladiator. But that was also why Dan-te wanted Ice to go with Reye. The changes in Reye, how she was reveling in her anger, frightened Dan-te.

Every member of The Remnant knew that there were two ways a person could die. Right now, Reye faced both of those ways, a physical death and a death of one's self. The latter referred to a point where a person changed so much that there was no way to *Know* them at all from the person that she or he had once been.

Looking at Reye, and then at Dan-te, Ice *Knew* what Reye was facing and also understood why Dan-te had told him to go with her. The wrathful energy that she was pulsing out of her was hurting her internally, as much as it was hurting the Tribe of Shadows externally. He saw the red energy corroding Reye's self, threatening to overwhelm her natural brown energy, and turn her into something ruled by rage and viciousness. The more Reye fought and spilled blood, the more her scent subtly changed from Hy-mun girl into horrible predator. If left alone, and assuming she wasn't physically killed, she would keep fighting until the Hy-mun Horror was the only person she could ever be.

"All right," Ice said. "I'll go with Reye. But you better get the Veil of Shadows. You know what's at stake." Ice looked grim. He turned to run toward Reye's side of the arena.

Don't worry, Dan-te thought to herself. *I haven't forgotten.* Dan-te stuck her dagger into her belt and began running at full speed toward the cross bearing the Veil of Shadows and the group of gladiators protecting it. About three yards before she reached the first of the attacking gladiators, she shifted her entire focus toward the ground, planted her first quarterstaff into it as she continued to run forward, and vaulted, sailing over the heads of the frustrated gladiators, who swung at her with their weapons, only to find her just out of their reach.

"Members of the Tribe of Shadows," the announcer boomed over the coliseum, "It seems that a coward, fearful of fighting our noble gladiators, has penetrated our Grand Coliseum." The announcer's words were accompanied by a stream of hisses and angry shouts directed toward Dan-te. "Pay no heed to her. Our proud gladiators will soon exterminate this Rodent before it can even touch the Veil's shadow."

Perfect, Dan-te thought, tucking herself into a ball as she landed from her vault, rolling a few feet over her second quarterstaff before pushing herself off the ground and breaking into a hard run. *If they start thinking I'm a coward, it will make it a little easier to get to the Veil.*

Most of the gladiators she'd avoided decided that instead of challenging a coward who refused to fight, they would rather head toward Ice and Reye, who were doing far more than their share of fighting. The remaining gladiators from the Veil's attacking team decided to turn and fight Dan-te. Now realizing she could vault, they weren't about to let her perform another one over the second guard team to reach the Veil. One group of gladiators started slinging stones at her to keep her off balance, while another rushed her to try and make the kill. Using the quarterstaff and the magma pools, she managed to keep the other gladiators at bay, but it was not easy. Some of them tried grabbing the quarterstaff so others could rush her and make the kill. Those gladiators, Dan-te either knocked into the magma pools, or pushed them close enough to burn them with the magma, forcing them back and into each other while others continued sending stones toward her, which she constantly dodged to avoid being stunned or killed. But Dan-te knew she couldn't hold out forever. She had to reach the Veil.

GONG!

The bone rattling sound echoing throughout the coliseum indicating the five-minute marker. It meant the traps in the Jac-ob Way were reactivated, and in another five minutes, the path leading to the Jac-ob Way would close. Dan-te was halfway to the Veil of Shadows, and Ice, right behind Reye, quickly glanced at his Hy-mun cohort, checking how she reacted to the sound of the gong. Time froze in that one instant.

Ice already *Knew* her as the Hy-mun Horror, but now she became an even more horrible version of that being. The gong, and the realization that there would only be five more minutes before the gate to the Jac-ob Way closed, caused the Hy-mun Ice recognized as both Reye and the Hy-mun Horror to change dramatically. A more intense form of her red energy, monstrously horrible and frightening, filled with rage and hatred for the creatures in front of her, pulsed from her with the intensity of a speeding heart, consuming her.

Ice could almost hear the stories in his head, about how the seven members of the Council who witnessed "The Coming" changed so much from anger and rage they became entirely different beings—the first Seven Vices and leaders of the Tribe of Shadows. Ice, now witnessing the same change in Reye as the horrible red energy surrounded her, almost paused to ask himself, "was this what the Seats of Courage and Hope witnessed." Reye also emitted the same kind of predator's scent, exuding scents of adrenaline, hunger, madness, and lust that the gladiators produced when they moved in for a kill.

The other gladiators *Knew* this change in her as well, and were struck with both fear and awe of her. Taking the opportunity of their hesitation, Reye began charging through them, killing them even faster, to the stunned silence of both the other gladiators and the audience.

Die! Reye thought. *Just die you bestial creatures. Give me back my family, my friends, my light!*

Confronted by the possibility of never returning to the surface, and living out the remainder of her life in this arena, Reye's mind became consumed with thoughts of killing as many members of the Tribe of Shadow as she could. Every gladiator standing in front of her only lasted a second.

I'm doing it Raymond, she thought, *I'm avenging you, just like you said, run and fight!* The two-handed war ax she picked up tore through one on the first swing and would take another two out on the return swing. The ax became weightless in Reye's hands as she continued to look straight ahead toward the Jac-ob Way. Meanwhile, Ice remained at her back, never noticed once by Reye, protecting her from any gladiators who tried to approach.

"The Hy-mun Horror is mine!" a voice shouted as another gladiator, armed with a rapier, jumped in front of the others and rushed her. Reye's first attempt to cut him in half with her ax didn't work this time. Ducking under the swing, quick as a mongoose, he hooked his arms around hers, and looked straight into her face.

"It's finally my turn to challenge you," the gladiator laughed. "My name is Gab-re. By Lord Tanas's order I led the attack on your encampment. By his order, I brought you, and other Hy-mun here to do with as we please, and now thanks to his order, I can have the benefit of facing you in a glorious battle on a proper field of combat, before sending you to oblivion, so let us enjoy ourselves." Gab-re quickly disentangled himself from Reye, slashing her shallowly across her arm with his rapier in a taunt before stepping back to begin his next assault. Reye, however, had different plans in mind than the "glorious battle" Gab-re wanted.

He led the attack that killed Raymond, Reye thought. *His Lord Tanas gave those orders. His Lord Tanas is the ones responsible for Hy-muns being used like cattle!* Those thoughts, repeating in Reye's head again and again, caused her rage to build even more. The rage was so thick Gab-re could feel, taste, and see it, adding to his excitement.

Now, thought Gab-re as he mockingly saluted Reye, *for the fight I envisioned, one that will only be bested by the retaking of the surface.*

Gab-re's dreams, however, were cut short, literally. As he saluted Reye in preparation to attack, he found himself falling to Reye's side.

But, my conquest...the surface... He looked up to see the Rodent looking at both him and Reye with extreme pity. His own body, still standing upright, cut diagonally upward by a quick cut from Reye's ax. The cut was so quick Gab-re didn't even feel or notice it, slicing across his hip, to his chest, through his griffin brand, and out of his shoulder, leaving the rest of him just a head, half an upper body, and an arm which still held his sword.

Dan-te never looked back at Reye, keeping her eyes focused on the Veil of Shadows. The moment the attacking gladiators stopped their assault to watch Reye, Dan-te used the opportunity to run and make one more vault, clearing the second defending team of gladiators—who were mesmerized by Reye's quick killing of Gab-re—and landing at the foot of the cross holding the Veil of Shadows. The stunned gladiators were still watching Reye while Dan-te tore the Veil of Shadows from its cross and put it on.

It will be safer if I'm wearing it instead of carrying it, Dan-te thought. *I don't want to risk anyone ripping it out of my hands.*

Dan-te took a breath, bracing herself, ready to run toward her brother and Reye, when a gladiator near the cross snapped out of his shock and noticed Dan-te wearing the Veil of Shadows.

"Defiler!" the gladiator screamed, lashing a whip, catching Dan-te's veiled arm, and tearing a layer of the fabric near a still glowing stone in a pocket of the Veil on her hand.

Sparks shot out suddenly from the rip, each one shinning with Light, burning the gladiator's face and throat, choking him. The sparks also brought the surrounding gladiators back from their daze, the closest gladiators burning black and squirming in pain from exposure to the Light.

The sparks, however, didn't affect Dan-te at all. Cringing at first when the sparks started to fly from the Veil, she quickly noticed she didn't feel any pain from the Light, and could look at it without being harmed.

The Veil must be protecting me, she thought. The Veil giving one more spit of sparks from her arm before a brilliant flash of Light from the tear illuminated the entire Grand Coliseum, and then Dan-te was gone.

P.J. Fenton

Chapter 17

The Light from the Veil of Shadows left its mark. The nearest gladiators were burned to death in a flash from exposure. The ones still fighting Reye and Ice—along with every spectator in attendance—were seriously burned, some even blinded. Others had attempted to shield themselves—recognizing the danger from the Light—and found their arms and hands burned black and in extreme pain, weapons dropping from their scorched hands. Thankfully, Ice had only small, yet harsh, burns on his back. The other gladiators, crowding around him to overwhelm him, actually shielded him from the worst of the Light. Ice *Knew* Reye also noticed the Light flashing through the coliseum. As the coliseum became illuminated, Ice noticed a small pulse of happy energy within Reye's heart, energy at peace with the light and radiating joy from it. Ice *Knew* some part of her, the person she once was, still existed. He had to continue on with her, to make sure that person did not die, for Reye's sake and for Dan-te's memory.

"Sacrilege!" the announcer boomed over the coliseum, as he and the rest of the audience began to recover from the flash of Light. "The Cowardly Rodent has destroyed the sacred Veil of Shadows and brought the cursed Light to Nis. Seal the Coliseum. Death to the Light Bringers!"

Reye cut down the last gladiator standing between her and the gate to the Jac-ob Way as the announcement was made. Reye and Ice ran through the gate and down the narrow torch lit stairway toward the Jac-ob Way just as the gate closed quickly behind them, the slamming sound of rock striking rock echoing around them. Ice knew it would only be a short time before the gate reopened and every able-bodied gladiator and soldier in Wrath Eras ended up on their trail.

We've really done it now, Ice thought to himself, moving along with Reye, paying Ice no mind as she charged down the stairs.

Ice knew the gladiators were always supposed to win in the end. If they killed their enemies, they were proclaimed heroes and great warriors. If they died, the Tribe of Shadows still considered it a victory because they had become martyrs. The latter of those outcomes was how all of Ice and Dan-te's matches had ended before. They would defeat their enemies, and the crowd would cheer for them as martyrs—like the millions of others who had died in the arenas before them. They would then be moved to another arena where stronger gladiators would try their luck against them.

This time, however, the three of them created a situation where they had managed to insult the gladiators, the Tribe of Shadows, and the city of Nis. First, they managed to escape, even if it was for only a short time, and no one ever *escaped* from the coliseums. Second, they managed to destroy the Veil of Shadows. The gladiators had certainly never expected Dan-te, Reye, or even himself to touch it. But Dan-te had put it on and was wearing it when it had been destroyed.

We really messed up on using the Veil, didn't we, Dan-te? Ice thought sorrowfully. Both Ice and Dan-te realized either one of them could die long before reaching the Veil, but loosing Dan-te, especially after obtaining the Veil, was harsh. Worse still, with the Veil of Shadows lost to them, they couldn't try to stop the Third Great Attempt from the surface. But they had discussed a contingency plan to use in the event that stealing the Veil did not work. He would have to put it into effect.

Lastly, by causing the destruction of the Veil, they inadvertently brought Light into the Nis. The announcer had called them "Light Bringers," the name of the leader of the Beings of Light who had led "The Coming." It was one of the worse insults to call a person. In fact, considering their situation, to be called a "Light Bringer" was an informal way of being sentenced to the worst kind of death the Tribe of Shadows could create. The idea quickly made Ice regain his focus.

"Reye, we have to keep moving. Don't stop for anything," Ice said forcefully to Reye, hoping she didn't ignore him this time.

Reye acknowledged Ice with a turn of the head and a frustrated grunt.

What do you think I'm doing? She thought to herself. *Just give me more of these creatures to fight and then a way back into the light.*

Ice *Knew* Reye felt that he was telling her something she already realized. When she turned her head to acknowledge him, he felt frustrated energy bristling from her. He also *Knew* that anger and rage had changed much of her into a fighting machine—one that kept going and going, powered by the red energy he felt beating from her, and stinking with an acrid smell. It shouted anger, fight, and kill louder than any voice could.

But there was still some of the original person that Ice *Knew* when they first met in the cells, a small beating heart of longing brown energy that yearned for the Light of the surface, and burned with a desire to go there.

Unfortunately, what Ice needed now was the Hy-mun Horror, a being that could be extremely helpful to the contingency plan Ice and Dan-te had discussed, and probably the best chance either of them had for staying alive. The notion sickened him because he knew if he did this, he would not only be using Reye, he would be betraying his sister's last wish by pushing her toward becoming the Hy-mun Horror, instead of trying to save the person she once was. And that would put him on the same level as the Tribe of Shadows.

But Ice realized what was at stake from the Tribe of Shadows' Third Great Attempt. If the Third Great Attempt succeeded, it wouldn't matter what happened to them. Also, he didn't have much time to consider any other options; as they quickly came to the end of the stairway leading into the Jac-ob Way.

Illuminated and heated by two magma streams along the floor where it met the walls, it forked in two directions from the stairs—left and right—leading further in and out of the city. Both the advantage and disadvantage of the Jac-ob Way was its directness. Now, the choice was which path to take.

"Which way leads deeper into the city?" Reye asked.

"Left," Ice replied, surprised, pointing down the passage, expecting Reye to head the other way toward the city's main gate as she bolted down the tunnel with Ice close on her heels.

"I thought you wanted to escape?" Ice asked.

"Not until I find this Lord Tanas, and tear him apart!" Reye shouted, almost like she wanted the entire city to hear she was coming for its leader. Reye remembered Gab-re's words in the coliseum, how "*by Lord Tanas's order*" he led the attack and brought her and the other Hy-mun to Nis to be used as cattle and sport.

"That creature said he ordered the attack that killed my brother. I'll destroy him!" Reye screamed in a murderous rage, surprising Ice, who felt the horrible red energy radiating off Reye as she talked about Lord Tanas. Meanwhile, Ice's head was also swirling. Reye willfully declared to head further into the city to kill Lord Tanas. It surprised him not only because she had chosen to do it, but because that was *exactly* what he wanted her to do.

We were right Dan-te, Ice mused, thinking of their contingency plan. *She will be a real help to us.*

The contingency plan Ice and Dan-te discussed, if they couldn't get to the Veil of Shadows, was to attack and kill Lord Tanas; a problem because no one was ever able to be in his presence for very long. They had hoped, if the Tribe of Shadows lost its leader, it wouldn't be able to execute the Third Great Attempt. It was a long shot, and one they knew would turn into a suicide mission, but they had already accepted they were going to die in Nis.

However, now there were bigger problems. The first problem was the Jac-ob Way. The traps were reactivated, traps that were difficult, if not impossible, to avoid because operators rearranged them or made them take up the entire passage. Also, all the Tribe of Shadows needed to do was turn off the traps, sending soldiers and gladiators at them from both directions, and they could catch them in the middle of a two-pronged attack.

We need to get out of the Jac-ob Way quickly, Ice thought to himself. *If we can reach the next circle, Greed U-Sez, I'll be able to lead Reye to Yam-Preen by feeling the residual energy on the roads and use that to get us through each circle. It will take more time, but it will give us the best opportunity to evade the Tribe of Shadows and go deeper into Nis.*

When Ice was led through the city, he felt different types of residual energy on the roads leading between circles; the energy that stayed in the circles, and the energy that traveled through them. The energy on the roads that lead between the circles felt like flowing rivers, while the energy that stayed in the circle felt like pools, and when another group approached them, the energy felt like a river flowing toward them. Ice had no doubt he could lead Reye through Nis.

The second and most difficult problem would be if they actually *confronted* Lord Tanas. Anyone from the Remnant who witnessed him was frozen on the spot. The only reason the Tribe of Shadows could get as close to him as they did was because of the "other blood" they had inherited from the beings that accompanied Lord Tanas when he first arrived. That was why Ice believed Reye, a Hy-mun and not a member either the Remnant or the Tribe of Shadows, could be the key to this backup plan.

After everything that has happened to her and her friends, Reye's become a killing machine, Ice through, examining Reye as they ran down the Jac-ob Way. *If no member of The Remnant can get close to Lord Tanas, perhaps she, a crazed Hy-mun, could.*

Ice hoped that Reye could kill Lord Tanas. Since his appearance, no one had ever seen Lord Tanas fight, so he believed any fighting skill he once had must be gone, and he was using both the paralyzing effect he emitted, and the Tribe of Shadows feeling of reverence, to make them follow him. But Reye didn't share any of those sentiments, so she should have no trouble attacking him. No Hy-mun, to the knowledge of The Remnant or the Tribe of Shadows, had ever been in the presence of Lord Tanas, so there was a chance she could do it. The idea still made Ice feel sick. He was breaking two of the strictest laws in The Remnant, "never use another," and "never change another." If he did live past this and succeeded, he knew he would not be able to return to The Remnant and expect to be welcomed. But he also knew what the Third Great Attempt would do to The Remnant if completed. If he failed, there would be no Remnant for him to return to.

Wherever you are right now, Dan-te, Ice thought to himself as the first trap activated, a series of spiked poles that shot through the floor and ceiling of the Jac-ob Way, *I hope it's a better place than I am.*

***

In a mixture of shock and relief, Dan-te found herself on the surface alive and unharmed. She stood in the shadow of a Hy-mun, who was standing at a doorway, in the "Reversed State," the world the First Envy witnessed when he used the Veil of Shadows. The Hy-mun in front of her looked as black as the darkest caverns and the walls around him as white as her own skin, but she knew that it really the opposite.

I made it, she thought to herself, *I'm on the surface, in the "Reversed State" from the stories.* But before Dan-te could do anything else, the Hy-mun closed the door between them. The moment the door was closed, cutting Dan-te off from the Hy-mun's shadow, the colors of the world instantly shifted back to their natural appearance. With a shock, Dan-te realized she had left the "Reversed State" and was back in the normal world.

What? Dan-te wondered to herself. She knew a little bit about how the Veil of Shadows worked from stories passed down in Rem. She should have been able to stay with the Hy-mun, hidden in his shadow, and encourage him to do things. That was the plan, to contact a Hy-mun and encourage him or her to move in a way that would stop the Third Great Attempt. Now, she realized the plan had changed, and for the moment, she would have to stay where she was. Thankfully, the room was extremely dark. Dan-te noticed the windows were closed with only a little Light coming in. She remembered how the Veil of Shadows protected her from the Veil's own Light, but decided to stay out of the Light's path, refusing to push her luck and see if the Veil would protect her from direct surface Light.

Dan-te examined her arm, looking closer at the rip on the Veil. The tear exposed strange ribbons that looked like veins, a few having burst open, bleeding an odorless, clear fluid near the still glowing stone on her hand.

It might be best to wait in this room until its occupant comes back, then I can try to slip back into his shadow, Dan-te thought to herself, not wanting to chance a direct encounter with a Hy-mun. *Staying hidden shouldn't be a problem, this room is full of shelves and books of all kinds. Whoever lives here must really read a lot.* She took a few steps and knocked over a small pile that she hastily restacked. *I just hope Ice and Reye will be able to get out of the Grand Coliseum in one piece.* She cast her eyes to the ground and thought of her brother and Reye, still underground in the city of Nis.

Part 4: The Emissary and the Guide

Chapter 18

It was mid to late afternoon at Spectral Academy and some of the students were eating dinner. The news around the academy was still gloomy. On the radio, Worm heard more talk about the disaster that claimed the lives of all but one member of the mining project, Sol. The radio was replaying the interview he gave after he got out of the caverns, and announcing another memorial service for the students who died in the tragedy. Worm had heard Sol's report enough times now he had it memorized.

"It all happened so fast," Sol said, his voice trembling and grief stricken. "Soon after we got down there and were given our initial orientation, I was sent to do some maintenance with one of the technicians on the emergency return rocket elevator. Then it happened, a minor earthquake right under our feet. It didn't seem like much, we just got shook up a little. One girl named Ann started asking about volcanic activity, but the instructor said it was nothing, and to not worry about it. But then there was this rush of heat. Some volcanic tube must have ruptured underneath us during the quake, and the cave quickly began filling up with lava. The technician pushed me in the elevator, hit the ignition switch, and I was off. The last thing I saw was the entire encampment being submerged in lava." Sol's voice seemed to drift away when he mentioned the camp being destroyed, almost like he had left a part of himself in the camp when the elevator returned him to the surface.

At first, Worm had a hard time believing it. He always had a streak of skepticism and paranoia in him, and Sol's story seemed rather convenient. His demeanor, his wide eyes and hollow words, was almost too textbook, as if he'd crafted it by reading up on trauma survivors. A minor earthquake just happened to cause a lava flood, wiping out an entire mining project except for one person who just happened to be near the emergency return elevator? Worm knew something about odds, and the odds of those events happening in that order were just too great for him to believe. Since the Project disaster, the company in charge of it immediately sealed the area around the caverns "for safety reasons," only adding to his skepticism. Closing the site meant sacrificing equipment worth millions, and completely disregarding the possibility of a surface eruption. It also went completely against the practices of other companies that tried to salvage their equipment, and investigate the possibility of future eruptions. Sol didn't even answer any other questions himself. After the disaster, and that one and only interview, he immediately returned to the Yellow Dominion; sending a note to Spectral Academy saying he was withdrawing, and a moving crew to bring his belongings back to the Yellow Dominion.

However, as the week wore on, and Worm's initial bout with paranoia started to wane, he realized that everyone he knew was probably gone for good, regardless what actually happened. He didn't doubt that Sol was lying about what had transpired. Worm was certain something had befallen the project, but he also knew he couldn't afford to dig into it—lest his own past come to light. Privately, he entertained the fantasy that they didn't die, but were caught by Cave Snatchers, hoping Reye would march out of the Demp Caverns, alongside everyone he knew, walk into class and shout, "Cave Snatchers exist!" in pure Reye-style.

But Worm also knew the harsher facts of life. He might have been a cheerful and quiet person most of the time, but he had seen dreams that meant more to him than anything else come crashing down around him, forcing him to start from scratch again. He witnessed friends and companions give everything and more for what they believed in, only to get nothing in return. It was a part of himself he didn't share easily with others, especially since one of Spectral Academy's goals was to help restore the world to pre-Rainbow War status. He didn't want to give anyone the wrong idea about their future. Worm, however, knew the kind of forces that were out in the world and had acknowledged it, and he was slowly becoming more certain, and more at peace, with the idea that his friends were gone—regardless of how much he didn't like it.

Hmmm, if it did happen as Sol said it did, Worm thought to himself, *I'll bet Ann would have screamed, "I was right," just before she died.*

Worm remembered the last conversation he had with Reye and everyone else at AB's. Ann talked about land-based volcanoes and magma flows. If they died that way, it probably would have been the high point of Ann's life, since it would have proven her predictions about the increase in magma flows.

Before the disaster, Ann and Reye both left books and charts with Worm. Even though the rest of their effects were collected, he still kept those books on volcanoes and land volcano theory. Personally, Worm liked volcanoes only when they were out to sea, where they would be less likely to hurt anyone, like the one near his home in the Indigo Dominion. He never liked the idea of one appearing on land. Still, he kept the books just so he could remember his friends better. But also in case Ann and Reye weren't dead and managed to come back; if that happened he wanted to return those books to them. Still, he knew the odds of that were even lower than Sol's story being true, and the mood of the students wasn't helping.

If the mood was somber, Worm would have accepted it easier. However, some students who were rejected for the project were actually giddy now over not being chosen, walking around the academy—a spring in their step and a sparkle in their eyes—glad to be alive. This giddiness made the disaster feel even worse for him, because these same students applied and were in tears over not being accepted into a project, which was supposed to have a degree of danger to begin with.

Show some respect for the dead, de mortuis aut bene aut nihil, Worm often wanted to scream out, remembering the Platin phrase which translated to "about the dead, either well or nothing," when he would walk by some of the giddier students. Worm's feelings were you never apply for anything risky if you can't accept the risk. And every one of these students, for him at least, never accepted the risk and were disrespecting the ones who did. As another couple walked by him, he could hear one of them talking about how glad he was to not be chosen for the project, a student he remembered crying his eyes out in the public bathroom when he found he wasn't chosen. Deciding he couldn't put up with the company of anymore students, he took the rest of his dinner back to his room.

***

Dan-te spent her time quietly looking around the large room she had found herself stuck in, examining it carefully, and making sure not to knock anything else over. There was a bed and other facilities she *Knew* were used for cleaning and relieving oneself from the sights and smells of water, fragrant bars, and other certain foul smells. Combined with the residual energy she felt throughout the room, she *Knew* a person must live here. Just as she was about to start examining the book titles, a click at the door alerted her that someone was coming into the room. Dashing to the side, she walked in between the large bookcases and was soon out of sight.

A Hy-mun male entered, the same age as Reye, but very somber. The feelings this Hy-mun carried were not for himself, but for others. The caring blue energy of his feelings rippled out of him like drops of water in a pool, seeking to reach as far as they could before dissipating. This blue rippling energy also had a soft and kind touch to it, the same way water felt when it gently touched someone. This was a very tender-hearted Hy-mun, and Dan-te *Knew* it. The fact that his energy only came out in ripples, instead of beating or pulsing like others, meant he kept himself guarded because he had been hurt before, and often felt the hurt of others.

Yet, there was also resolve in him, and a combat instinct that made her want to keep her distance. As she watched him, she could feel that resolve and instinct like a sleeping energy, lying dormant, and not to be tampered with lightly. The Hy-mun knew how to fight, and she realized she needed to be very careful with how she dealt with him.

***

Worm put his food on his desk and was about to sit down to eat when he noticed something.

142

Worm's dorm room was a mess, but he took pride in it being his own mess. He knew where every book was, what every stack, shelf, and display ought to look like. If he had to, he could be blindfolded, given a list of books, and walk through his room and collect every book without disturbing any others. So, he knew that one small stack had been knocked over and restacked. Looking at both the door and the windows, Worm saw the bolts that locked them from the inside hadn't been disturbed. If someone did come into his room and knock something over, he or she could still be there. Another person would have told him it was an insane idea, but he had already seen enough in his life to make him believe in the insane.

***

Dan-te *Knew* the Hy-mun was alerted, she felt his blue energy shifting from a gentle ripple to a rapid ripple, seeking her out. The Hy-mun also oozed a sharp-smelling fear and excitement scent—the same scents she smelled on Reye and the Tribe of Shadows' gladiators before combat. However, the energy this Hy-mun generated was the same natural blue caring energy he possessed—shifting to prepare himself for possible dangers—instead of changing energies, like Reye, who generated a new and hateful red energy that was slowly degrading and corroding who she was—turning her into something else. Regardless, as the Hy-mun got up and checked the locks on the door to his room and windows, closed all the curtains, and blocked out all the natural light—which made things both easier and more difficult for her—she realized slipping back into his shadow and making contact was going to be harder than she originally thought.

***

This should make it harder for whoever could be in here, Worm thought to himself as he began making his way through the room toward his closet. The room was now almost pitch-black. A little light shone through the edges of the doors and windows, but it didn't do much to improve visibility.

***

This Hy-mun knows this place better than I thought, Dan-te realized. The Hy-mun never stumbled, tripped, or collided with any of the stacks of books on the ground. He moved through the darkness like she did, *Knowing* everything that needed to be done—the moves, the pace, everything that allowed him to go from one end of the room to the other. When he got to the closet though, she felt

143

the Hy-mun's energy and scents change, the dormant energy she felt earlier beginning to stir and pulse within him like a tremor, rising to the surface. Taking a long pole with a blade at its end out of the closet, he returned to the door, assuming a defensive stance.

"All right, who's in here?"

Dan-te looked at the Hy-mun from her hiding place. He held the weapon tightly, and she *Knew* if provoked, he would fight; she could sense he had been attacked before. The way he appeared to her now reminded her of her brother, during their times in the coliseums.

He is generating the same protective violet energy, mixed with his own blue energy, that lets an opponent know he's ready to fight, unwilling let anyone past him, just like Ice, Dan-te thought, lost for a moment in memory.

From what Dan-te had managed to *Know* from the Hy-mun's energy, she thought the Hy-mun would relax if she showed him she meant no harm. But after seeing the way Reye suddenly changed, she didn't want to simply reveal herself to him. Dan-te knew she was still robed in the Veil, but had no idea how the Veil had been altered after the gladiator struck it before coming to this room. However, if the Veil offered her some protection, and let her slip back into his shadow, then it would be best to keep it on. Stepping slightly from the bookshelves, moving slowly toward the Hy-mun's shadow, she accidently kicked a pile of books on the ground, causing the Hy-mun to turn toward her. But his sudden reaction, looking straight at her with a flash of the golden energy of shock and awe, beaming from his equally stunned face, was something Dan-te never expected.

Dan-te *Knew* the Hy-mun could see her. While in the "Reversed State," she could see and feel herself just fine, but touch nothing else. When she left that state, she quickly realized she could touch things, something she knew she couldn't do in the "Reversed State" according to the Stories of Rill, but didn't know if she was still protected by invisibility. Somehow, the damage to the Veil had canceled that ability as well.

***

Though the light was low, Worm could still make out the being that emerged from between his bookshelves. It was covered in a dark cape, or veil. The veil, wrapping the entire body, almost clinging to the skin, gave off the appearance of being made from some kind of silk that would still be comfortable to wear despite how tight it might be. The being had all the distinctive feminine features about her to indicate she was a woman. The woman was taller than him by a head, and from that head it seemed like there was a protrusion, but the covering kept him from figuring out what it was. The woman put her hands up in a surrendering gesture, and spoke in Worm's language with a strange accent.

"Fear not, peace be with you," she said, wanting to make Worm realize he didn't have anything to fear from her. However, she would rather have been the one to get the reassurance from Worm; he held the weapon.

She doesn't seem to want any trouble; if she did, it would have already happened. She's also putting herself at my mercy, Worm thought, considering what she said, and how she was acting. From what Worm could make out from beneath the veil, she seemed extremely frail, possibly half starved. Her voice also trembled with a little fear, but also a genuine desire to talk.

"I am called Worm," he said, placing his weapon down at his feet and repeating the same surrendering gesture with his hands, showing her he also didn't mean to threaten her.

"My name is Dan-te," she replied, keeping the line of communication open between them. Just then a smell caught her attention, an odor that made her realize something she had attempted to put out of her mind the moment she first approached Nis. The smell of food not made from the flesh of The Remnant.

Dan-te's stomach growled so loudly it echoed throughout Worm's entire room. Dan-te had ignored and fought hunger—almost to the point of starvation— during the long fights she and her brother had endured in Nis. Now that food was available, food not made from dead bodies, her instincts were overtaking her endurance.

"Uh, would you like something to eat, Dan-te? I have pasta and vegetables if you're hungry," Worm offered, gesturing to the food sitting on his desk.

As soon as he made the offer, Dan-te quickly moved from the bookshelves to his desk, took the Veil off of her head, and began to eat vigorously. While she ate, Worm took his first real look at his visitor's head. Her facial features were mostly the same as any other Hy-mun, except her short, messily-cut hair was pure white, as white as her skin. Not fair-skinned like himself or others from the northern dominions. Her skin looked chalk-white, like it had never seen the light of the sun. Then there was the coronet, or at least it looked like a coronet. Two bony horns, one silver and one gold, wrapping around her head, just above a pair of large pointed ears, and joining together at the center of her forehead, where they created a small two colored horn from their fusion.

Yet, the thing that captivated Worm the most about his guest were her eyes, irises of bright silver that almost glowed in the darkened room. He didn't have much time to admire them, though, because it wasn't long before Dan-te finished Worm's entire meal, exhaling a long-held breath, followed by a look of complete satisfaction.

"Thank you," she said.

"You're welcome," Worm replied, still a little taken aback by his strange guest. "But I would like to know more about who and—forgive me if this sounds rude—*what* you are. I've never had a guest like you before."

"I am not surprised," Dan-te said, turning to look at Worm directly. "My people can't stand the Light."

Worm suspected there was a lot to it than simply that, when Dan-te mentioned "Light" he recognized something in her eyes, an emotion he was all too familiar with—fear. Worm didn't know why she, or any of her people, would have a fear of light, but decided to let her explain it when she was ready.

"My people call themselves the Remnant of the Tribe," she said, answering short and simply. "We used to live on the surface when there was no Light at all, until 'The Coming.' Then we were forced underground and our people divided into two groups, the Remnant of the Tribe, and the Tribe of Shadows."

"Who forced you underground?"

Dan-te *Knew* Worm's curiosity was starting to rise, white inquisitive energy was radiating from his head the same way it did when a child learned something in Rem. But she would have to be careful about what she told him, Dan-te didn't want to upset him—and change him—like she had Reye.

"According to the stories passed down over the generations, 'The Coming' was caused by Beings of Light and their leader, the Light Bringer."

"Light Bringer," Worm repeated. Dan-te heard a note of curiosity and recognition in his voice. He had heard it before.

"What is it?" Dan-te asked.

"The term 'Light Bringer' is in our creation story. It was the title given by the Great Master Ash Addiel to his closest friend, who later betrayed him and was imprisoned underground with his legions. The current translations call him, 'a true friend,' but the older texts in Platin name him Tanas."

"Tanas!" Now it was Dan-te's turn to be surprised, her face twisting with grim realization.

"What's wrong?" Worm asked, confused by how she looked: frightened, angry, and upset.

"It was him. The whole time it was him. The Light Bringer has been leading the Tribe of Shadows!" Dan-te fell to her knees, crying, realizing an extremely sick joke had been played on her and her people for generations.

Worm knew that there was far more to this story than he was aware of. If he wanted to help this woman, he needed to hear it all.

"Dan-te, listen to me. Whatever it is, it's all right." Worm put his arms around her in a comforting embrace. "But before we move on, we need to, as they say here, compare notes. I need you to tell me everything you can about your people and their history. We have already found one point where our pasts connect. I am guessing that there are more, so we need to find them before we can do anything else."

P.J. Fenton

Chapter 19

Ice thankfully *Knew* where the spears were going to come from by the energy flowing through the walls and floor, so he was able to tell Reye when to jump, stop, and sidestep—avoiding the traps—but it took a lot of time. Finally, the trap operators activated a trap Ice *Knew* they couldn't avoid, because its energy felt like it could fill the entire Jac-ob Way. Pulling at Reye, straining his arm in the effort, he stopped her just as a wave of molten heat and energy approached them. A stream of magma suddenly poured down in front of them, blocking their way forward, followed by another magma stream behind them, leaving them few options about what to do next. Thankfully, by then they reached a stairway going up into the next circle.

"I hoped we would make it this far," Ice said shakily. The moment he and Reye started down the Jac-ob Way, Ice realized it would only be a matter of time before the Tribe of Shadows either activated the unavoidable traps, or sent troops down both directions of the Jac-ob Way to catch them. He hoped they could make it to the next circle before that happened, and they did.

Reye, however, wasn't wasting any time. Once she saw that she could only go one way, she made her way up the exit stairway with Ice close on her heels. But as he neared the exit of Jac-ob Way passage, he lost sight of Reye, leaving him to follow her by the acrid smell of sweat and blood clinging to her, leading back up into the city.

"AH!" Reye screamed in the distance, making her way to the top of the staircase.

At the top of the staircase was a door leading into a guarded checkpoint. The crashing noise of an ax colliding with men and metal further alerted Ice that Reye was already hip deep in combat. She had already smashed the door in, destroying the phone in the process, and was currently attacking the guards with the ax she had taken from the Grand Coliseum. The red energy and acrid smells she produced told him she was still changing for the worse. More of the horrible and evil red energy—the characteristic of the Hy-mun Horror—was radiating and further corroding the remaining traces of her own energies. Sadly, he needed her like this if they were going to attack Yam-Preen and best Lord Tanas.

Reaching the scene of the battle, Ice caught up to Reye just in time to stop a guard approaching her from her behind, slashing the guard's sword arm, and interrupting his attack. Before the guard could recover, Ice stepped around him and slashed his leg. Teetering for a moment, the guard fell to the ground.

"Play dead," Ice whispered, hoping to save a life. "It's useless to keep fighting, so play dead and survive. Just give up for now."

"I will never give up!" the guard shouted in reply, staggering back to his feet, and drawing Reye's attention who turned around and finished him with a blow from her ax, cutting a line down from his left shoulder to his left leg. Ice already *Knew* not to get in front of Reye when she was more the Hy-mun Horror and less herself, it could cost him his life. But as she turned her back to him, he had to ask her.

"Is it necessary to kill the injured?"

"Ask the ones responsible for my friends," Reye replied, burning with the energy of the Hy-mun Horror. However, Ice did notice that at the mention of her friends the small brown natural energy inside her burned a little brighter.

With the fight over, the horrible red energy diminishing, and her own natural brown energy increasing, Reye became more herself again and less the Hy-mun Horror.

Was it the mention of her friends that caused the shift, Ice wondered, *or maybe the feeling of satisfaction over hurting members of the Tribe of Shadow?*

"Where are we?" Reye asked Ice, breaking him out of his thoughts.

"We are in the Sixth Circle of the city of Nis, Greed U-Sez," Ice said, slightly exhausted after leaving the Grand Coliseum, running through the Jac-ob Way, and the recent fight.

"Greed U-Sez?" Reye asked, confused.

"That is correct," Ice replied, sounding as confident as he could be. "Anyway, we best get moving before more soldiers come. Follow me."

"And what makes you my guide," Reye asked, annoyed at being told what to do.

"For starters," Ice began, "I was already led through the first five circles. The entire city is a maze of streets designed to stop intruders, which works both to our advantage or disadvantage if we get separated. If you don't live here or can't *Know* and feel the residual energy that flows through the streets and circles, it's easy to get lost."

Reye grumbled when he mentioned *"Know"* again, like it was a special way for anyone to see anything.

Yet with all that knowing *they can't know right from wrong,* Reye thought to herself, not caring if Ice *Knew* it or not.

"Also, there are bound to be a lot more soldiers, guards, and gladiators coming real soon. Despite how much you might want to fight them, if you want their leader, *Lord Tanas*, we have to get moving." He made sure to punctuate the fact that the leader of the Tribe of Shadows, Lord Tanas, was their real goal.

"So, in other words, we leave now, you lead, and you'll get me to the boss," Reye said, summing up what Ice said in a way that she accepted.

"Yes," Ice responded, realizing if Reye believed him, she would not only follow him, but avoid most of the trouble she could find. In order for Reye to face Lord Tanas, Ice needed her to be more like the gladiatorial Hy-mun Horror than a Hy-mun girl, but that didn't mean she had to be the Horror now. If that did happen, there might not be any way for her to be brought back after the deed was done. But by avoiding trouble, keeping her from generating the horrible red energy of the Hy-mun Horror, he hoped she could be brought back to the Reye she used to be after it was over. Ice was certain he could nurse her natural brown energy; energy that was strengthened through memories of her friends, and the satisfaction she felt from achieving a goal, until it overcame her horrible red energy.

"So, which way?" Reye asked.

"This way," Ice answered, feeling for the residual energy leaving the Jac-ob Way that flowed, like a river, into the next circle. Together, they left the checkpoint and made their way into Greed U-Sez.

Reye quickly realized Ice was right about the city being built like a maze; she felt she must have doubled back three times already, yet they had only been walking for a short while now. Ice, on the other hand, seemed to know exactly where he was going. He walked through Nis like had been born there.

It sure is quiet, Reye thought, thinking about how Ice said more soldiers would be coming. But it didn't stay quiet for long. After their first hour of traveling, they arrived at another checkpoint, similar to the one they encountered when they left the Jac-ob Way, only this one was more heavily guarded.

"This shows we're heading in the right direction," Ice said to Reye. "There are checkpoints like this only on the way to—"

Ice didn't finish his sentence; Reye plowed into the checkpoint with her ax swinging. But this time, the guards were better equipped than the ones at the Jac-ob Way exit, and were expecting them. Meeting Reye with smiling faces, the guards were ready to take on the Hy-mun Horror. Ice, barely able to get behind Reye to cover her back, made a mental note to watch out for the next time she took off. The better equipped and more seasoned warriors didn't seem to matter too much to Reye as she bathed herself in the horrible red energy. The harder the soldiers from Nis fought, the more her anger increased, and the stronger and better fighter she became.

"This noise is going to bring more soldiers coming at us from both sides," Ice said to Reye, urging her past the checkpoint. "We have to move."

Reye, however, wouldn't leave until she had finished off every last warrior. Ice *Knew* that arguing with her when she was like this was not only a bad idea, but possibly a fatal one. He stood back and let her work.

Over the next few hours Ice and Reye went through two more checkpoints with at least the same amount of commotion as the first one. However, not long after passing through their third checkpoint since entering the circle, they heard the approaching thunder of soldiers running towards them from both directions.

"They know where we are," Ice said, realizing now why they hadn't heard the soldiers before in the maze of pathways leading through Greed U-Sez. Instead of madly sweeping all of the passageways like he hoped they would, they waited for them to make their way through a number of checkpoints to determine the path they were on, and then move accordingly.

"Let them come!" Reye screamed.

Reye wanted to take them all on, but Ice knew she was getting tired and needed some rest, or a slower pace at least, or she would pass out—but she wasn't going to admit it.

"I know you can beat these soldiers, Reye," Ice said, trying to be as convincing as possible. "But if we don't find a way to dodge them, you'll never get to fight Lord Tanas. He will have left the city by then."

"My brother's final words were fight and run," Reye barked, still intent on fighting.

"Then run for now," Ice said, pulling her arm, "and fight later."

Reye turned on him, preparing her ax—for a moment, Ice thought she was going to kill him—until she lowered it. Ice felt the tension leave Reye's body as she relaxed and her red energy subsided.

"Fine," Reye grated, clearly upset over not getting the chance to fight the oncoming forces. "But I get to lead this time." Reye took off down one of the side streets with Ice in hot pursuit.

This is very bad, Ice thought to himself. Because of the maze-like pathways of Nis, running around could end up putting them back where they started. Since Ice focused on Reye's red energy and acrid scents to keep from losing her, he had no way to tell where they were going. Thankfully, they ended up someplace he heard of.

In front of Ice and Reye, a building, bigger than the others around them, stood out alone and separate from the other parts of the circle. Engraved on each of its sides was a depiction of a large bird, with griffin statues adorning its roof. Hundreds of cables streaked out of windows from each level, connecting to boxes along the roofs on the upper levels of the other buildings, giving the larger one the appearance of being covered in cobwebs.

"What is that?" Reye asked, confused by the weirdly marked building.

"It's one of the three E-gle Buildings," Ice said, slightly surprised about where they ended up. "I have heard about what they look like, but this is the first time that I have seen one."

"What are they for? Are they important?" Reye asked.

Very, Ice said to himself, fully aware of their importance for Nis, but knowing what Reye's reaction would be if she found out. She would want to charge in and wreck the place, costing them precious time.

On the other hand, the E-gle Buildings were essential to running all the functions of Nis, including the current pursuit of them. Telecommunications between circles were conducted by them. When guards and warriors reached checkpoints, those on duty would have to call the designated building for permission to let them through. Ice, while locked up in Wrath Eras, often heard plenty of guards complain about it and could imagine how much trouble it would be if Nis lost just one of them.

"Yes, they are," Ice said, deciding to tell Reye what he could about them. The information made Reye's heart beat loud enough that he could hear it in her chest. He also felt Reye's energy shifting again, become more aggressive and battle ready as the horrible red energy of the Hy-mun Horror encircled her, choking her natural brown energy.

"The Circle of Greed U-Sez is one of the ruling circles," Ice continued. "In this particular circle, decisions are made that focus on Nis itself, and those decisions are both made in, and communicated through, one of the three E-gle Buildings."

"So, we wreck the place, and the city loses a third of its communication and decision-making capabilities?" Reye asked.

"Yes," Ice answered.

Reye charged into the E-gle Building, ax swinging, taking down as many members of the Tribe of Shadows she could find. The facility was built in an extremely compartmental fashion, each floor filled with workers, working in cubicles overseeing the decisions of Nis while they operated massive switchboards to run the telecommunication network. But while the workers might have been geared toward the administration and running of Nis, they were still trained fighters, having fought in the arenas, and fully willing to fight and die against her. Ice traveled close behind Reye, keeping her back clear of anyone trying to approach, and keeping himself clear of her ax.

I still think she is the best hope we have of defeating Lord Tanas, Ice realized, regardless of whatever misgivings he had about using Reye. *The way she moves is ferocious, yet also incredible and awe-inspiring.*

Ice also realized he must be changing, in a way larger than he could imagine, if he actually felt that way about Reye. The horrible and savage red energy she displayed was extremely addictive.

I could just watch her and nothing else, Ice stared, quickly chastising himself, knowing that the same alluring red energy making Reye this way was wrong, and that he shouldn't be feeling this way. He needed to keep her from drowning in this energy.

Ice's internal debate was quickly cut short. Watching Reye open a side room, she paused at what she saw. Now at Reye's side, he caught a glimpse of her eyes bulging wide before feeling the horrible red energy of the Hy-mun Horror suddenly challenged by her own brown natural energy and a new mental white energy. Rising to the surface, the two new energies broke through the red energy, and began mixing with it.

"Don't let anyone in here!" Reye shouted in a commanding tone, running into the room, and leaving Ice at the door. Ice, turning his back to Reye, did what he was told. Not out of fear, but because he *Knew* she had a plan. Her natural brown energy surfacing meant something triggered memories from before she came to Nis, and that energy was nothing compared to the white mental energy radiating from her. Before now, Reye had been charging in and cutting down anything that moved on instinct, but this was different. The Reye he now *Knew*, while still possessing the same desire to hurt the Tribe of Shadows that made her the Hy-mun Horror, included her mind's awakened mental white energy. She was thinking and planning, using all the strength her mind possessed. The E-gle Building's workers also felt the white energy from her mind, as they rushed the door with increasing vigor. Ice stood his ground in the doorway, holding off each worker that approached—made easy since they could only approach him from that position one at a time—and did not let anyone through, waiting patiently until Reye finished whatever she was doing. Thankfully, he didn't have to wait long. Reye soon ran out of the room, wearing an extremely large and loaded pack on her back and knocking Ice and a few workers over in the process with it and her ax. Freeing one of her hands, she grabbed Ice's arm and pulled him to his feet.

"Run!" Reye screamed.

Ice didn't need to be told twice. Reye's entire image had changed. Her voice contained fear and her energy had become wild—quickly changing from red to brown to white and back again.

Ice and Reye started running from the workers, down the stairs, and eventually out of the E-gle Building. Soon afterwards, a loud hissing sound began echoing around them. Ice's guessed it originated back in the room where Reye was working. Feeling the stone walls, he *Knew* there was danger—the energy rapidly dropped, becoming null and lifeless, something was attacking it. Feeling heat on his back, he looked back up the stairs and saw what could have been magma, except instead of giving off the reddish-orange glow and sulfur smells of both magma and the magma tubes around and under the city, this material glowed bright white, like the light from the Veil of Shadows after it had been torn, but didn't cause pain. The other members of the Tribe of Shadows weren't so quick to make the realization, jumping for cover, and giving them the chance to escape. Once outside, Reye quickly dragged him down one of the streets. Ice *Knew* she also wanted to avoid the white magma, it wasn't until she stopped running, letting him go, that he was able to ask.

"What did you do? What was that?" Ice, looking back at the E-gle Building, saw the white magma eating straight through it, eating into the ground the facility stood on. As the material sank lower into the ground, the structure sank with it.

"Magnesium Mining Charges, or MMCs for short," Reye replied with a grin, opening the backpack and pulling out a strange device, a small metallic cylinder about a hand's span in diameter and height.

"They've been used in mining and deep surface exploration since before the Rainbow War. They use magnesium and special compounds to create a high-heat liquid that will eat through just about anything. That room I was in had a whole stockpile of them. After grabbing a pack of them, I rigged them to go off and then…boom." Reye flashed one of her hands open to illustrate of the effect, but it was nothing compared to the actual event that followed.

A loud boom from the direction of the ruined E-gle Building furthered Reye's explanation. Turning back, Ice witnessed the destruction. The MMCs were exploding throughout the entire place, liquid magnesium melted the floors and walls, dumping more MMCs that hadn't exploded everywhere, then those bombs detonated, adding to the chaos, and eventually leaving nothing but a hole in the ground that the cables and debris were drawn into. Workers caught or covered by the liquid barely had any time to scream before melting down to nothing. As the remaining walls crumbled in on themselves, and the griffin insignias melted down into the ground along with the liquid magnesium, Ice felt the ground shake and heat begin building under his feet; focusing itself at the center of where the E-gle Building once stood, and where the liquid magnesium continued melting into the ground. Soon after that, a geyser of magma erupted from where the E-gle Building used to be in a miniature volcanic eruption.

"One other thing about MMCs," Reye said with a gleam in her eye that made Ice shudder, "when they hit anything, including magma, the chemicals in the charges blow everything up to the surface."

Ice looked at Reye. The wildness he felt from her was gone, something new had taken its place. She still generated and wrapped herself in the horrible red energy that made her the Hy-mun Horror, but now it had started to mix with the two other energies she was generating instead of corroding them. One, the emotional brown energy from her heart and self that made her who she was, the other, the white mental energy she produced when she thought and planned. Ice realized by the familiarity on her face, a look he recognized on emissaries after they returned to Rem from Nis—knowing they were back in their home territory, that Reye was used to generating these mental and emotional energies before she came to Nis. Only now she found a way to use them with the horrible red energy that made her the Hy-mun Horror. The destruction of the E-gle Building had given her something else that she needed to come to this point: satisfaction, revenge, and a sense of familiarity.

"Reye, how do you feel?" Ice asked cautiously.

"Satisfied, for now," Reye answered.

Reye did seem that way. She hated the Tribe of Shadows for killing the other Hy-muns and turning them into food she ate. She hated that the creatures in this city could say, "You are fighting this gladiator to the death." She was glad she took away a third of their ability to do that, using skills she learned to become a terranaut, and was extremely proud to have the tools of a terranaut instead of just an ax. And she would be even more satisfied when she reached Lord Tanas, who ordered all of this, and finished him herself.

It won't be for nothing, Raymond, Reye thought to herself. *I'll do what you told me to do, I'll run and I'll fight all the way to the leader of these creatures. Then these creatures will be the ones running, they'll be running whenever they see a Hy-mun again. They are going to know how it feels to lose someone. I'm going to keep running and fighting over each and every one I can get to until there isn't a single creature left that can hurt us.*

"Okay, Ice, get us back on course," Reye said.

The destruction of the E-gle Building will have multiple consequences throughout Nis, Ice thought. *Confusion and chaos will increase as every warrior with a weapon is sent to the ruins to look for us, but they will have to wait at checkpoints for clearance from the remaining two facilities. They will also need to pick up the telecommunication work from the destroyed one. It's the perfect distraction for moving on with little to no opposition.*

Taking the lead again, and remembering not to challenge Reye—because even if she was more at peace, it didn't mean she wouldn't kill him—Ice felt and found the energy that continued onto the next circle.

"This way," Ice said, turning down a side road with Reye right behind him.

Chapter 20

Dan-te and Worm talked for hours. Dan-te, after learning about Tanas, decided not to hold anything back and told him about her people—The Remnant of the Tribe—and their history from before "The Coming," when the world didn't have the Light, but all creatures produced the Glow.

"All by themselves?" Worm had asked, intrigued.

"Yes," Dan-te replied.

She told Worm how after "The Coming," the Tribe split between the Tribe of Shadows and The Remnant, and the two cities they would build—Nis and Rem. She told him how Tanas came to lead the Tribe of Shadows and provided them with the Veils of Shadows that allowed them to travel to the surface without harm, and about the first two Great Attempts that had been used to retake the surface, and lastly how she came to be in his room. Dan-te noticed Worm radiated extreme interest when she mentioned not only Tanas, but the past two Great Attempts. "So, *that's* what happened," he had mumbled.

Worm also told her about the Hy-muns' myths and legends. Dan-te was clearly disturbed to hear the Nag-el praised as good beings. Worm told her the

159

history of the Dominions' technological skill and how it was nearly lost during the Great Rainbow War, a war he now knew was instigated by the Tribe of Shadows, also realizing that the First Great Attempt—instigated by the Tribe of Shadows—ended up resulting in the origin myths of the Hy-mun people.

"So that is why the Nag-el left," Worm said, after comparing the story of the First Great Attempt with the legend of the Nag-el departure. He was also glad to learn that Reye was still alive when Dan-te had last seen her. But disheartened when he heard about the kind of person she was turning into.

After talking with Worm for a while, Dan-te *Knew* that he had also suffered losses like Reye, losses that pushed him to extreme conditions, both mentally and emotionally. When Worm talked, his voice became edged with sadness and fatigue—the same way an elder's voice sounded after a lifetime's worth of loss. Worm also radiated the same deep blue energy as an elder, as if the entire world rested on his shoulders, yet he kept smiling so he wouldn't worry others.

They continued talking throughout the night. By then, Worm started to use candles—with Dan-te's permission—to see, discovering candlelight didn't affect Dan-te the same way sunlight did.

"Let me see if I understand a few things correctly," Worm asked, "this ability to *Know* other things or beings. You said you can *Know* things about buildings, plants, and even the ground we walk on, not just living beings, and it's not so much mind reading as it is seeing with all of your senses."

"It also involves studying," Dan-te added. "Learning how to read and tell what those sensations are telling us."

"So, while Hy-muns see things just through their eyes," Worm continued. "You use more than that; you use your eyes, ears, sense of smell, taste, and touch, to create a composite image through which you see, or *Know*, the nature of things. A nature you are able to read after studying under a teacher. Is that correct?"

"That's pretty much it," Dan-te answered, impressed Worm could understand what she told him, unlike Reye. "The image I have of you is not just made up of what I see, but also from the scents you give off—no matter how miniscule they might be, the sounds you make, what I can taste in the air around you, the kinds of energy I can feel off you, and my own skill at reading those sensations. I'm actually surprised you believed the feeling part."

"It's not that unbelievable," Worm said. "I studied martial arts back home and one of the disciplines of it is feeling where your opponent is going to direct an attack, and what they might do, based on the energy that they emit. A simple example is when one person walks past another, and the first person simply gets a bad feeling off the other. What you're describing is the same idea, just taken much further. Your description of the world prior to 'The Coming,' a dark world with none of what Hy-muns refer to as light, actually supports that idea."

"And how is that?" Dan-te asked.

"Because any people developing in a low-light environment would need to learn other means of perception. Otherwise, they wouldn't be able to survive," Worm answered.

"What do you mean by 'low-light?' There was no Light, just the Glow. And why were you so interested when I talked about the world before 'The Coming?'" Throughout the entire story, Worm kept stealing glances to his bookshelves. Dan-te felt his white mental energy and desire directed toward something in the shelves—there was something in them he wanted. She had thought about letting him get what he wanted, but she *Knew* from the way his white mental energy was radiating and processing the story that he also wanted to hear the story in its entirety.

Dan-te's description of "The Coming" also had a similar effect, causing Worm to look through the beginning of a black book with a seven-colored snake biting its own tail outlining a white circle on its cover that was sitting on his desk. A book he called the *Tome of the Ouroboros*, the mainstream sacred text for all the Hy-mun Dominions.

"Well," Worm began, "first of all, I don't believe that the world before 'The Coming,' is it alright if I refer to the world that way?"

"Just 'the Land' will do," Dan-te responded.

"Alright, I don't think the Land was without light. It was without sunlight but not without 'Light.' Just a moment, let me grab a few books." Worm went to the bookshelves. He wasted no time, picking book after book from his shelves without even bothering to look at the titles, knowing where to find each book he needed and pulling it out quickly. When he returned to Dan-te—who was admittedly puzzled—he quickly took one out of the stack and paged through it until he found what he was looking for.

"This book is by an undersea explorer from the Blue Dominion who lived prior to the Great Rainbow War," Worm explained. "In it, he describes something he witnessed in the deepest parts of the ocean, where practically no sunlight shines whatsoever. He witnessed sea plants and fish glowing through a process he dubbed bioluminescence."

"Bio-what?" Dan-te asked.

"Bioluminescence," Worm said the word again, more slowly so Dan-te could catch it. "It's a process where, in extremely dark conditions, certain forms of life can generate their own light. You said before 'The Coming' the Land was dark and emitted the Glow. I think the Glow might have been bioluminescent plants and animals that once covered the world until 'The Coming' happened."

"And this explorer saw them?" Dan-te asked skeptically.

"Unfortunately, the samples brought back by the explorer were confiscated and then lost shortly after he returned and published his findings." Dan-te *Knew* that when Worm said "lost," he really meant that they were either destroyed or buried, triggering memories from Worm's past. His voice turning bitter, as he started to emit slivers of the same hateful red energy Dan-te recognized as being similar to the energy Reye was generating.

"What happened to this explorer has happened to you?" Dan-te asked.

"Yes, but that's another story," Worm sighed, the red energy dissipating. "It's actually happened throughout Hy-mun history. Life, order, and good are believed to be the products of Ash Addiel's light—sunlight—and the light of the Nag-el—starlight—covering the surface of the planet. Whenever something happens that challenges the religious beliefs of the Hy-mun people—like, for example, light or life where it shouldn't exist—someone comes along and attempts to bury it. Back in my home, there is a saying in the old language of Platin, "condemnant quod non intelligunt," meaning "they condemn what they do not understand." Throughout history, we Hy-muns have had a bad habit to either fear or destroy anything we can't understand or that challenges our beliefs. That's why your stories of the world before 'The Coming' and 'The Coming' itself are not only important, but dangerous."

"Because they challenge your beliefs?" Dan-te asked, realizing that her presence in the Hy-mun world could be far more hazardous than she originally thought. She hadn't lost her trust in Worm, though; she *Knew* no matter what he learned about her, her people, the Tribe of Shadows, or the world underneath their feet, he wouldn't turn on her. One type of energy he generated since they started talking was the indigo energy of loyalty, an energy she often felt between friends and loved one. She had the right Hy-mun as a companion, he was not going to turn on her or abandon her regardless of what he learned.

"That's right," Worm said with a serious expression on his face. "If you revealed yourself, and tried to tell your story, the first thing people would ask for, if they asked at all, is proof—beyond your testimony—that your story is real, which you don't have. All you *can* prove by your existence is that there are non-Hy-mun beings living underground and can't stand sunlight. A supporter of the Tome's story would easily claim you were one of Tanas's followers trying to tempt Hy-muns with lies."

"I would rather die than serve Tanas," Dan-te spat.

"I believe you," Worm said, trust echoing in his words. "But others won't, and since your story shows the Nag-el, whom you refer to as the Beings of Light, as conquerors instead of creators, the powers that be would not want to risk a story like that getting out. Anytime something is found relating to the Nag-el, it causes a commotion. The movement that led to the Great Rainbow War began with the discovery of artifacts in the Yellow Dominion believed to be the property of the Nag-el."

"The Yellow Dominion," Dan-te mournfully echoed the Hy-mun name she learned from Worm with a sigh. She remembered the stories passed down in Rem, of what their world looked like before "The Coming." But since then, it was "a great desert where, according to your history, nothing has grown or lived except in the Grand Oasis, and down the Great Line River. The place that was once the Ancient Tribe's homeland, until the Beings of Light first came to this world and started butchering them."

"The people of the Yellow Dominion thought something similar as well," Worm replied, recalling his history lessons. "Except without the knowledge of your people. After documents believed to have been owned by the Nag-el were discovered in their dominion, documents containing what they believed were instructions from the Great Master Ash Addiel on how he wanted us all to live on this world—in a word, simply—the Hy-muns of the region took the notion to heart and attempted to imitate it. That idea grew into an anti-technology fervor that nearly destroyed the world in the Great Rainbow War."

"The Second Great Attempt," Dan-te said, remembering what she and Worm had discussed about how the Tribe of Shadows acted in the Great Rainbow War. The Tribe of Shadows prodded leaders, and then stole technology from the secret underground bunkers each dominion hid for after the war. The technology from those bunkers allowed the Tribe of Shadows to make greater strides toward completing the Third Great Attempt in the more recent generations than in all of the past generations combined.

"However," Worm began, "those artifacts began another movement, one almost wiped out by the war, yet survived until recently."

"A movement that you are very familiar with," Dan-te said, noting Worm's change when he started to talk about this movement. His voice becoming gentler, and his overall energy more joyous, losing its prickling sensation, and turning softer, smoother, feeling almost like a watered down stone against her skin—he was recalling happier times.

"Indeed, the Ancient Astronaut Movement, or AAM for short. They believed the Great Master Ash Addiel and the Nag-el were real beings from another world, separate from our own, instead of divine beings." Worm picked up the black book with the serpent on it and showed it to Dan-te. "They examined the *Tome of the Ouroboros*, the stars, and our world in different ways, thinking they could discover where the Great Master and the Nag-el came from, and what happened to them. Your story proves some of their theories."

"How does it do that?" Dan-te asked.

"For starters, you said that there was no sunlight. The *Tome of the Ouroboros* says: *Light Bringer searched and found a world shrouded in darkness and chaos, a world in need of the glory of the light. Light Bringer brought his people to that world to make it ready for the coming of the Great Master, bringing light to the darkness and shaping order out of the chaos that he found.*

"We now know that the Light Bringer spoken here, the Light Bringer from your story of 'The Coming,' and the Tanas ruling Nis and the Tribe of Shadows are all the same person," Worm said, excitement building within him. Even though the mention of Tanas's name brought a hiss from Dan-te, thinking about all he brought to her people throughout the generations, first as the Light Bringer who led the Nag-el against her people, and then as Lord Tanas who still ruled Nis and the Tribe of Shadows.

"Second, it says that he came from one world to another, indicating travel between worlds. Third, and this is important, the world they found was one that was *'shrouded in darkness and chaos.'"*

"Our world was many things, but not chaotic," Dan-te said defensively.

"That depends on how you define chaos," Worm said. "It's because of these claims that the AAM, who claimed to only be 'seekers of truth,' got in trouble in the first place. Chaos can simply mean without order, and order is defined by the one making the definition. From what you have told me about Tanas and Nis, after he came to power, he completely restructured the city. His definition of 'order' might be a civilization similar to his own. Anything else, he would have seen as chaotic. Also, while your world might not have been chaotic, I do believe it was shrouded in darkness. Personally though, I don't think that Ash Addiel became the sun. I think it was always there, but your world was just naturally shielded from it, by dark matter."

"What's dark matter?" Dan-te asked, her face twisting in confusion.

"Dark matter is an invisible substance, and it can only be detected with specialized telescopic equipment," Worm answered, now in the role of a scholar. "It was first discovered in small patches just beyond the planet's atmosphere. Later, more was found along the planet's orbit, the path it travels around the sun. It's theorized a ring of dark matter once existed everywhere along and around this planet's orbit. If that is true, the world would have been shrouded in darkness, so if someone looked at the planet from space, it would be invisible. Not only that, if anyone living on the planet looked up, they would see nothing."

"Until Tanas comes along," Dan-te continued, putting Worm's thoughts together, seeing where he was going. "Finds the planet, kills everyone on the surface, and removes the dark matter, 'bringing light to the darkness and shaping order out of the chaos that he found.'" She *could* see how the passages in the Tome matched her history. "But that doesn't explain why my people are not mentioned, or why this movement's beliefs would challenge the mainstream Hymun beliefs."

"To answer the first question, I would guess ignorance—they didn't know," Worm said.

"They didn't know!" Dan-te shouted, fighting to keep her voice down.

"History is always written by victors," Worm replied, shaking his head and hanging it low. "The first Tome was said to have been written by the last Nag-el on Prism before leaving the Platinum Throne. Now, whether the writer was a Nag-el or not, I doubt he would have included your people in the story, regardless if he knew about them. Ego and pride can be powerful and dangerous things. I highly doubt that the writer would have wanted to place the Nag-el in a negative context."

Dan-te calmed herself, realizing that Worm was right. She often heard the story of "The Coming," and how one of the seats of the Tribe's council became so consumed with ego and pride he became known as The Pride, one of the first Seven Vices, whose name lived on in the Eighth Circle of Nis. Even now, pride was often used as a means to inspire the members of the Tribe of Shadows. She could still remember hearing the teachers in Envy Opal-Lo, screaming to the Tribe of Shadows' children to take pride in who they were, where they came from, and what they were doing; that the legacy passed down from their ancestors was something to be proud of. Everything was done with a measure of pride.

"That same ego and pride are also the answer to why the movement's beliefs would challenge the mainstream's beliefs," Worm said. "The belief is that the Hy-muns were created by the Great Master Ash Addiel 'from where his light seeped into the ground,' creating 'a new race of beings...born from the mixture of the earth and the light.' The mainstream thinkers love this verse because it turns the Hy-muns into a unique creation formed by the joining of the Great Lord Ash Addiel with the land itself. Ash Addiel then takes those first Hy-muns under his wing, and then gives this world to them. It presents Him as a responsible creator who takes care of his creations—like a father caring for his son. The AAM's theories however lower the Hy-mun status to the point where, at worst, the Hy-muns' creation could have been an accident, or the equivalent of a science project. His care for us is also called into question."

Dan-te knew that while Worm understood this, it also unsettled him, and she didn't blame him for that. Like he said, "Ego and pride can be a powerful and dangerous thing," and after talking to him, she realized most Hy-muns would probably die instead of swallowing their pride to accept an idea like that. Dan-te imagined if she had to face a possibility similar to the one Worm was describing, it would be just as difficult.

"Pride causes problems for everyone in one way or another," Dan-te said. "The dividing of the Tribe, Tanas's rise to power, and everything that the Tribe of Shadows has done since—cannibalism, forced breeding, everything—can be traced to some form of pride. Why they just couldn't swallow their pride and live in peace, I don't know?"

"The Tribe of Shadows has been, excuse the pun, living in the shadow of two invasive races, the Nag-el and the Hy-muns, for an uncountable number of years," Worm answered, his own voice filled with pity for the Tribe of Shadows. "They were driven from their homes, forced underground where they had to develop new survival tactics, and constantly reminded about how they ended up there by their first leaders, continuing under Tanas's influence—which only made their pride and hatred grow even more. It's no surprise the Tribe of Shadows seems unredeemable, that kind of environment could warp almost anyone's mind." His expression changed as Dan-te felt cold sadness wash over him. "Personally, I feel bad for the Tribe of Shadows' children," he said mournfully, his voice echoing pain, pity, and sorrow for the Tribe of Shadows' young.

"You wouldn't be the first one," Dan-te sighed. "Growing up in Rem, I often hear other emissaries and elders speak about how the children in Nis only know what they are taught. I've also had a hard time believing it. I used to think that all members of the Tribe, regardless of where they come from, should be able to *Know* to a certain degree. So why couldn't children *Know* their elders are wrong. But when I reached Nis, saw their children in coliseums, turning out just like them, I just didn't know what to think."

"You told me you can *Know* whether something is right or wrong through its composite image," Worm replied, looking at Dan-te challengingly. "You can *Know* someone or something through the way you feel its energy, and see it with your external senses, but you still need to learn how to read it. So tell me, how do you understand what you are reading; what is 'right' and 'wrong,' really?"

Worm's question caused Dan-te to stop and think. What he asked aimed beyond a definition of right and wrong, transcending examples of both concepts, looking for something deeper. She quickly realized that this kind of question didn't have an easy answer. In fact, it was the kind of question a member of the

Council would give her.

"I can think of examples of right and wrong," Dan-te said. "But I *Know* you are looking for something deeper than that, and I'm sorry, but I don't have an answer for you."

"Taken alone, right and wrong are simply words that we intelligent beings simply assign definitions to, no different than how we assign left and right." Worm held up his left and right hands as he was talking to make his point. "Now, if an innocent generation, one that doesn't know, or perhaps a better word would be understand, what 'right' and 'wrong' is, and has no other way to tell how an older generation defines it, the innocent generation is left to the mercy of the older one. Now if the older generation raised the innocent one to understand 'wrong' as 'right' and 'right' as 'wrong,' despite what that older generation was raised to believe, wouldn't the younger generation now understand and know 'wrong' as 'right' and 'right' as 'wrong,' teaching it to future generations as well?"

Dan-te couldn't respond. In the hours that they had talked, they had shared some of largest events of their histories, 'The Coming,' the first two Great Attempts, the Great Rainbow War, the rise and fall of Hy-mun civilization, and the Tribe of Shadows and The Remnant's own civilizations. In that short time span, she knew Worm had a deeper level of understanding to some of the aspects of her own world than many of her own people did. If there were any more people like him around, people who were willing to help, willing to understand, she might be able to stop the Third Great Attempt yet. She felt her hopes beginning to rise as she imagined a larger group of Hy-mun similar to Worm returning with her to Nis to stop the Third Great Attempt.

"Are there others like you around this school of yours?" Dan-te begged, excitement and anticipation building in her voice.

"Like me how?" Worm asked.

"People who are able to understand like you can, or perhaps a part of this AAM. Are there more people that are just like you? If there are more like you, I would really like to meet them." Dan-te could hardly keep her voice in check now, but unfortunately, Worm's response was not what she was hoping for. She actually felt herself lean back from the pain carried in his voice, her ears practically burning from the sadness in it.

"I don't think so," Worm answered sadly. "The movement was at its peak prior to the Great Rainbow War, but after that, it was all but eradicated. The last small pockets of members did come together in secret a couple of years ago to attempt completing one of the great projects of the movement—sending a Hy-mun into space. All prior attempts at space travel were deemed taboo, because it was believed to be violating the territory of the Great Lord Ash Addiel and the Nag-el. These members, however, still wanted to try and see if they could send someone up there."

Dan-te *Knew* from the torment in Worm's voice that these memories were not only personal, but also extremely private, the kind that Worm would not share with just anyone.

He must either be placing a lot of trust in me, or he's positive I won't talk to anyone else about this, Dan-te thought, *or that no one would ever believe me.* Either way, Dan-te decided that no matter the reason, she would keep whatever secrets they shared to themselves and not divulge them to anyone, not even her own people.

"You were friends with those AAM members, weren't you?" Dan-te asked, fully anticipating both Worm's reaction, and the answer to her question.

"Yes, I was friends with them. My mother's side of my family had ties to the AAM before the war, so when they needed support, they came to her. I worked and studied with the AAM members for a long period of time, and was even training to go into space."

"What happened?" Dan-te asked, her concern growing for Worm, Dan-te *Knew* it was getting harder for him to retell this story. She could hear the pain in his voice as he talked about his friends, and could feel a red painful energy—similar to the energy Reye released when she was unconscious in her cell—begin to bubble out of Worm's blue energy.

"The Hammers of the Orange Light happened." Worm pulled out a brown book and opened it to a page showing a Hy-mun robed in orange cloth carrying a large hammer. Other illustrations showed teams of the same robed Hy-muns attacking and destroying temples, factories, and homes. "They were an extremist group founded prior to the start of the Great Rainbow War, and during the war they went about destroying anything, and anyone, thought to be an enemy of the Great Master Ash Addiel, or an ally of Tanas. It didn't matter if it was technology, people, or ideology. They were intent on purging away anything they thought didn't fit with what they believed was 'proper,' for lack of a better word."

"Proper" may not have been the best word Worm could have used, but Dan-te *Knew* what he was talking about. These Hammers seemed to be the complete opposite of someone like Worm. They were intolerant and inflexible. If they were confronted with something they didn't understand, they would destroy it, instead of trying to learn about it.

"Officially, they were wiped out after the war. However, there were rumors that squads of them survived and were being used to remove 'harmful political elements.' I found out the hard way that those rumors were true when they came to the AAM camp and destroyed it, killing all but one person."

"You," Dan-te said.

"Me, a certain situation with my family made it necessary for me to wear a mask when I was there, and use an alias. Because of that, only a handful of people knew who I was, and they were all killed getting me safely home. Everyone else just knew me as the kid in a mask called Uni." Worm closed his eyes briefly and Dan-te could feel his white mental energy drifting, returning to the past and the events of the attack. "It took me a year and a half before I had the courage to leave home again. Soon afterwards, I came here."

"So, no chance about finding anymore AAM members here, but what about people who can understand like you can?"

"I can't name anyone who could be like me since I can't *Know* another person like you can," Worm said. "You would have to reveal yourself to every person here, and that would do more harm than good."

Dan-te knew Worm was right, based on what he told her about the Hy-mun world, especially with groups like the Hammers around. If she made herself publicly known, she would be captured at least, and at worst be killed before anyone could listen to her. Worm was probably the only ally she would find on the surface, who might actually listen to what the Tribe of Shadows are trying to do, and also try to stop the Third Great Attempt—instead of ignoring it, calling it a myth like the First Great Attempt, or a war like the Second.

Chapter 21

"So, tell me more about the Third Great Attempt?" Worm asked, trying to get their discussion off his past, and back to the more immediate problem that brought Dan-te to his room in the first place. "You told me that if it comes to completion, it would mean the end of all our races, and that you came here looking for help to stop it, but you still haven't given me any details on exactly what it is."

"Of course," Dan-te said, realizing she and Worm spent enough time on history. It was time to start focusing on the future. "The attempt is actually older than the previous two; it's just called the Third Great Attempt because the others were tried before it could be completed. It began soon after Tanas joined the Tribe of Shadows, when they started digging."

"Digging?"

"You know the piece of land covered with volcanoes?"

"The Red Dominion, I know it."

"For generations now, Tanas and the Tribe of Shadows have been digging a great tunnel from Nis to the main magma veins of those volcanoes. Once there, they plan on setting off a charge that will cause a massive volcanic eruption. Powerful enough that the volcanoes themselves will darken the sky, removing Light, and returning the world to the way it was before 'The Coming.' The Tribe of Shadows will then march up from the caves, without fear of Light, and overthrow the Hy-muns. That is Tanas's plan, but the Remnant *Know* that it will not happen that way, instead it will end up destroying all of us. We *Know* this from the Land, the ground radiates a fearful pink energy that only increases the closer the attempt come to completion. The Land is scared for its very life, and the lives of everyone who lives on and within it, a fear I can still feel beneath us now."

"The land itself is scarred?" Worm asked.

"You don't think the Land itself is alive?" Dan-te shot back accusingly. Worm, blushing with embarrassment, realizing his stupid remark, decided to move the conversation along.

"Forgive my stupidity. Does the Tribe of Shadows *Know* this as well?"

"Not as clearly as we of the Remnant do," Dan-te answered. "As far as the Tribe of Shadows is concerned, the fearful energy they *Know* is the Land's fear of failure. They think the Land is afraid of failing the Tribe of Shadows, that the volcanic eruption won't be enough to complete the transformation."

"And both of your groups would be right," Worm said, his eyes confused, white mental energy radiating from his head, indicating to Dan-te he was trying to make sense out of the attempt. "A large-scale volcanic ash cloud would block out the sun, and without the sun's rays, the temperature would drop dramatically to the point where life on the surface is impossible. But it doesn't make sense."

"What doesn't make sense?"

"Well, the volcanoes of the Red Dominion have been studied for centuries, and the possibility of large-scale volcanic ash clouds have been examined, but considering both the size of the volcanoes and their location, even if all the volcanoes went off in one massive eruption, it still wouldn't make a large enough ash cloud to cover the entire continent and block off all sunlight. The type of volcanic eruption needed to achieve the level of devastation you're describing would have to come from a volcano more powerful than all of the Red Dominion's volcanoes put together, and need to be located on a different part of the continent. It also doesn't explain how it would hurt your people. Do you know how the eruptions are going to be triggered?"

"Yes, I do. Do you have something to draw with?" Worm handed Dan-te some paper and a pencil, who quickly drew a picture. When she was done, she handed it back to Worm. "There are charges like these being set up at the vein; the Tribe of Shadows has been stockpiling them throughout Nis for a long time now. There are at least a few crates of these charges in almost every building in the city."

Worm looked at the picture Dan-te had drawn. He recognized it instantly from some of Reye's books, a Magnesium Mining Charge. Worm often heard about how they worked from Reye. A picture began forming in Worm's mind.

MMCs, cavernous city, everyone dying, tunnel to magma vein, ash cloud, ANN! Worm's thoughts about what Dan-te had told him suddenly collided with the memory of Ann's talk at AB's before they left for the Mining Project. Pieces began falling into place in Worm's mind, forming a gruesome picture of just how the Third Great Attempt would work.

Dan-te also *Knew* Worm figured something out. He radiated a grim understanding as he quickly turned to his desk, cleared it, emptied a bag of books from the side of his desk onto it, and unrolled a large sheet of paper—placing other books on corners the table to hold it down. Dan-te glanced at the paper, it appeared to be a map of the Hy-mun world with markings on it.

Dan-te watched Worm examine and work on the map. She *Knew* he was getting scared—the acrid stench of fear was rolling off of him in increasing waves—the harder he worked. She *Knew* Worm understood something about the Third Great Attempt, what it was supposed to do, how it worked, or how it was going to be the end of all of them, and it terrified him. Finally, Worm turned from the map to Dan-te.

"All right, now look here, and tell me if I'm wrong in any way," Worm said, pointing to a part of the map. "These are the Prison Caverns, they're the deepest caverns in the world and where, it is believed, Tanas was imprisoned underground. From what you told me, it's also where your people escaped to when Tanas and the Nag-el first came here. It is also the place where the first reports of cave snatching took place, which I now know was done by the Tribe of Shadows at Tanas's command. They should lead straight to Nis, correct?"

"Correct," Dan-te said, wondering where this was going.

"And Nis has magma running all through and under it, right?"

"Right."

"Okay. If this is where your people and Tanas came in, and this is the city of Nis, and the Tribe of Shadows dug this tunnel to here, then…" Worm stopped talking, his face contorting into shock and terror.

"Worm, what's wrong?" Dan-te asked, trying to get Worm talking again.

"You were right, Dan-te," Worm said, his voice thick with fear. "The Third Great Attempt *will* destroy everyone. Surprisingly enough, Tanas is right about how the Third Great Attempt is going to do it. And you were also right, there won't be anyone left once it's over."

"What do you mean?" Dan-te *Knew* the Third Great Attempt would destroy them all, but Worm's sudden reaction told her he must have figured out how.

"Tanas is trying to set off a volcanic eruption, but it's not in the Red Dominion. He's trying to set off a supervolcano, in the city of Nis itself."

"What?" Dan-te asked in surprise. Dan-te never heard of a supervolcano before, but she *Knew* from the way Worm said the word, it was dangerous.

"A supervolcano is a theoretical type of volcano that a friend of mine named Ann was working on. In theory, an extremely large amount of magma pools in one large area, then an earthquake, or some other seismic event, causes the pool to erupt out of a single fixed point, forming an ash cloud over the planet's surface that blocks out the sun, causing temperatures to drop to the point where nothing can survive. Now, you said magma runs throughout Nis. There must be a magma pool beneath it. If not, then the blast at the magma vein in the Red Domination will allow magma to flow through the tunnel to Nis, flooding both the city and the cavern that it's built in, creating one artificially—like a bucket filling with water. As for the eruption, Tanas already prepared the city to 'erupt' once the magma hits it."

"How?" Dan-te asked.

"This is how," Worm replied grimly, indicating Dan-te's picture. "This is a Magnesium Mining Charge. They burn hot, fast, and eat downward until they hit magma. They then create a reaction that causes the magma to force its way up in a miniature eruption. You told me Nis is stockpiled with these charges. Once the magma hits, all the charges go off and then, boom! It's all forced through the roof to the surface in one supervolcanic explosion."

"And Rem and the Remnant…" Dan-te began.

"They will be destroyed as the magma flows throughout the tunnels."

Dan-te felt like she was going to throw up, a feeling Worm shared. Now she understood the danger her people *Knew* was coming. If the Third Great Attempt happened like Worm was predicting, all of the members of the two Tribes beneath the surface, and all of the Hy-muns on the surface, would either meet their end in a volcanic fire or an ice age.

"Wait, why would Tanas do this?" Dan-te asked suddenly. "Wouldn't he be killed as well?"

"I think he's trying to free himself."

"Free himself?" Dan-te whiffed, turning even whiter than she already was over Worm's notion that Tanas was sacrificing countless lives just to free himself. However, she also knew Worm wasn't the first person to suggest this. Throughout Rem's history, members of the Council thought Tanas wanted the Tribe of Shadows to do his work because he couldn't go to the surface anymore, the possibility that they were right made her dizzy.

"According this is a passage in the Tome. *'Eight sentinels took watch across the land to make sure that Light Bringer would never return. Should he try, the sentinels would ensure that he suffer an even worse fate than what he had already been condemned to.'*

"There has been numerous speculation as to who or what these eight sentinels are, but considering what we have discussed about the previous Great Attempts and the Great Rainbow War, I'm betting that the eight sentinels are the Seven Ziggurats and the Platinum Throne."

"You mean where we are now, and the seven capitals of each dominion?" Dan-te asked.

"That's right, both the Seven Ziggurats and the Platinum Throne predate Hy-mun history. To this day, the amount that any Hy-mun has ever been able to discover about the deeper reaches of them has been minimal at best. What Hy-muns do know, is that once a year they have an automatic reaction on the Day of Rainbow Light, when the sun causes the Platinum Throne and Ziggurats to cover the land in light. During the previous Great Attempt, the Great Rainbow War, it's a little known fact that there was talk in some of the extremist movements—like the Hammers of the Orange Light—to destroy the Ziggurats and the Platinum

Throne entirely, claiming they were scientific constructs. I understand now that those talks were instigated by the Tribe of Shadows on Tanas's orders. Now, the Third Great Attempt is trying to create a disaster that will affect the sunlight that must power the Ziggurats and the Platinum Throne. I'm betting they are what's keeping Tanas imprisoned and he either needs them destroyed, or in some way disabled, to get past them. Maybe, if he can get to the surface without being stopped by them, he knows a way of undoing whatever the Great Master Ash Addiel did to him so he can leave this world. Unfortunately, I'm still just theorizing based on what you've told me, passages in the Tome, and my own knowledge of supervolcanoes, which is based purely on reading Ann's work. Ann is the real expert."

"Well, if your friend Ann knows so much about supervolcanoes, maybe she could help us?" Dan-te asked, regaining some of her composure.

"That would be impossible. She went on the same mining project that Reye did, and unless you know if she escaped or is still alive—"

"I don't," Dan-te answered regretfully. She had already had that conversation before with Reye, and the result didn't turn out so well. Thankfully, Worm took the news differently, but now that she understood a little of his own past, she realized getting past the deaths of people he cared for was something he had done before.

"So, what do we do now?" Dan-te asked, trying to turn the conversation constructive again. If the only person she could count on was Worm, it didn't give her much hope at stopping the Third Great Attempt.

"You are going to get a few hours of sleep," Worm replied firmly, pointing toward his bed.

"What?" Dan-te exclaimed, shocked that Worm suggest sleep after learning about all of this. "I don't have time to sleep. We need to make plans, we need—"

"To get moving and stop the Third Great Attempt," Worm said. "But if we are going to do that, like you just said, we need to make plans, and arrangements. That is something only I can do, so let me do that while you get some sleep and regain your strength. From your story, you need as much as you can get, but still, we don't have a lot of time. Let's use the time we have in the best way we can."

Dan-te knew Worm had a point, even though she didn't want to admit it. Also, she still didn't have any idea how damaged the Veil of Shadows was, or if it would work now. Worm was right, only he could make any plans for them to travel across the surface world.

"All right then, I'll get some sleep, and leave it up to you to lead me across the surface, but tell me one thing first."

"What's that?" Worm asked.

"What's your real name? You said you used an alias before, and I *Know* that Worm isn't what you're really called. The way you say it sounds like a self-made lie, so what is your real name?"

Worm looked at her again the same way he did the first time he saw her. He had always been told to keep his real name a secret, and use an alias or a nickname for various reasons, it helped him out more than once in the past. Dan-te was now one of the few people who ever asked him directly for his real name, instead of settling for the nickname he gave her.

However, Worm also knew he had told Dan-te more about himself than anyone else at Spectral Academy. If he was going to trust her this much, especially considering the trust she put in him, he knew he could trust her with his name.

"Virgil," he said, the tone in his voice clear and unmasked. "My real name is Virgil."

"Thank you. Wake me when we're ready, Virgil." Dan-te quickly fell into a sound sleep. Virgil was right, she needed sleep, and considering what was still to come, she needed as much sleep as she could get.

Virgil looked over the map he received from Ann. He knew that the Prison Caverns in the Yellow Dominion—near the Violet Dominion's boarder—were the closest caverns to the Platinum Throne and would lead directly to Nis, just like they did for Dan-te's ancestors. However, considering the Yellow Dominion's security, and the still tense relations between the Yellow and Violet Dominions, Virgil knew there would be no way to make it there quickly even with his family's connections. After the Prison Caverns, the next best cave system would be the Tri-Dominion Caverns outside Tri-Dominion City, a place Ann actually predicted to be ground zero for a supervolcano eruption. Tri-Dominion City was also a tough city to enter, usually needing either guides or passes because it rested on the Yellow, Green, and Violet dominions' borders, but it was far easier—and quicker—to get to than trying to go to the Yellow

Dominion and the Prison Caverns.

Virgil took a deep breath and looked around his room. Ever since coming to Spectral Academy, he was surrounded by people from all over the continent. He knew he had to remain anonymous and keep certain parts of himself, his family, their connections, and especially his involvement with the AAM and the Hammers of the Orange Light hidden. But once he started moving across the continent, using his family's connections to gain passage to the continent and Tri-Dominion City, it meant leaving a trail that he knew could be traced all the way back to his family in the Indigo Dominion if he was ever identified—knowing full well what that would mean for his family. However, after hearing Dan-te's story, he also knew that the time for anonymity was over. If the Third Great Attempt succeeded like Tanas envisioned, then who Virgil really was, and why he needed to keep himself hidden, wouldn't matter to anyone anymore, now was the time for action.

Virgil sat down at his desk and prepared to write the first in a series of letters and requests needed for the journey. He needed transportation to the continent and Tri-Dominion City, entry into Tri-Dominion City and the Caverns, spelunking gear, and numerous other things. Yet, with all of those needs, his room and home still lingered on his mind.

"One way or the other, I'm going to miss this place," Virgil said to himself, quietly so he wouldn't wake up Dan-te. He began to write his first letter to the Head of Spectral Academy.

Chapter 22

"Sis, I really have to thank whoever destroyed the E-gle Building, if I ever meet them." Met-on huffed. "Practically no one paid any attention to someone like me before, because of my Rodent Blood. Now they don't notice me at all, and I can see you as often as I like."

Stella couldn't tell how many times the boy called Met-on had come to be with her, or how long they were together. Since the attack on the camp, Stella's memories—both painful and dreamlike—led her to try and convince herself everything happening to her was just a bad dream. Waking up clean, but naked, all alone, and groggy on a simple bed in a room lit by a red-orange light looked weird enough that she had no problem believing it was a dreamscape. The rosy and odorless hissing gas filling the room that made her hot and sluggish, either just another part of it, or her own drowsiness acting on her. Finally, the ash grey boy who turned the dream into a nightmare, the pressure and sharp pain he caused in the lower half of her body, and the fact that he showed no guilt over it at all, only cemented Stella's belief. Only in a dream world could such a boy exist. She still didn't know who—or what—the boy was, only that he was a boy, and that she had multiple chances to examine him better.

This boy, "Met-on," Stella thought, trying to process both his image and what he's told her so far. *He's about half a head shorter than me, he doesn't look quite like the other creatures that I dreamed attacked the camp. He has the same pointed ears, but the skin is the wrong color, the others were bluish. Then there are those horns. He has two black horns growing around his head, it looks like they form a coronet, and entwine together to make a small horn on his forehead; I dreamt that that blue creatures didn't have horns.*

Stella's mind may have been working slowly, but since that first encounter, the same questions kept buzzing through her mind.

Is this really *happening to me?* Stella buzzed, her mind attempting to stir her lethargic body into action while trying to make sense of her surroundings. *This is just a dream, isn't it? Am, I alive, or am I dead, is this what happens to Hy-muns after they die if they don't join the Nag-el?*

The questions, like the gas in the room, flowed constantly throughout Stella's mind. Unfortunately, the gas kept leaving her in a lethargic and dreamlike state, barely able to move, or tell time, only think, and even that was limited to the same questions. The boy, Met-on, could have returned anywhere from two to twenty times by now. Stella couldn't tell, time blurring into a single experience filled with questions and pain. Yet she did know who was responsible for her pain, a revelation that only added to how unbelievable the situation was. As the gas became thicker, the nightmarish dream continued. She would feel hot, Met-on would come to her, talk a little, and following what he did, leave.

At least he is the only one who comes, Stella realized, remembering the first time he came, and how he said he would try and "reserve" her.

What am I saying? This isn't reality. I'm dreaming, right? Stella thought, chastising herself for even considering that what was happening to her was real. *I mean, how could this be real, there are no creatures* really *living underground, right? I have to wake up.*

Stella refused to admit to herself that what was happening to her was real. She knew she was becoming resilient to the gas, slowly regaining both her strength and her mobility, but no matter what, she refused to accept the reality around her. The moment she did, she knew her life—as she knew it—would be over.

If this was real, Stella knew she would never be able to go home again. Her best friend Reye understood she came from a strict family, but had no idea just how strict they actually were, and how much traditions were ingrained in them. After Met-on's first visit, Stella knew what her family's traditions required of her.

I'm only supposed to submit myself to another from the Violet Dominion. Stella remembered the words without even trying; she had been brought up thinking that way since birth. *To do otherwise would mean disownment and banishment from my entire family.*

She remembered her elder sister, after falling in love and marrying a man from the Blue Dominion, had to leave home without any of her belongings in order to join him. At the time, Stella wondered how her sister could have been so foolish to fall in love with someone from another dominion, knowing full well what the consequences would be, but later at Spectral Academy, she found herself developing feelings for Sol from the Yellow Dominion. Feelings that scared her, not only because she remembered what happened to her sister, but because they forced her to reevaluate her own sister's choice, and ask herself if she could do the same. It didn't help that Reye was always pressing the issue. One thing Stella always hated about Reye was that she always pushed where she shouldn't, and let her imagination run wild when it came to pairing people up.

Stella knew if she accepted this reality, her choices—by her family's traditions—would be to either join a holy order, or make a life with Met-on. Neither choice a good option, especially from her current point of view. Stella could hardly see herself in a life alongside this boy, a boy who came to her constantly, acting completely innocent, like it was the most natural way for him to behave.

I can't accept this. This has *to be a dream, a nightmare, there* must *be a way out of it. It's* my *dream after all. I must have given myself a way out.* The sound of a door closing, breaking Stella's train of thought, alerted her that Met-on had entered the room again.

My way out! Realization dawning on Stella as Met-on approached her.

Outside of this room, Stella imagined, *is a nightmarish dream world I have no knowledge of, nor guide, nor do I know any way out of it and back to reality, except for Met-on. He seems to come and go as he pleases, and he really is the only source of information I have about this dream world. If I want to escape this dream, wake up, and get back to the reality where I know my friends are waiting for me, I have to do whatever it takes. No matter what has to be done to me in the process.*

"Well, I got to go, Big Sis." Met-on puffed, straightening himself after finishing his business. This time, however, Stella grabbed his hand, holding it with all the strength she could—which was not much—to get his attention.

"Please, stay, talk to me," Stella squeaked. Those few words drew Met-on's his face closer to hers than ever before.

"You want to talk to me?" Met-on's face was brimming with both delight and excitement. He looked like he had waited for Stella to say those very words to him.

Perfect, Stella thought, determined not to let this chance slip away.

"Want to… learn… about you, your people."

Met-on was ecstatic, his silver eyes shining like stars. Quickly going to the door, he opened a panel above it and pulled a rope inside. The hissing sound from the gas quieted, the gas flow was slowing, while around them the room's surroundings became clearer.

Good, Stella thought to herself, noting the panel's location after he closed it. *I've learned something already.*

Met-on laid down next to Stella and began talking about himself. Stella listened intently, making sure to remember every word he said, if she was going to wake up, she needed to use this boy to do it.

I'll wake up soon, she thought to herself, listening to Met-on's story. *And then this will be nothing but a bad dream.*

Chapter 23

The destruction of the E-gle Building worked better than I could have imagined, Ice realized, running just behind Reye. Damage control from the miniature volcanic eruption took far more effort from the Tribe of Shadows then they originally thought. Reye and Ice had no trouble escaping their pursuers, leaving the Sixth Circle, and entering the Seventh Circle—Sloth Cur-Nos.

"This Circle is the planning center for everything that goes on outside of the city," Ice explained, making their way through Sloth Cur-Nos.

"I would like to melt this circle down to the ground," Reye replied.

Everywhere in the circle, staircases of one style or another dotted the architecture. Polished marble ones lead into large rectangular planning halls, and within them metal and stone spiral ones wound into smaller chambers leading everywhere. Reye and Ice crept up, down, over, and under multiple staircases of various designs, passing through each of the halls connected by them—everyone with its own set of smaller chambers joined to it by even more staircases. Reye clutched her pack of MMCs as she walked, a lifeline to her sanity and herself, constantly stopping to privately hide under a staircase and look into her pack.

Each time they stopped, Ice *Knew* she felt comforted by the MMCs' sight, she would release a breath and relax her muscles slightly, before picking herself up and start walking again. He could guess what must be on Reye's mind.

"You don't have enough charges for it," Ice said, jokingly, not to upset her. "The best thing to do would be to keep moving forward to the next circle."

"Killjoy," Reye said disapprovingly.

Ice knew from the way Reye was right now, it would be best not to put her into a violent situation. She clutched her ax, which now carried a lingering odor of blood on it, as tightly as her backpack. The Reye Ice presently *Knew* still had all the savageness of the Hy-mun Horror, radiating the same horrible red energy and giving off the acrid smell of blood. But now, that energy mixed freely with her own natural brown energy and her mental white energy, creating a calculating and thinking predator who believed—as long as she had her tools— she could do anything. The strike Reye made at the Tribe of Shadows, by destroying an E-gle Building, had given her the stimulus she needed to combine those energies; a mixing Ice realized he also needed, if he wanted to keep Reye's old self from dying and being replaced by a new self. As long as Reye's natural and metal energies were still alive instead of being corroded, it would be easier to help her let go of the horrible red energy completely, once Lord Tanas was finished.

"Okay navigator, which way do we go?" Reye asked, putting her backpack back on after another stop. They had climbed, descended, and ducked under so many staircases now, she started to think Ice had lost the trail.

"This way, to the Great Staircase leading to Pride Aster," Ice answered, pointing to his right, up another small flight of steps.

"The Great Staircase, what's so great about it?"

Reye quickly found out, coming to the single largest set of stairs she had ever seen, possibly bigger than the Amber Ziggurat back in her home, the Orange Dominion. It reached up to the top of a large wall, dividing Sloth Cur-Nos from Pride Aster, and extended so far from the base of it that she didn't even try to guess the distance from the first step to the wall itself. The stone stairs were wide enough so that she could have easily driven three of her family's farm carts side by side up the staircase with room to spare. The stones making up the staircase were polished white marble, reflecting the flickering red and orange glow from the magma so that the whole structure glowed with those colors. The Great Staircase was also covered with members of the Tribe of Shadows, some going up, others down, but all armed, and waiting for them.

"Okay, so it literally is a 'great staircase,'" Reye said, examining it from where they hid. "But is it the only way to move on to the next circle?"

"Unfortunately, yes. With the Jac-ob Way still blocked, this is are only way in. The next circle, Pride Aster, is the ruling center for anything that happens outside of Nis. Beyond that is Circle Emporium, where the Inner Council and the chosen of Lord Tanas live. After that is the center of the city, Yam-Preen itself.

"When the city was first expanding outwards, many functions now handled by the other circles were the responsibility of just one circle, Pride Aster. When Sloth Cur-Nos was first constructed, it was the Tribe of Shadows' first outer defense fort. There are stories among the Remnant about how many of the planning chambers in this circle were once prison cells—similar to Maestri. That's why they built the circle with only one way in or out, so it could be easily defended in case a large number of prisoners escaped, or if there was a large scale invasion from the surface."

"On the other hand," Reye chuckled, her lips curling into an evil smile. "Melting this entryway to the ground could give us an overwhelming advantage over our pursuers." Ice *Knew* Reye's mental white energy was beginning to pulse and mix with the horrible red energy from her rage. She was creating a gruesome mental picture of cleverly conducted destruction.

Ice didn't enjoy Reye slipping further down the path leading her towards the Death of the Self, becoming someone new who delighted in both the planning and execution of ideas that caused massive devastation and the death of others, but he knew she was right.

The destruction of the E-gle building did set our pursuers back, Ice reflected, thinking about what they had already done. *But I doubt that it's over. The bulk of our pursuers will be here in Sloth Cur-Nos, waiting at the one place we* have *to go through if we want to reach Yam-Preen by the normal city routes. Destroying the Great Staircase would increase our lead over them, leaving the Jac-ob Way as the only way to get into Pride Aster, and according to that group of soldiers we hid from while Reye checked her MMCs, it is still being cleared.*

"Well," Reye laughed, "it's time to make another diversion."

At first, Ice assumed Reye might charge headlong up the Great Staircase, cutting down every soldier in her path. But his time, Ice *Knew* Reye had a plan. She pulled a small metal cylinder from her backpack and pushed a button on top of it.

BOOM! BOOM! BOOM!

All around them, Ice heard explosions going off. Buildings and stairways collapsed at random points, followed by mini-eruptions from the magma flowing beneath the buildings. Seeing the explosions, the soldiers from of the Tribe of Shadows rushed down to investigate. Ice *Knew* Reye had somehow set this up with the MMCs while they traveled through Sloth Cur-Nos, and that she was delighted with both herself and the chaos.

"Reye, how did you…"

Ice, wasn't able to finish his question as Reye suddenly took off for the Great Staircase. Running to catch up, Ice noticed that almost all of the soldiers had either abandoned it to investigate the explosions, or were waiting at the bottom of it. Reye wasted no words, swinging her ax at the surprised soldiers—who were slow to react after witnessing the explosions—and carved a path leading up the Great Staircase.

Ice recovered his composure quickly, positioning himself behind Reye's back to cover her from the surviving soldiers. As Ice climbed the Great Staircase, he also noticed MMCs scattered on the ground.

Reye has been dropping them on her way up the Great Staircase, Ice thought to himself, realizing how Reye caused the earlier explosions. *Every time we hid behind a corner or under a flight of stairs, when Reye removed her backpack to look at the MMCs, she planted one before putting it back on.* Ice also realized that the higher he climbed, the easier it was for him to fight the soldiers.

So that was it, she was planning for this, amazing. Reye first triggers the explosions, brings the soldiers on the high ground down to us, allowing us to pass them, then we take the high ground, and force them to fight an uphill battle.

"Catch!" Reye cried, throwing the bisected remains of another member of the Tribe of Shadows behind her.

Ice, catching the body, immediately noticed something different about this member of the Tribe of Shadows. He wore a satchel over his shoulder with the symbol of an E-gle Buildings on it.

A *"Runner,"* Ice thought to himself. *Not surprising. With one E-gle Building destroyed and the Jac-ob Way still being cleared, the Tribe of Shadows must be using Runners to send messages and transport documents between circles.*

"Come on, Ice! Get up here if you want to live," Reye screamed.

Ice could hear both the honesty and seriousness in Reye's words and *Knew* she wasn't joking when she said he would die if he didn't join her at the top of the Great Staircase quickly. Ice raced up the stairs, taking the satchel from the runner's body, and killing any remaining soldiers that faced him until he finally caught up with Reye at the top; noticing her backpack was emptier, and that she held the metal cylinder again.

"Boom," Reye said, pushing the button.

All at once, the MMCs she had left on the way up exploded with a brilliant flash. The Great Staircase was suddenly all aglow, pieces of it melting down under the heat of the charges, taking the soldiers with it.

Ice, speechless as the Great Staircase melted from the MMCs, watched until only small bits of undamaged pieces remained, jutting up from the ground. Once the melting reached the floor, more mini-eruption caused the remaining pillars to shake, and in most cases collapse to the ground, killing any soldiers still around the base.

I'm doing it, Raymond, she thought to herself, delighted. *I'm running and fighting.* She remembered the last words she heard Raymond say to her before the creature from the Tribe of Shadows killed him. And ever since the Grand Coliseum, Reye had been doing just what he said, "Run…Fight."

If you can hear me Raymond, thank you for those MMCs in the E-gle building, Reye prayed, thinking of her brother. *As soon as I saw them, every lesson and practice session I ever took with them for demolition and mining— part of my terranaut courses—came back to me and I'm using that knowledge to its fullest.*

Reye also knew that Ice was looking at her with mixed expressions, it annoyed her.

He's probably trying to Know *something about who I am again,* she thought, but nothing was going to dampen her mood now. She was doing what her brother asked her to do. She was making these creatures pay for turning Hymuns into their food, and they were going to keep paying until as many of these creatures, and their leader Lord Tanas, was dead.

"Reye," Ice began.

"One of the things about MMCs," Reye said, reciting a lesson from Spectral Academy. "They can be easily set to explode on a timer or with the simple activation of a detonator like this." Reye held up the metal cylinder that she was holding. "I planted numerous MMCs as we traveled through this circle, set to go off at different times after I pressed this button. Then, as we climbed the staircase, I dropped a few more that would go off instantly once detonated. Now, will we be able to keep going, or what?"

"Yes, we will."

By destroying the Great Staircase, Reye's effectively sealed off the main way into the inner circles. Ice knew that moving forward through the remaining circles of Nis would now be far easier than Reye realized. *The only way to reach us now would be through the Jac-ob Way, and with the chaos we already caused, I can't imagine that the Jac-ob Way will be cleared to allow the number of warriors needed to mount a full-scale chase. All we really have to worry about now are the forces past it. Formidable yes, but nowhere near as bad as having to face all of Nis.* Ice didn't want to say it, but he was deeply thankful for Reye's actions.

Since escaping the Grand Coliseum, Ice witnessed Reye's horrible red energy grow and spread across her like moss on a stone, threatening to cover and corrode her own natural brown energy, which slowly rotted away with every life she took and every drop of blood she covered herself and her ax in. But as soon as she found the MMCs, they opened the door to her thinking mind, allowing her mental white energy to join with her natural brown energy, creating a mixture of the three. Using the knowledge she brought from the surface, knowledge she deeply enjoyed using, she created a mixture of the energies which let her cause even greater carnage throughout Nis, but not fall too deeply into the form of the "Hy-mun Horror."

It's for the greater good, Ice thought to himself watching Reye. During their entire time together, Ice didn't try to stop the horrible red energy from being produced. Ice wanted her to be covered in it, the new energy and scents becoming a part of her, giving her the strength to take down Lord Tanas for him, in hopes that it would stop the Third Great Attempt. Yet looking at her, Ice still felt a tinge of guilt.

The Third Great Attempt and Lord Tans have to be stopped, he said to himself again. *It is the right thing. It's for* all *our survival. It's for the greater good.*

"So where do we go now, navigator?" Reye asked.

"Oh, yes, this way." Ice left his guilt and thoughts behind, leading Reye down the other side of the Great Staircase. Even with the bulk of the forces trapped in Sloth Cur-Nos, Ice realized it would only be a matter of time before the forces here came to meet them.

And it would be better to face them if they can't push us back to the top of the wall.

With that thought in mind, Ice quickly led Reye forward into Pride Aster.

P.J. Fenton

Chapter 24

"Are you ready, Dan-te?"

"Yes, Virgil, let's get going."

Virgil opened his room's door, letting the light shine in. Dan-te rested for almost half a day before Virgil woke her to make the final preparations for the journey to Nis, starting with disguises for both of them.

"Other members of the Tribe of Shadows can see me while I am veiled," Dan-te explained, "and could recognize me either by my horn or female body. Do you have any ideas?"

Virgil did, wrapping her in tight cloths, using blankets to bulk out her form, and adding an extra wrapping around her head to mask her horn, he created the illusion of a masculine Tribe of Shadows body for Dan-te. As for Virgil's disguise, combining a pair of dark sunglasses, a white and red cane, and a quick change of clothes, Virgil took on the appearance of a blind Hy-mun.

"No one pays attention to the blind," Vigil said. "I'll change into this costume after we leave, we should encounter less trouble from other Hy-muns that way."

"I've also heard during my time in Nis that Tempters—members of the Tribe of Shadows active on the surface—don't pay much attention to people with disabilities," Dan-te said, agreeing with him. "Your disguise will work there too.

"The next thing to prepare for is what to do if a Tempter does look at us suspiciously. If I say the word 'Tempter' in your ear, put your hand on your head and stress out over something. When I was captive in Nis and moved through the circles, I overheard some of the Tempting lessons. If a Tempter's words can cause a Hy-mun to generate a grey energy of confusion or stress, they are tempting correctly. So, stress out over something."

"That will be simple enough," Virgil laughed, quickly demonstrating his ability to produce grey stressful energy immediately after Dan-te asked him to, "stress out over something." She *Knew* he was no stranger to stress.

The final and most important preparation was determining how the Veil of Shadows worked in its damaged state. Using the light from the window as a test, Virgil and Dan-te discovered the Veil did protect her from sunlight, but with restrictions. Unless Dan-te stayed in Virgil's shadow, she couldn't move. She also couldn't jump from shadow to shadow, like the Tribe of Shadows did with their veils.

Thankfully, the damaged Veil also provided advantages for them. Dan-te could clearly touch and speak to Virgil while veiled, allowing her to keep in constant contact with Virgil. Unlike before, when the Veil of Shadows only let the veiled person's voice be heard as a whispering thought and prevented contact. It was a benefit they both enjoyed. With their preparations complete, they left the dorms, Virgil leading and Dan-te following—veiled within his shadow, into the late day sun at Spectral Academy.

Spectral Academy was busy during the end of the day. Everywhere a person looked, someone either came or went from one place or another amidst the different reflections and refractions of light coming from the Platinum Throne. But for Dan-te, robed in the Veil, the Platinum Throne appeared entirely different. The Veil's altered perception, and her own way of *Knowing* through the image her senses created, revealed Spectral Academy to be a black place. Where Virgil saw different shades of colorful light, she saw different shades of black. Grass, trees, and plant life looked dead, slowly wilting in the blackness. Each of the building radiated cold inky black energy, feeling lifeless and unwelcoming. As for the other students, Virgil's belief about himself being the only one at Spectral Academy who could understand the way she *Knew* he could turned out to be correct.

They are all the same, Dan-te realized, *Knowing* each of the students as they past. The energy produced by their emotions, the only source of color in the "Reversed State," radiated stress, anger, pain, and disbelief.

How could anyone live in this kind of world, Dan-te wondered. *Knowing* all the differing emotions of the students at one time made her both homesick for The Remnant, and thankful for having Virgil's hand to hold onto. Unlike the other students, Virgil was the only student who appeared differently to her.

"Tempter!" Dan-te whispered quickly into Virgil's ear, shaking off the effects of *Knowing* the other students and tugging on his hand. Virgil stopped mid-stride and moved to sit down. Placing his hand on his head, he started radiating grey stress and the same worries Dan-te *Knew* the other students possessed.

Dan-te then realized that there were Tempters all over Spectral Academy. Like her, they were wrapped in black veils and following other Hy-mun in their shadows. She overheard some of them tempting students to cheat on tests, destroy property, and start fights as a way to relieve their stress. The Tempters usually ignored one another, but once one took an interest in what Dan-te and Virgil were doing, Dan-te used their code word to alert Virgil and act tempted. Neither of them wanted to run the risk of having another Tempter ask questions about them.

Thankfully, Tempters on the surface moved with their Hy-muns, moving fast thanks to the quick pace of Spectral Academy. After passing the third Tempter who almost stopped them, they reached the carriages that would take them to the airship port. Sitting alone, they talked freely for the first time since they left Virgil's room.

"You said people are happy to come here?" Dan-te asked, still shocked at *Knowing* the other students.

"Yes, Spectral Academy is the most prestigious school in the Hy-mun world. It offers just about every class imaginable, and is the best place to learn about the world prior to the Great Rainbow War. Why, how did you *Know* it?"

"For me it was a gloomy, stressful place that lacked belief."

"I can understand the stressful part. But what do you mean by gloomy and lacks belief?" Virgil, no stranger to the stress Spectral Academy put on its students, never thought the school was gloomy.

"Most of the people I *Knew* generated a gloomy green energy, filled with dread and fear over their futures—immediate and distant—magnified by a hollowness I felt from within them, a hollowness from lack of belief. They don't believe this place to be all it was supposed to be, or in themselves, or that they are going to do anything with what they learned here. The hollowness from that lack of belief only made the gloomy green energy they generated worse."

No one ever *talks about Spectral Academy the way Dan-te does*, Virgil realized, thinking about what Dan-te said while they traveled to the airship port, and about every student, alumni, and scout he had ever heard talking about Spectral Academy. But in the short time he had known her, he learned to trust her judgment, especially when it came to her ability to *Know* something or someone else through her senses. As the carriage pulled into Minos Airship Port, a thought occurred to him.

I wonder how Dan-te might Know *the rest of the Hy-mun world on this journey.*

Minos Airship Port was the second busiest place on the Platinum Throne after Spectral Academy. Shaped like a large capitol "T" pointing out toward the Seraph Sea, the port gleamed and sparked as light reflected off the platinum walls embedded with diamonds. All along the port, gleaming bronze airships added to the glittering kaleidoscope as the light reflected off each of them as they rose and descended from the sky. Inside the port, people came and went almost as fast as they did at Spectral Academy. But unlike Spectral Academy, there were many more people from the different Dominions, and many more Tempters from the Tribe of Shadows that Dan-te and Virgil had to look out for, especially once inside the port's terminal.

Minos Airship Port was divided into two sections, the first—and busiest—was the main public terminal. It contained offices for buying tickets, food, sending messages and packages, as well as arranging transportation around the Platinum Throne and to the other dominions. Once inside, Virgil headed straight for an office that had a snake with wings on it, giving the attendant a long case he had carried with him since leaving Spectral Academy.

"Would you please send this to the address listed on the label?" Virgil asked.

"Of course." The attendant looked at the destination and the mailing instructions. "This is a C.O.D. package correct?"

"It is," Virgil replied, the attendant taking the package and carrying it away.

Dan-te had seen the package when she had woken up. Virgil packed it while she was asleep, and when she asked him what it was, he answered, "An old friend, one who's saved me more than once and one I think might save me again before this is over." He wouldn't say anything else, but from those words alone, Dan-te *Knew* that whatever Virgil put into that case was important where they were going, giving her a few ideas of what it could be, yet deciding not to press the issue. She hadn't felt anything dangerous from Virgil that made him untrustworthy, and they both knew they had far bigger problems to worry about.

Returning to the main terminal, they headed to the gate separating the two areas of the port where Virgil presented a ticket—the last piece of mail he received at Spectral Academy before leaving—to the Hy-mun at the gate. The Hy-mun looked at the ticket, ripped a part of it off, and ushered them into the second part of the terminal.

The second part of the terminal—where Hy-muns arrived and departed from airships—looked, from the inside, like a long hallway with blocks of chairs near multiple gates. The terminal provided transportation to every Dominion on the continent. There were also more Tempters, but this time there were so many they didn't notice Virgil or Dan-te. Reaching their gate, the two sat down for a second when Virgil heard someone call him by his nickname.

"Worm?"

Virgil looked to where the voice had come from, and saw the distinctive grey and red hair of Professor Bridget Heart—who had recognized him despite their limited encounters. Next to her was a heavily loaded backpack, and two over the shoulder haversacks; it looked like she was also going on a trip.

"Professor Heart, how are you doing? Are you going on a vacation?"

"I'm okay, and yes, I am going on a vacation, of sorts." Professor Heart's eyes looked past him as she talked, staring into the distance. Virgil could tell by her voice, and the look on her face, that she wasn't okay.

"After the mining accident, I need to go back home and sort a few things out. I was the one who acted as a moderator for the students who went on that project, and sent every one of them off with congratulations. I've been looking at all the information I have at the Academy, and something about what happened in the Demp Caverns just seems wrong to me. But enough about what I'm doing, what about you? Are you also going on a vacation? Is that why you're outside for a change?"

"More like a journey, Professor," Virgil replied. "With everything that's been going on in my life lately, I need to get out for a bit."

"All right then," Professor Heart said, slightly disturbed by Virgil's remark. "Well, have a good trip." She started to walk to another gate when Virgil called back to her.

"Professor?" Professor Heart turned around. "Can you spare a minute? I would like to ask you a volcanology question."

"Okay," she said, worry crossing her face, and entering her voice, as she took a seat next to Virgil.

"I was reading through some of Ann's papers on supervolcano theory," Virgil said. "I was wondering, if a supervolcano was ever detected, how you would stop it from erupting?"

Professor Heart looked a little puzzled, and pained, the memory and loss of her student—whom she worked extremely close with—still fresh in her mind.

"Stop a supervolcano from erupting? As far as we know it's impossible," Professor Heart's answered simply. She knew she was stating the obvious. "I looked over Ann's theories with a fine-tooth comb, and the bottom line is that once the eruption starts, there is no way to stop it, only diffuse it."

"Diffuse it?" Virgil asked. While stopping the Tribe of Shadows from starting the eruption was Dan-te and Virgil's plan, he realized they had to be ready in case they failed. Any advice about what to do when they reached Nis would be helpful.

"Yes, diffuse it. You know how in the Red Dominion there is one central volcano and multiple smaller volcanoes ringing it? Well, some theorists, Ann and myself included, think that the central one was once a possible supervolcano. However, during its eruption, a series of smaller eruptions occurred at its base, causing the formation of the other volcanoes around it, letting the ash, lava, and most importantly pressure, diffuse through those smaller volcanoes. That diffusion exponentially reduced the damage the one volcano would have caused if it erupted as one supervolcano."

An idea began forming in Virgil's head, a crazy idea, and one that could only work if the conditions were right. But if Nis had the supplies Virgil thought it did, then it just might work. He would have to talk to Dan-te about it. Just then, the speakers around the terminal crackled to life, issuing an announcement.

"Attention, Air Cruise 215 for Wanton City now boarding at Gate 2."

"That's my cruise, Professor Heart. It was good to talk to you again."

"It was good to talk to you again as well, Worm. Have a safe journey."

Virgil got up from where he was sitting and felt the familiar tug from Dan-te, signaling she was with him, and proceeded through the gate, walking out onto the airfield grounds and toward the airship. The airship, a large metal gondola attached to a massive airbag, had multiple propellers and engines keeping it floating just above ground. Once they walked up the entry ramp and were onboard, they took up residence in a private cabin Virgil reserved for them.

After the airship was on its way, Virgil drew all of the shades down, darkened all of the lights, and put a "Do not disturb" sign on the door so Dan-te could unveil and they could talk in privacy.

"It should take a day to get to Wanton City," Virgil said. "That business dodging Tempters can be exhausting."

"You don't know the half of it. I'm actually thankful that you couldn't see me."

Now that Dan-te unveiled herself, Virgil knew she wasn't exaggerating. She looked exhausted, almost like she had run a marathon and tried doing ten other jobs while running at the same time.

"Virgil, when you were talking to that older female Hy-mun, the one you called Professor Heart, you were talking about how to stop a supervolcano. Something came to you, didn't it?"

Virgil knew he couldn't keep secrets from Dan-te for long. As soon as he got an idea, she *Knew* from the white mental energy spark that he had one. And considering both he and Professor Heart were talking about supervolcanoes, it wouldn't be hard to figure out what his idea was about.

"Yes, I did. Sorry, I know it's risky to talk about an aspect of the Third Great Attempt in public, but Professor Heart is the best expert on volcanoes at

Spectral Academy. I would have suggested we talked to her sooner, but the day before we met, she took a leave from all activities at the academy. Running into her when we did was an extremely good stroke of luck and I didn't want to waste it."

"And I don't blame you for it. Any information we can get that could stop the Third Great Attempt is a blessing. Also, the Tempters in the terminal seemed less interested in us and more interested in the rest of the Hy-mun they were following. I doubt any of them were paying attention. You were just asking a teacher a question about a friend's theories. So, what was your idea?"

"Well, according to the Professor, once the eruption starts it can't be stopped."

"I heard that all too clearly," Dan-te said, fearful for what could happen to them.

"Well, I was thinking about what we might have to do in case the initial explosion does goes off in the Red Dominion. Now, you said that the Tribe of Shadows has been stockpiling both technology and mining equipment that they have been stealing off Hy-muns for years, right?"

"Right."

"Well, if we could—and this is a big if—get our hands on some of that equipment once we are down there, then perhaps we could create more points before Nis where the lava can burst through and defuse the supervolcano."

"But that would devastate your world!" Dan-te shouted, realizing what Virgil was suggesting and shocked he would even think of an idea like that.

"You think I don't know that!" Virgil shouted back, mental and emotional anguish radiating off his face. Dan-te *Knew*, inside of his mind, something else was waging its own private battle, the battle between choosing the lesser of two evils.

"If we can't stop that eruption, and life has taught me that being pessimistic is the safest course of thought, then all life, both on the surface and below it, will die. I'm just trying to figure out how to save as many lives as I can."

"But if adding more points for the lava to burst through is the idea, wouldn't the best place to do that be where the initial blast is going to happen, in the Red Dominion?"

"Yes, it would be, with Nis itself being the next best choice since that is where the magma has to break through to the surface. But if I were Tanas, and I had been planning this for more years than I could count, then I would have also planned for every kind of obstacle that could end up stopping me from bringing this attempt to completion, especially after two failed attempts."

"What do you mean? How?"

"The place you showed me on the map that is going to serve as the detonation point has no direct routes to it, other than the Demp Caverns, and that is sealed off from the surface, so we can't use it. Since Reye's group was attacked there, Tanas must have guards stationed near there. I'm also betting that there are more guards posted everywhere along the lava's route to ensure no one approaches the blast site. Guards that are fully committed to the completion of the Third Great Attempt, even if they have to die for it.

Next, before the detonation, I would remove all mining equipment from the work area once the tunnel is complete, in case someone figures out the real plan. Then I would rig the bombs and equipment, so if they're tampered with prior to the time of their detonation, they would explode automatically, and that's still just the start of my preparations."

Dan-te thought about what Virgil said. She didn't think he was overthinking, in fact, she agreed with him. She knew Virgil was trying to understand what was going through Tanas's head, assuming that was even possible. At the very least, she didn't doubt the Tribe of Shadows would willingly sacrifice their lives for Tanas and the Third Great Attempt. When Virgil said he wanted to save as many lives as he could, she *Knew* he was not only thinking about Hy-mun lives, but about the lives of everyone who lived beneath the surface as well—both the Tribe of Shadows and The Remnant.

"So, you think making vents along the path of the magma is the best option to stop the supervolcano from destroying the world, assuming we are unable to reach the detonation site?" Dan-te asked.

"Yes, *if* we can get our hands on the needed equipment once we reach Nis." Virgil answered, knowing that obtaining the equipment was going to be extremely difficult.

I know my family has connections to mining companies, Virgil thought, considering other ways to get the equipment. *But the kinds of arrangements we need to get both the equipment and manpower from the powers that be to put everything in place would require too much time.*

"So, what you are planning to do is return to Nis with me, find a mining machine, and then we use it to drill holes in the magma's path from the city to the detonation point, leading close enough to the surface so the magma and pressure can exit through them." Dan-te had a hard time believing Virgil's plan. It didn't just sound crazy, but the way she just presented it, made it sound too easy.

"If we can't just stop the blast itself, then yes. If you got a better plan, Dan-te, I'm listening."

Dan-te couldn't answer. From the moment she and her brother Ice started their plan, it had been about getting to the surface, influencing the Hy-muns to face the danger that she and the rest of The Remnant *Knew* threatened the world, and getting them to do something about it. However, the actual "what to do" once they reached the surface was something neither she, nor her brother, had seriously considered. Truthfully, they both though they would either die in the coliseums, or be forced to use their alternative plan, the assassination of Tanas, spending more time planning how to assassinate Tanas than what to do with any help they might find on the surface. In the end, they just decided that if they did make it to the surface, they would trust the decisions made by whatever Hy-mun leaders they influenced. After talking with Virgil, Dan-te realized that idea was doomed to fail from the start.

"No, I don't have any better ideas," Dan-te said despairingly.

"Let me guess. You were expecting to come up here, talk with our leaders, and try to get them to 'do something,' maybe send a large army down to Nis to take care of Tanas for you, weren't you?" Virgil asked smugly.

"Does it show that much?" Dan-te asked, slightly embarrassed.

"It didn't take much imagination to figure that one out," Virgil said.

"So, what do we do now?" Dan-te asked, wondering what their next move was

"Now, we relax while we can. We are going to be doing plenty of traveling once we reach the continent. We should also practice getting better into costume and character for when we arrive. It might help to throw off the Tempters better."

"Agreed. I'm still sore from some of the stunts that I had to perform to make it look like I was tempting you."

"As to where we're going, the port town of Wanton City is the entertainment and commercial capital of the Yellow Dominion, and the only place there that is easy to get into because of the amount of business that takes place there. It is also the biggest port city on the continent; it has all kinds of transportation going to and from all the dominions all the time. We'll be able to get transportation to Tri-Dominion City, and from there to the Tri-Dominion Caverns, they should lead us back to Nis."

"But for now, we relax?"

"We relax, eat, practice, and plan our next move."

Dan-te was already beginning to stretch and relax on the bed before Virgil finished his sentence. Dan-te knew they would have to come up with more plans for when they were on the ground again. Yet, Dan-te found it easy to relax in the rocking motion of the beds as the airship began lifting off the ground.

Just like the hammock beds back home, she thought to herself. But in the back of her mind, she worried about whether or not they had enough time to do anything to stop the Third Great Attempt before it was implemented.

If we only knew when they were going to start the Third Great Attempt.

P.J. Fenton

Chapter 25

Judgment Halls, council chambers, and planning halls dotted Pride Aster. Built with specks of quartz embedded in them, and lit by the magma, they looked like fixed stars set into the ground. Normally, the circle would have been a hub of activity, each chamber and hall—with its own unique purpose—filled with members of the Tribe of Shadows as they deliberated new plans and projects to be carried out beneath the surface. Those plans would then be reviewed by the various councils before being judged about whether or not they would be implemented. But now, the chambers were nearly empty, filled with nothing but the lingering energy of the members who worked there, and the strong rush of the left-over energy heading back toward the Great Staircase. It made Ice feel eerie.

So many, Ice thought to himself, a nagging sensation constantly reminding him of what happened after Reye destroyed it.

After Reye's MMCs exploded on the Great Staircase, almost every member of the Tribe of Shadows in Pride Aster stopped what they were doing and ran to their side of it, hoping to catch them. Reye however was already lobbing MMCs to the base of the Great Staircase long before they reached it, so by the time they did, MMCs were scattered everywhere.

"Okay navigator, which way now?" Reye had asked, producing the detonator again and placing her thumb over its button.

Ice knew exactly what Reye was planning before they even reached the bottom of the Great Staircase, but he also knew he didn't have time to dwell on it. The crimson energy of anger from almost every inhabitant of Pride Aster was pouring down on them in waves from practically every direction. Instinctively, Ice ran down a path with no energy coming from it. As soon as they were far enough away, Reye pushed the button, causing another series of explosions, and screams.

All gone, Ice thought to himself again bitterly, the two of them now moving virtually unnoticed throughout the circle. Ice, feeling his way through the latent energy to find the path leading to the next circle, was constantly reminded by it of just how many came after them. Since then, he had been studying the documents in the Runner's satchel—an easy way to take his mind off the number who died, and his own role in their deaths—and was glad that he did.

This is a timetable for the final phases of the Third Great Attempt, Ice realized as he studied the documents intently. *According to this, the Third Great Attempt is going to begin after a "Purging Event." Is the Tribe of Shadows going to attack Rem? There is also a map leading to Rem in the satchel. Do they plan on purging all traces of what they were before become the Tribe of Shadows? I wish there was more information about this event.*

"How long are you going to keep reading those silly papers?" Reye asked, slightly annoyed at the attention Ice was giving to the documents instead of her goal of getting to Lord Tanas.

"They are not 'silly papers,' this is a timetable, and it's got important information on it," Ice answered. He *Knew* the ease of their movement through Pride Aster left Reye feeling disheartened, she wanted more members of the Tribe of Shadows to fight. Ice however, was glad for the reprieve, realizing it would give Reye more time to recover, and give him time to focus on the documents he picked up and the path in front of him—instead of the dead behind him.

"Well, what does it say?" Reye asked sarcastically.

"Just that we don't have much time left until you lose your chance at Lord

Tanas. I *Know* that's all you care about right now," Ice said, continuing to read.

That answer almost made Reye take her ax and swing it into Ice's back. Reye hated being ignored. Ice was also using the accented *Know* again, which she realized meant he was figuring things out about her, and he was assuming that whatever was on the papers didn't have anything to do with her goal of killing Lord Tanas and avenging Raymond and Stella. Reye was getting more anxious with every step, she could feel her ax itch, waiting for the moment when she would sink it into Lord Tanas. After that, she knew her brother could rest in peace, there wouldn't be any more Hy-muns made into food, and then she could leave this dark world behind her and return to the light.

Ice, however, found the information priceless. He was so intent on reading that he could almost forget about the person Reye was becoming, part her old self and part Hy-mun Horror, as her multiple energies mixed together and her scent noticeably changed. Also forgetting his own personal guilt from the role he played in that change.

According to the timetable, when the attack on Reye's camp happened, the Tribe of Shadows was reaching the magma vein, Ice thought as he reread the timetable. *They were about to start moving MMCs to the Keyblast Point to start the eruption when Reye was first brought here. By now, the Tribe of Shadows should have finished stockpiling their explosives. Next, they are going to start removing the equipment from the site, bringing it back to just beyond the city limits. After that, is the purging event, then the bombs will be set off, officially beginning the Third Great Attempt, and ending all of our lives. Time is running out.*

Just keep Reye and yourself focused toward Lord Tanas. We have almost reached him, once we do, Reye can finish him, and then it will be all over.

Ice *Knew* that if he gave Reye the details leading up to Third Great Attempt, it would waste time and still come down to her having to kill Lord Tanas.

It's better if she just knows she's running out of time, Ice mused. He believed Reye should be focus only on Lord Tanas.

However, as he led Reye through the Eighth Circle, a sight caught his eye and caused him to suddenly stop, making Reye bump into him.

"Now what's your problem?" Reye asked.

"That building, we have to get in there take it out."

Reye looked at the building. It looked no different than the other buildings in Pride Aster, except that it had the words "RODENT CONTROL" written above the door in the Hy-mun language.

"What's the deal with rodents?"

"The Tribe of Shadows considers The Remnant of the Tribe nothing more than rodents." Ice took a document from the runner's satchel, the map from Nis to Rem—the home of The Remnant. If they were making maps to Rem, then they could be planning an attack. "Taking that building out will set the Tribe of Shadows plans back even further."

And protect my people, Ice thought, the lie tasting bitter on his lips.

"So, going wild in there will hurt the Tribe of Shadows?" Reye asked, slightly curious about this detour, because Ice was the one who always said they should keep moving or they would miss their chance at Lord Tanas.

"Yes, but no MMCs!" Ice exclaimed. "We don't want to give away our position." *Or destroy anything that could tell me the Tribe of Shadows' plans for Rem.* If Ice had any remaining doubts about whether or not he was using Reye before, they were gone now.

I'm lying to her, the realization worming into his head, *I'm lying to her and I'm purposely using her now strictly for my own reasons. Not to stop the Third Great Attempt but for my own personal reasons, condemning who knows how many members of the Tribe of Shadows to die just for my own gain.*

"No promises," Reye said smiling. Lifting her ax, she ran off toward the building with Ice close behind. Ice realized that by telling her the building's destruction would hurt the Tribe of Shadows—which he knew was a lie—Reye would attempt to take out everyone she could find. However, after reading the timetable, seeing the "Purging Event" written on it, and finding a map back to his home in the Runner's satchel, he needed to make this detour. He needed to know if the Tribe of Shadows was planning to exterminate The Remnant before beginning the Third Great Attempt. If they were, then he knew what he would have to do after Lord Tanas was killed. He would have to get back to Rem fast and tell The Remnant to evacuate further into the caves; they would listen to that, at least, before banishing him from The Remnant.

I'm using her for my people, Ice said to himself, trying to stomp out the nagging feelings of guilt inside of him. *For my people, it's all for* my *people.*

The attack turned out to be easier than Ice thought. There were only a few members of the Tribe of Shadows present, so the fatalities were few, meaning no one could set off an alarm. Unfortunately, all Ice found in the building were notes on how to train Tribe of Shadows/Remnant offspring, nothing about what the "Purging Event" was, and nothing about any possible attack on Rem. Walking through the corpses, Ice couldn't squash his guilt.

I am responsible for this, Ice thought sickly, *I sent Reye in here on nothing but a lie, telling her it would hurt the Tribe of Shadows when I knew it wouldn't. And for what, nothing! I'm no closer to finding out if the Tribe of Shadows is going to destroy Rem before starting the Third Great Attempt than I was before. Only now, lives had been lost pointlessly, by my choice.*

"Are you satisfied?" Reye asked, a little angry that she couldn't fight longer, but also happy over what she considered a "job well done."

"Yeah, I'm satisfied," Ice lied again grumpily, since he didn't find anything about the "Purging Event" or Rem. Leaving the building and the bodies within it, Ice led Reye back to the path leading to the next circle.

The rest of the journey through Pride Aster was quiet. The greatest source of commotion came from the still-burning remains of the Great Staircase behind them. Ice knew the chaos Reye caused was the principal reason for the ease of their journey, no one had ever done what they had accomplished—leaving more than a few soldiers confounded. However, Ice also knew it wasn't going to last. Before leaving Pride Aster, there were still challenges they had to get through, and after rounding a turn, he quickly backed up and grasped Reye—holding her with all his strength—at the sight before them.

"Now what?" Reye asked, both shocked and angry. Ice quickly shushed her and pointed around the corner.

The biggest gate Reye had ever seen stood before her. It actually looked more like a small fortress from an old walled city than a simple door. One large entry was sealed with three rows of spiked iron bars. At either side and above the entryway were windows that guards constantly watched from. On top of the structure were two more guards, and around it was even more heavily armed guards.

"The first of the Three Examination Gates," Ice said, looking at the compound before quickly ducking back behind the corner. "We're lucky they didn't see us. You may or may not have noticed, but members of the Tribe of Shadows have various kinds of brands on their bodies. These gates, separating Pride Aster from the Ninth Circle—Circle Emporium—are where members of the Tribe of Shadows have to present those brands in order to pass."

"I have noticed that some members of the Tribe of Shadows have been branded," Reye said, remembering the griffin brand on the chest of the gladiator who told her about Tanas. Of course, she assumed it was a griffin; it was hard to tell after she bisected it with her ax. "But how do you prove that the brands are real?"

"The branding is done at these gates, and the written records and actual branders live here as well. The guards you just saw outside of it were probably all branded at this one, after receiving the same kind of training the soldiers receive, and that's nothing compared to what happens once we get through them."

"What do you mean?" Reye asked, excited over what was going to happen after she made it through them.

"Once we hit the gates, they'll know we're here. There are more than enough guards to set off an alarm to alert the entire circle. Then all of the forces in Circle Emporium, as well as the forces making their way through the Jac-ob Way, will be able to close right in on us."

"That just means that there'll be a lot more targets to hit."

Reye's eagerness to attack and charge into the first gate was building. Ice could feel the anticipation rolling off her in the waves of red energy and sharp smells of excitement. Ice knew it wouldn't take much more for her to go right through them, regardless of whoever stood in their way. In fact, considering that the first gate was right in front of her, and she had hardly moved, actually surprised and scared him. Reye had a plan, the mental energy she was giving off proved that, and it involved explosives.

"So, how do you plan on attacking them?" Ice asked, wondering what it was she was planning.

"I don't," Reye said, and Ice knew from her voice she was both honest and serious.

"You don't?" Ice replied, slightly shocked over Reye's non-aggressive attitude.

"You said that a lot of soldiers would be taking the Jac-ob Way, which I'm assuming will be cleared now. Those soldiers will leave the Jac-ob Way and come here. So, let's take the Jac-ob Way ourselves. We can make our way to Yam-Preen, or at least to the next circle, and not only bypass these forts, but also set up a few surprises of our own for any soldiers following us instead."

Ice knew the word "surprises" meant the cool cruelty that he had come to expect from Reye, but he was more shocked at himself for not thinking about using the Jac-ob Way as a quick means of bypassing the Examination Gates. From the Jac-ob Way, there would be only two gates to worry about, the one entering Circle Emporium, and the one that left the Jac-ob Way and entered Yam-Preen. When the Jac-ob Way was constructed, the Tribe of Shadows didn't think to place more than one gate in it at those two locations because the traps would serve as its greatest defense. Now, Reye wanted to turn that strength into a weakness. She was becoming strategic, a new aspect of herself that was part Hy-mun Horror and her old self. Ice seriously believed more and more this "new" Reye might be the one who could help him complete this mission, hopefully stopping the Third Great Attempt in the process.

"So, how do we get to the Jac-ob Way?" Reye asked.

"This way," Ice said, turning around and doubling back.

P.J. Fenton

Chapter 26

I created Met-on to help me, Stella thought to herself, struggling to convince herself that she was in a dream. *He has all the information I need about this world and is willing to talk about it.*

Met-on did like to talk a lot. Through him, Stella learned more and more about where she was. Not only that, but each time they talked, the amount of gas lowered further, and Stella's senses and strength slowly returned. Unfortunately, both the information and the weakening of the gas came with a cost, each time he visited her, he joined with her first. But if joining with him meant regaining her strength, learning more about her surroundings—whatever those surrounding might be—and gaining information she could use to escape—and by escaping, waking up—then the price for acquiring it was well worth it.

Stella learned she was being held in Nis, a city made up of nine outer circles surrounding the original city at its center. She was in the Third Circle, Lust Atrophied. In this circle, Met-on's people, who called themselves the Tribe of Shadows, kept their women so they could serve the Plan by providing future generations for the Tribe of Shadows.

"Is the Third Circle the third one from the center of the city, or the third one from the edge?" Stella asked, after learning about the multiple circles.

"Third one from the edge," Met-on told to her, making Stella extremely thankful for the fact he didn't have any concerns about sharing information.

Great, Stella thought. *Once I get out of this cell, I won't have to go far to get out of the city. But I need more information.*

"What is the Plan?" Stella asked.

"That's a long story," Met-on said, reciting to her the history of the Tribe of Shadows. Stella found it enlightening, but also tragic, and frightening.

"We used to live on the surface until the event known as 'The Coming,' when Beings of Light came to our world and all but destroyed it, forcing the survivors underground. Those survivors then split into two groups, the Greater Tribe and The Remnant of the Tribe." Stella realized the "Beings of Light" were the Hy-muns' Nag-el, but didn't mention it.

Am I really this creative? Stella thought to herself. The way Met-on talked, the honesty to it, seemed too real for a dream.

My parents always said reading religious fiction would give me nightmares, Stella flinched, listening to Met-on talk about the Nag-el as destroyers. *They weren't kidding.*

"I have a black horn and ash-grey skin because my mother came from the Remnant," Met-on explained. "The Remnant live like rodents beyond the Greater Tribes' borders. The Greater Tribe, however, began rebuilding what was lost to them, and looking for ways to defeat the Beings of Light. During that time, the practice of keeping women separate to provide children began, as well as the tradition of referring to the women as 'sis,' because of the relationships some of the first generations had with their partners."

Met-on's culture practiced incest, Stella shivered, forcing herself not to show it. *I'll bet it still happens. If every woman of childbearing years is kept separated from men in general, including their offspring, there's a good chance of it. That would explain a few things.* Stella remembered the dangers of close breeding from some of her classes. The implications of what Met-on told her, his people practicing incest—even if it was necessary—would have consequences.

Future generations would eventually develop weaker immunities, deformities, and potentially become more aggressive, Stella reflected. *Someone must have realized the practice was becoming self-destructive; otherwise the entire civilization could have wiped itself out by now.*

"It was also during this time that the Great Savior, Lord Tanas, first came to the Greater Tribe with his Legion of Shadows to lead the Greater Tribe against the Beings of Light. That was when the Greater Tribe took the name, 'the Tribe of Shadows.'"

Stella immediately recognized the name Tanas. Like Virgil, she also knew how the older versions of the Tome referred to Light Bringer as Tanas, but said nothing about it to Met-on.

Tanas, the traitor to the Great Master Ash Addiel, a savior, that's impossible! Stella whiffed at the thought, and the doubt Met-on's story was casting on her own belief. *If this isn't a dream, and he is here, alive, then he must be pulling one of the biggest con jobs in history.*

"With the help of Lord Tanas, and the tools he provided, the Tribe of Shadows restructured itself into the civilization it is now. We have secretly attacked the surface and made two great attempts to reclaim it. The First succeeded in driving the Beings of Light from the surface, but the Hy-muns remained. The Second destroyed much of the Hy-mun civilization and technology during what they call the Great Rainbow War, but it didn't finish the job. Yet, it did create massive stores of technology underground that the Tribe of Shadows still steal from and use to complete the Third Great Attempt, which is going to be initiated soon. It's an attempt that will make the surface world livable for the Tribe of Shadows again, and allow us to retake our ancestral home."

"Why didn't you return to the surface sooner?" Stella asked.

"The Light the Beings of Light brought into the world is lethal to us. If it touches us, it burns us black, eventually burning us to death." Met-on's answer awakened a vague memory. Stella remembered blue creatures, members of the Tribe of Shadows, burning black from exposure to light. Stella quickly tried forcing it from her head, but that image wouldn't leave her, nor would her feelings of pity.

Wait, why am I feeling pity? Stella wondered. *Why should I feel sorry for the way they've been forced to live?*

But Met-on's story did move her to pity his people. While she despised how they forced others, like herself and Met-on's mother, into this role, she felt sorry that they needed to do this to themselves because of anger, hatred, and the need to survive.

They must have been taking members of the Remnant, and Hy-muns like me, to counter the self-destructive effects of their breeding practices. Wait, why am I even thinking about this? THIS IS A DREAM! Stella roared her last thought in her mind, again chastising herself for even thinking that everything around her was real instead of imaginary.

If I'm even considering this is real, it only means I need to find a way out faster. This dream city is on the path to self-destruction. I have to get out, I have to wake up. Stella frantically tried pinching herself and willing herself to wake up when she was alone, but it didn't work. All it did was force herself to reaffirm that she was dreaming, strengthen her desire to escape the room—and the things happening within it—and get back to what she considered reality.

I am not going to die like this; I will wake up from this nightmare.

The memory of the attack also stirred another memory inside Stella. The last sight of Reye's brother Raymond, and a final word he spoke, "Live." Stella couldn't remember much besides that one word, but it was enough, she was determined to live.

I already know I'm near the outer edge of the city, Stella thought to herself. *Now I need to find out how to get out of it.*

Stella decided the Tribe of Shadows feelings—born out of hurt, genocide, and banishment, with generations compounded on them—could be reflections of her own desires to wake up and return to the surface, only intensified and turned against her.

The Tribe of Shadows is going to be difficult to get past, Stella realized, thinking about how badly she wanted to leave the city. *If the Tribe of Shadows' feeling are even a tenth of what I'm feeling, it's going to be almost impossible. This nightmare really is "Tanas-sent."*

Tanas's name also reawakened Stella's doubts about whether or not she was dreaming. Met-on identified Tanas someone who *lived* in Nis.

But if this isn't a dream, Stella shuddered, wondering again if she was wrong, and if everything happening to her might actually be real. *If Tanas is here, like Met-on said...*Stella let that thought drift in her head for a second before deciding. *I can't tell Met-on, or anyone, what I know about Tanas. Dream* *or not, he can't know that I'm onto him.*

Stella knew from her own upbringing that Tanas, the closest friend to the Great Master Ash Addiel, discovered the world of Prism—bringing the glory of Ash Addiel's light to it. However, following the creation of the Hy-muns, Tanas rebelled against Ash Addiel and was imprisoned underground. After hearing the story of "The Coming" from Met-on, she started to realize how Tanas could fit into the Hy-mun creation story.

Tanas is Light Bringer, Stella thought, piecing together the Hy-muns' story and Met-on's story. *He leads the extermination of the Tribe of Shadows' ancestors in what is referred to as,* "bringing light to the darkness and shaping order out of the chaos he found" *in the Hy-mun texts. Whoever wrote the* Tome of the Ouroboros *either didn't know about the annihilation of the Tribe of Shadows' ancestors, or considered their destruction part of the* chaos *that needed to be shaped into an* order *the Nag-el would recognize. Later, after Tanas's failed rebellion and banishment, he reappears—changed beyond the point of recognition—to the survivors of "The Coming." He now looks like a savior, with the means for the Tribe of Shadows to strike the Nag-el, who may not even be aware of who they are, or why they are attacking them, and begins the conflict with the surface.* Stella knew if she told Met-on what she was knew about Tanas, it would not end well for her. She knew from the way Met-on spoke of him that he, and all of the members of the Tribe of Shadows, held him in godlike status.

Okay Stella, let's try to get a grip on your feelings, Stella thought to herself. *Either I'm trapped in a strange city with Hy-mun like beings, beings that die in light, that want to physically use me for their own purposes and pleasures, beings that I'm actually feeling SORRY for,* the idea made Stella shake, *or I'm in some kind of dream, one I can't wake myself up from normally.* Stella looked at Met-on, he still seemed as honest and strangely innocent as when she first started talking to him, and he still had a weird look in his eyes—like he was seeing more than Stella realized.

Dream, defiantly a dream, Stella concluded. *No one—even if they were raised to do it—could do the kinds of things Met-on has done to me and still look completely innocent about it. My parent often told me 'If you're trapped in a dream sent by Tanas, head for the light and you will wake up. But don't let Tanas know, or you will never wake.' I always thought that was a superstition, but it looks like it's true. So, I have to get out of here and head for the light.*

"What else would you like to talk about?"

Met-on's question snapped Stella out of her thoughts.

"Uh, is it okay for you to be here this long?" Stella asked, realizing Met-on had stayed longer then he usually did.

"It's okay for me to be here. Actually, I wasn't gone that long. The gas makes us feel time slower so we can enjoy ourselves more. Also, as soon as I get my first brand, brands are marks we get after completing missions from the circles granting us greater citizenship into the Tribe of Shadows, I'll be able to use the Jac-ob Way, and then I'll really seem to be here all the time. Since I'm only half-Rodent though, I might never get one, but I would do anything for one. Besides, with all of the madness going on in the city right now, especially after the Great Staircase's destruction by the Hy-mun Horror, no one is going to notice a half-Rodent like me missing from anything."

"The Hy-mun Horror? Who is that? And what is the Jac-ob Way?" Stella wondered.

"The Hy-mun Horror is a crazy Hy-mun that was released into the Grand Coliseum alongside two full-blooded Rodents," Met-on said. "In their match against two teams of gladiators, one of the Rodents destroyed the Veil of Shadows worn by the First Envy; the other Rodent escaped with the Hy-mun Horror into Nis. Since then, they have been creating chaos and martyrs from Wrath Eras to Pride Aster. My guess is that they're trying to challenge Lord Tanas himself in Yam-Preen."

"You don't seem worried," Stella said.

"I'm not Sis, no one has ever been able to defeat Lord Tanas. Attempts have been made, but no one has ever put a scratch on him."

Stella didn't doubt Met-on's confidence about Tanas.

Why would you doubt Tanas? Stella thought to herself, attempting to relate the "Hy-mun Horror" to her dream world belief. *I wouldn't doubt Tanas, and you were created by me. If even half of the myths and stories about Tanas are true, then whoever this Hy-mun Horror is, he needs the luck of Ash Addiel if he wants to challenge Tanas and win. I must have created the Hy-mun Horror to symbolize my struggle against Tanas.*

"As for the Jac-ob Way, it's the underground passageway that connects all of the circles of Nis," Met-on explained.

"All of the circles?" Stella asked, immediately curious. This could be the information she was waiting for, a way to get to the light and wake from this dream.

"Yes. I can't go into it since I don't have my first brand yet, but its entrance is near here. If you entered the Jac-ob Way and turned right, you could run all the way to the center of the city, and if you turned left you would reach the city's main gates. And with the traps disabled because of the Hy-mun Horror, it would be even easier, just a few guards."

Yes! Stella mentally exclaimed. It was the information she needed. If she could get to the Jac-ob Way, she could escape the city. Stella didn't doubt once she passed Nis's gates, she would either reach the light, wake up—finding herself back in the mining camp with everyone safe and sound—or find her way to the surface. Either way, Stella knew she would be out of this room and away from the city, and right now, that was the most important thing.

"Of course, getting to the Jac-ob Way is hard enough; it's a maze of streets outside this room, and if you don't know the way or have a guide, it's easy to get lost."

No! Stella exclaimed again, realizing now she couldn't just walk out of the room and go to the Jac-ob Way. But on the other hand, the chaos Met-on mentioned gave her an idea.

"So, Met-on, would you like to join again?"

"Would I?"

Met-on started coming to her and Stella smiled at the idea forming in her head. Stella believed Met-on would provide her a way out, and now he had done that. She knew she was being kept near a passage called the Jac-ob Way which led to the city's main gate. She knew the way she needed to go once she entered it, and that it was safe to travel in because the traps in it were turned off. The problem now was getting to the Jac-ob Way. According to Met-on, outside her room was, "a maze of streets," but with the chaos going on around the city, now might be the best, if not the only, time for her to chance an escape through them.

It's soon going to be now or never, Stella realized, waiting for the opportunity to present itself.

P.J. Fenton

Chapter 27

"This is too easy," Ice whispered, confused as he and Reye ran down the Jac-ob Way. "There should at least be guards, a sentry, a trap, anything. It's almost like they want us to get into Yam-Preen unobstructed."

"Or, considering we have gone straight through Nis and whatever soldiers and gladiators the Tribe of Shadows have thrown at us so far, they don't think we'll do anything differently," Reye replied. Chuckling as she stopped, put her ax down, and fixed another MMC to the roof of the Jac-ob Way. "Just tell me when we're past Circle Emporium."

Ice had been with Reye long enough to know what she was planning. Once they were through the Jac-ob Way, she planned to detonate the MMCs and cause a massive explosion running right down the center of Circle Emporium.

"Circle Emporium is one of the most important circles for the Tribe of Shadows," Ice explained. "If it is destroyed…"

"Just be quite already." Reye huffed, tired, and ignoring Ice's explanation about the importance of Circle Emporium. "The only things that matter to me now are taking another step closer to Lord Tanas, and hurting the Tribe of

Shadows. I want each one of them to know what it feels like when something precious to them is crushed from the neck up. I want every one of them to know what I am feeling. What it feels like to watch a brother, who followed me on every crazy stunt and challenge, kept me from getting punished by tight teachers and parents, only to end up getting his own dreams of adventure smashed like an egg and taken from him. I'll make sure of that."

Ice could feel the horrible red energy radiating off of her so powerfully that it felt like it could burn him. Exactly the state he wanted Reye to be in, it would be the only way she could take down Lord Tanas.

"Are there any more checkpoints that we have to go through?" Reye asked, setting another charge.

"Only the last gate that's at the end of the Jac-ob Way, once we get through there we'll be in Yam-Preen, the center of Nis."

"And that is where the boss of this place is, right?"

"That's right, Reye."

"So, let's take that gate!" Reye shouted.

Just you wait Raymond, Reye thought. *It will all be over, soon you'll be avenged, no more heads smashed open, no more corpses turned into food, and no more fights to the death for a mob's amusement. No more Lord Tanas means no more Tribe of Shadows and no more Nis.*

Ice *Knew* Reye was excited, more excited than he had ever seen her before. The three energies mixed wildly as she psyched herself up, storming down the Jac-ob Way to the last checkpoint. Her body, now covered and stinking of blood, also stank of adrenaline as excitement seemed to course through her veins. The drug's smell, continuously coming from every pore on her skin, made it hard to not want to get just as excited as she was.

"Where's the gate?" Reye asked, taking another charge out of her bag.

"I don't think it will be that much farther now," Ice answered. Looking up, he barely felt the energy flows from the city above them. "We should be just under the boundary between Circle Emporium and Yam-Preen. Of course, with the way you were screaming just now, I wouldn't be surprised if they heard us there."

Ice immediately regretted his choice of words. Reye suddenly turned on him and barreled straight toward him.

I forgot who I'm dealing with, Ice realized with a fright. *Is she going to kill me?*

Reye didn't kill Ice, but instead ran past him after fixing her last charge, leaving him extremely relieved. She had spotted the gateway. It was manned by only a few members of the Tribe of Shadows that were arguing amongst themselves as Reye charged toward the gate. However, once Reye reached it and started attacking, they quickly remember their post, trying to raise a panicked alarm.

"The Horror is here! Call back the troops! The Horror is here!"

"Well," Reye's frenzy boiled in her eyes as she tightened the grip on her ax, "I guess it's time to start this party." Reye cried, launching herself deeper into the soldiers.

This is almost getting boring, Reye through, plowing through the guards and the gateway with ease. *I can feel where these creatures are going to come from next. I can smell and taste their retched breath—fouled by eating corpses—in the air. I can also feel how they move now, thanks to the nonstop fighting throughout Nis. And it's all preparation, leading to what's next, the final fight with Lord Tanas.*

Continuing on, Reye and Ice ran up the stairway in front of them toward a small arched opening, the exit of the Jac-ob Way. Once outside the Way, Reye noticed that the exit was part of a colossal wall that stretched in both directions.

"The wall of Circle Emporium," Ice said, answering Reye's unspoken question. "It encircles Yam-Preen completely, the only two ways through it are the main gate in Circle Emporium, and the Jac-ob Way."

Reye could see a large door in the distance, as big as the wall.

The main gate, she realized.

Outside the Jac-ob Way, Reye braced herself against the wall of Circle Emporium. Crouching down, flattening herself against it on the right side of the Jac-ob Way's entrance, she waved for Ice to join her. Ice didn't need to *Know* anything about Reye to guess what was coming next, he quickly joined her against the wall.

"This is it," Reye shouted, taking out the detonator and pushing the button.

***

The devastation from the MMCs quickly revealed itself as each charge went

221

off in a continuing sequence, starting from the last checkpoint in the Jac-ob Way—between Circle Emporium and Yam-Preen—and stretching back to where it met with Pride Aster. As each charge exploded, a part of the Jac-ob Way collapsed in on itself. Luxurious homes—reserved for The Seven and the chosen living in Circle Emporium—crumpled, collapsed, or melted as the MMCs created small volcanic eruptions, geysers, and pools of magma connecting together into one great canyon, just like Reye planned. The multitude of soldiers in Circle Emporium, many of whom expected Reye and Ice to charge through the Examination Gates, were struck dumb at the destruction laid out before them as Reye's volcanic canyon leveled council chambers, homes, and everything in its path.

The destruction was so great that many of the soldiers dropped to their hands and knees at the sight of the devastation. Not only because Circle Emporium was broken, but for many, it felt like a dream had been broken as well. Ice tried telling Reye that many members of the Tribe of Shadows viewed living in Circle Emporium as the highest reward, bar martyrdom, one could achieve in life. Now, Reye had ripped a canyon-sized tear in that reward, and every member of the Tribe of Shadows present felt it.

***

The force of the explosion almost shook Reye and Ice to their feet, nearly breaking them in half. The two of them ended up backing away from the wall, and the opening to the Jac-ob Way, for their own safety as debris and magma poured out from the tunnel, effectively sealing it. With the Jac-ob Way sealed, and no guards in sight, Reye didn't need Ice to tell her which way to go this time. Turning away from the wall, Reye looked out upon Yam-Preen, home of Lord Tanas and the center of the city of Nis.

Part 5: Confrontations

Chapter 28

"This is Yam-Preen?"

Reye stared, shocked at the ruin before her. Ice understood her surprise. He had already told her the Tribe of Shadows considered Yam-Preen the most holy of holy grounds. But what Reye saw in the dim light of the magma flows was hardly something she would have considered sacred.

Rot and decay surrounded her as far as she could see. In the other circles, all of the buildings were well-kept, but here, none of that maintenance seemed to exist. Reye knew the Tribe of Shadows worshiped Lord Tanas, and Yam-Preen—their original city—was his home, but this wreck could hardly be called a city. It couldn't even be called a ghost town, tomb, or even a graveyard. There were no monuments, or people, just absolutely nothing. It looked like the Tribe of Shadows simply abandoned Yam-Preen, leaving it to crumble after building Circle Emporium. Walking toward a two-story building, Reye slightly touched it.

The side of the building felt like dust mixed with ash, and just as week, swallowing her hand and crumbling around it. The whole building soon followed, dissolving in front of her and collapsing with barely a sound.

It's like the whole building is made of dust. Everything in Yam-Preen is made of dust and shadows, Reye thought to herself, unable to understand how anyone could feel any spiritual connection to this place.

As the dust from the collapsing building cleared, Reye could see one real building resisting the decay in Yam-preen, a single tall black obsidian tower, magma flowing out from its base, stuck in the middle of the city.

"Let me guess, that tower is where I'll find Lord Tanas," Reye asked dryly, but tingling with excitement.

"Decca-Ju Tower," Ice nervously replied. "We'll be able to get there without any problems now. Lord Tanas is the only one who is there constantly. The attendants only serve part-time."

"He doesn't have any guards? This will be easy!" Reye shouted, running across the landscape of Yam-Preen. She didn't even try avoiding the buildings, running straight through them instead. Ancient buildings, now little more than dust, quickly collapsed behind her as she continued toward Decca-Ju Tower. The glow of the magma becoming brighter as she approached their source, just as her own energy radiated brighter as she approached the tower.

So, this is the Reye that will kill Lord Tanas, Ice wondered to himself, his thoughts marred with feelings of guilt and accomplishment.

When I first saw Reye in the cells, felt the horrible red energy pulse out of her, only to see it in action later, I knew I found an inexhaustible well of strength. I told Dan-te, "she might be the key to defeating Lord Tanas and stopping the Third Great Attempt." I knew it meant breaking the laws of the Remnant, but I needed to take her, use her, and her horrible red energy—an energy born from her loss and suffering—and aim her at Lord Tanas like an arrow, a goal Reye was primed to accomplish with little prodding from me. The Tribe of Shadows gave her the desire for revenge, and the soldier Gab-re gave her a target in Lord Tanas. All I've ever done was point her in the direction she wanted to go and let her do what she wanted; it's for the greater good.

Ice told himself, "it's for the greater good," more times than he could count, watching as Reye made her way through the circles of Nis, becoming more destructive along the way, and loosing herself in her horrible red energy. However, after finding the MMCs, Reye's mental white energy awakened, allowing her original brown energy to resurface and mix harmoniously with the horrible red energy. Ice slowly began *Knowing* the image of the Reye who, after finally reaching Yam-Preen, was now racing toward Decca-Ju Tower.

"Soon Raymond," Reye said in anticipation. "Soon nothing like what happened to you will ever happen to anyone again. First, I'll kill Lord Tanas, and then I'll fight my way back to the light to bring the whole might of the Seven Dominion back to wipe these creatures off our world for good. They'll never bother us again."

This is Reye, Ice realized sorely to himself, her three energies mixing perfectly, and aimed directly toward Lord Tanas. She reeked of blood, but also felt full of joy and excitement, the way someone feels when they are about to reach their goal. Her words rang with truth. Ice *Knew* she wouldn't stop with Lord Tanas, she would keep going until every *creature* beneath the surface was gone.

It's for the greater good, Ice repeated again in his head.

Reye stopped running a few feet before the stairs leading up into Decca-Ju Tower. The stairs, like the rest of the tower, were pitch black, reflecting an eerily red glow from the four rivers of magma oozing out from its base. Standing at the foot of the stairs, Reye called out with all the strength in her voice.

"Tanas, come out and face me!"

The doors of Decca-Ju Tower, twin doors made of black stone with griffins engraved on either side, remained shut as Reye's cries went unanswered.

"Remember why you've come here," Ice encouraged nervously from behind her back. "He's in there."

Reye, frustrated at being ignored, didn't need to be told by Ice why she came here and called again. Ice had done his job getting her here, and while he was busing himself—stuffing the documents he found into his clothes, Reye knew she didn't need him anymore, she just needed to beat Lord Tanas.

"Come out! I have fought my way through this infernal city and all of its creatures to fight you. Come out!"

Again, Reye's cries went unanswered. Challenging Tanas once more, she screamed again.

"Come out, coward! In the name of the Great Lord and Master Ash Addiel, come out now!"

Whether it was because Reye invoked the name Ash Addiel, the third time she challenged him, or he simply wanted to be dramatic, Reye's third attempt provoked a response. One of the stone doors of Decca-Ju Tower screeched open slowly—the stone door rubbing against the floor of the tower—and the black robed figure of Lord Tanas exited the tower, calmly descending the stairs. Once Lord Tanas left the tower, all of the heat vanished from the surrounding air. Even the magma rivers, which warmed the surroundings, suddenly felt freezing cold in Lord Tanas's presence.

Lord Tanas's approach forced Ice to collapse to his knees, frozen in fear of *Knowing* him. The descriptions of him, of *it*, from the Stories of Rill had not been exaggerated.

If anything, the stories don't do it justice, Ice thought, gazing upon Lord Tanas.

Lord Tanas seemed like an outline of a person, but within that outline was a gaping void of nothingness, pulling Ice into it. Worse yet, with every slow step Lord Tanas took toward them, the pull became stronger and stronger. Ice was barely able to turn his head away from that abyss to look at Reye, hoping to find the strength and determination he *Knew* in her, but it was gone.

At the sight of Lord Tanas, all of the fight, the hatred, and need for vengeance left Reye, leaving her nothing more than an ordinary girl. From Reye's perspective, Lord Tanas wasn't the void of nothingness that Ice *Knew*. Lord Tanas was a hooded man with black eyes, black as obsidian, cold, and deadly. His skin was an extremely dark blue, it looked like ocean water at the depths where it was about to lose its color completely and turn black. He also radiated the same cold found at those depths, deep and penetrating, reaching into her body, into the deepest reaches of her molecules, freezing her bit by bit until she felt like a piece of ice about to shatter.

Until now, Reye had charged through each of the circles of the city of Nis on brawns, brains, and explosives, with the purpose of reaching this one being. However, now that she finally reached him, she suddenly knew, in much the same way Ice could *Know*, that there was no chance she would even be able to fight against him.

Submit, Submit, Submit…

The word echoed coldly through Reye's mind and body, freezing her in place with fear. Lord Tanas radiated such a cold, lethal presence that the pointlessness of any action she could make against him hit her like a tidal wave.

I can't fight him, Reye mentally sobbed to the echoing "submit."

I can't even detonate the MMCs I have in my pack and try to take both of us out at the same time. Not only will he kill me before I can use the detonator, but I know he could still get clear of the blast. Reye knew now that this was an entity, and *entity* was truly the only word that could describe him, who had existed for ages, and was ready for anything.

Seeing Reye frozen, Ice realized his desperate gamble failed disastrously. The documents Ice found and tucked into his clothes told him the Third Great Attempt was going to start soon, and that the Tribe of Shadows could get to Rem. The idea to stop the Third Great Attempt by using the Veil of Shadows to influence a Hy-mun failed, so he gambled on using Reye to take out Lord Tanas. But that plan failed even more miserably. Against Lord Tanas—who stood before Reye, reaching out to grasp her—Reye was just as susceptible, if not more susceptible, to Lord Tanas then he was. Ice *Knew* the part of her that was the Hy-mun Horror was gone. There was no horrible red energy, no harmonious mixture of horrible red, mental white, and natural brown energies, no new versions of her. It was all drawn out. Confronted with the sheer magnitude of Lord Tanas, and the gaping void that made up his being, the red energy was pulled out of her and drawn into it. Without that red energy, Reye was left no different now than before she came to Nis. But whatever pain she suffered in the past, planting the seeds of the Hy-mun Horror's energy in her, it was nothing compared to what happened after Lord Tanas grasped her.

The moment Lord Tanas's hand took hold of Reye's neck, all of her body heat was drawn out of her and into Lord Tanas. Ice could see and feel the heat leave her body in waves and enter Lord Tanas. Yet, most frightening, was no matter how cold she became, she didn't die of it. Lord Tanas wouldn't let her die of it. Also, body heat wasn't the only source of warmth being drawn out of Reye, so were her warm thoughts and emotions. All the warm memories she made and shared with her family and friends slipped from her mind and into obscurity. The connection between Lord Tanas and Reye opened a drain, drawing her feelings to it. Reye could only catch a glimpse of them before they were gone, and replacing those warm memories and emotions were all the cold ones. All of the cold horrors she witnessed and committed from the death of her brother, her rampage through Nis, to facing Lord Tanas were suddenly played back before her again in vivid detail. Only this time, they wouldn't go away. Worse, she was facing them in all of their full gory detail without the hot zeal of a crusader and avenger.

Throughout her journey through Nis, Reye's hot-blooded desire for revenge changed her, allowing her to live, and quickly move past all the death and destruction she caused. In Reye's mind, it would be justified to avenge Raymond, and to ensure that what happened to him would never happen to anyone again. But now, stripped of those hot emotions and zeal, facing Lord Tanas, she knew in all certainty she couldn't beat him. Her entire body screamed "submit" from the first moment she saw at him. Finding herself facing all the members of the Tribe of Shadows she killed, the destruction she caused, and the cold emotions of guilt, shame, and regret buried deep within her; her entire spirit shattered like ice. Finally, Lord Tanas tossed Reye to the ground alongside her sack of MMCs.

How did Rill break free from this state, Ice wondered. He knew he should move, do something to help Reye, but remained stunned from Lord Tanas's appearance. Reye curled up on the cavern floor, next to her sat the bag of MMCs, and a pin that fell off her clothes after Tanas dropped her.

The moment Reye's body hit the ground, Ice stirred at a sound behind him, soldiers were cheering. While locked in the abyss of Lord Tanas, the soldiers of Nis had arrived in Yam-Preen and had gathered a distance away from Decca-Ju Tower, stopping out of both fear and divine reverence for Lord Tanas. The cheering was the loudest Ice ever heard.

"All hail the Lord Tanas!"

"Praise be his name!"

"He has destroyed the Hy-mun Horror with his own hand!"

"None can defeat him!"

The cheers for Lord Tanas were deafening. Ice could barely move to cover his ears. Yet, despite all of the cheers, all Tanas did was raise his hand and the entire congregation fell silent.

"My people, you now see before you the so-called Hy-mun Horror, reduced to nothing from my touch and presence. Soon the Third Great Attempt will begin, and what has happened to this Hy-mun will be visited upon all Hy-muns, like a curse of destruction a thousand times over!"

The crowd became more excited as cheers for the destruction of the Hy-mun, the reclaiming of the Tribe of Shadows' ancestral lands, and the praises of

228

Lord Tanas rang throughout Yam-Preen. This time, however, Lord Tanas didn't silence them. Instead, he beckoned two members of the Tribe of Shadows to come to him.

"What are your names?" Lord Tanas asked the two, who had approached both excitedly and reverently.

"I am Jem-sa, my Great Lord," one replied. Gesturing to his companion he said, "This is my brother, Ho-jn."

"Jem-sa, Ho-jn, take this Hy-mun and Rodent out of this sacred ground and have them imprisoned in Maestri. But when you get there, tell the guards to take the Rodent and use him for Tunnel Construction. After being so helpful to this Hy-mun, he can certainly be helpful to us now."

"Yes, Lord Tanas!" the two brothers said in unison, taking hold of both Reye and Ice, and dragging them through the deafening crowds.

"I must retire to make preparations for the Third Great Attempt's commencement," Lord Tanas said, climbing back up the stairs to the stone doors of Decca-Ju Tower. "The rest of you do the same. Worry not about city repairs. We won't need this city anymore, because soon we will be returning to the surface where we will take the Hy-muns' cities, and they will learn our pain."

Lord Tanas turned his back on the Tribe of Shadows, the stone doors grinding close behind him. Returning to his chamber at the tower's apex, he reviewed his own private instruments and calculations using the devices he brought with him when the Nag-el banished him, making his own special preparations for the Third Great Attempt. However, his current thoughts also drifted to the recent events, and how they not only aided in his plans, but how they worked out so perfectly he would have thought he planned them himself.

In a matter of hours, Lord Tanas mused, *everyone in the city will be praising "Lord Tanas's power,"* working even harder *to trigger the eruption that will give me my freedom. If I wasn't going to wipe out all of those Rodents, I would* thank *that Rodent for using a crazed hybrid mutant in a useless attempt against me. The genetic programming installed in them doomed his plan before it even begun.* Lord Tanas burst out laughing at Ice and Reye's attempt on his life, his mind drifting back to the time before his banishment, when the Hy-muns were first created. As well as the events that eventually led him to his long campaign for freedom. One that was almost complete.

P.J. Fenton

Chapter 29

When Tanas and his followers were first sent out, they were told to find a new planet for their people, but to leave inhabited planets alone. Constantly searching for battle, conquest, glory, manipulating their own genetic code, and creating biological and viral weapons to beat better soldiers eventually destroyed their planet. Ash Addiel, their ruler, wanted to start a new world for his people and make a fresh start.

"We must put the old ways behind us and live simply," Ash Addiel said. "The ways of our ancestors have betrayed us and we cannot let it happen again. We must leave our warlike ways behind us and live in peace."

However, Tanas and his followers did not want to give up the glory and thrill of battle and conquest as easily as he did. So, when Tanas and his forces found the Tribe's planet, cloaked in dark matter, making it invisible to their ships—finding the planet by chance, flying through the Dark Matter surrounding it and discovering the planet within it. They were not going to let the chance of glory, conquest, and a new world pass just because it was inhabited.

"Are the native animals wiped out Ethos Primes?" Tanas asked.

Ethos Primes, Tanas's second in command, was outfitted in the same full-body armor as Tanas. Designed to emit heat to keep animals away, each part of the body armor had a small motion sensor mounted on it to detect incoming movement, and a laser. If any animal approached him, the closest laser would incapacitate or kill the animal, depending on the suits setting.

"The native plants and animals are wiped out; Scorching Protocols are nearly complete. It should be noted that a part of the continent sunk into the ocean and a landed ship sank with it."

"The ship and territory can be written off easily enough." Tanas said, surveying the piles of dead bodies waiting to be incinerated. "Just make sure the planet is ready for the genetics and bio-engineers."

After wiping the planet clean of its native life, and destroying the dark matter that blocked the sunlight from it, Tanas and his advance party welcomed the rest of the Nag-el. The new arrivals worked tirelessly, recreating the surface of the planet so that it would resemble their own lost world. Using the plant and animal DNA from the seedlings and blood samples they carried from their home world—a world that had quickly died as a result of biological warfare—they created plants and animals that were now native to their new world. The Nag-el also mined precious materials—creating volcanoes to force the materials up from the ground—to build cities to live in, and slightly cool the surface in the process. During that time, a small group of newly-arrived bioengineers began experimenting with combining the DNA of their own race with various blood samples from their home world to create a hybrid creature. The idea was to create something that could be used as a beast of burden, a gladiatorial creature—providing an outlet for the Nag-el's need for combat, or both. The creature's intelligence would be limited, higher than a simple animal to provide a challenge, but not to the point where it could be called sentient.

The experiments were all failures, except for one that came from combining the DNA of their own leader, Tanas's best friend Ash Addiel, with an unknown DNA sample—one of many uncategorized animal samples from the home world evacuation—found in the DNA bank. The hybrid mutant creatures were genetically programmed with an internal submissiveness program that would make them submit to the sight of any Nag-el—a programming that would be passed on from generation to generation—and turned out to be more intelligent than its creators originally intended. The hybrid mutants were not only capable of fighting intelligently, they could also follow instructions, act on their own, and perform menial tasks and light work.

However, for Tanas and his advance force, who were with him when they first arrived on the new planet, the hybrid mutants—or Hy-muns—brought an eerie reminder of the creatures that had been there when they arrived. The Hy-muns' appearance was so similar to the creatures they wiped out that Tanas himself researched where the "unknown DNA sample" came from, discovering it was from one of those creatures. The revelation was unsettling. Tanas was fully aware of what would happen to him if it was discovered he and his forces wiped a planet clean of life for their own use, the punishments that both Ash Addiel and the Nag-el would demand of him, and began making his own plans to erase any remaining evidence.

Tanas's first step in his plan was the assassination of anyone who worked on the Hy-muns' development, so no one could ask why they were successfully created, or where the unknown DNA came from. Tanas's first target was one of his own men, his second in command Ethos Primes, who submitted the blood sample under the label of an unknown DNA sample for his own "personal study and amusement." The assassination, similar to the murder of the bioengineers who selected the sample and worked directly on it, was conducted by Tanas personally with little or no assistance. In fact, Tanas not only assassinated all of his targets at once, but used a method similar to the idea he would later employ in the Third Great Attempt. Tanas's three coconspirators, Cassius, Brutus, and Judas, brought each of their targets to a lab—all under different pretenses— located near one of the newly crafted volcanoes. Once they were all there, Tanas used explosives to trigger a minor eruption. Destroying the lab, targets, and his three coconspirators in one move, leaving him the only person who knew the Hy-muns' genetic origins.

Unfortunately, the destruction of the lab and the bioengineers didn't cause Tanas's fears to subside. Instead, the loss sparked an interest in the Hy-muns. With the bioengineers that created them dead, other scientists began wondering why their experiment worked when nobody else's did. But with the data and original genetic samples lost with the original team, all the other bioengineers could work with were the Hy-muns themselves. This caused the people to take a closer look at both the Hy-muns, and what they could accomplish. Soon after, they were placed on an isolated island off the coast of the continent, given a form of education, and were soon found to mentally develop similar to Nag-el children, but still extremely submissive and loyal to the Nag-el despite the advancing education in science and self-defense.

The Hy-muns are even more intelligent than they *realize,* Tanas often thought. The Hy-muns' intelligence made Tanas even more afraid that his secret would be revealed. Worry tormented him, thinking about how others might begin examining the Hy-muns' genetic origins, discovering something Tanas might have missed when he erased the records of where the Hy-muns' base DNA came from.

If the Hy-muns are declared sentient beings by Ask Addiel... Tanas endlessly worried to himself. *It's only a matter of time at this rate; there will be no stopping a genetic investigation of them, and then they will find out the truth.*

Knowing that he couldn't assassinate every bioengineer who could study the Hy-muns, he began making plans for the Hy-muns' extinction, which would erase all the remaining traces of life that existed on the planet before their arrival.

The first phase of the plan was simple rumor spreading. Because of the Hy-muns' intelligence and submissiveness, some Nag-el were already using Hy-muns to perform menial tasks. All Tanas did was simply whisper the right words to the right people—about how the planet was for the Nag-el alone, and that the Hy-muns were replacing Nag-el workers—to whip up a frenzy of prejudice against the Hy-muns. The frenzy grew into a movement against not only the Hy-muns, but also against Ash Addiel himself, who publicly, and at the secret suggestion of Tanas, endorsed the Hy-muns' safety and right to live. The Anti-Hy-mun Movement eventually turned violent, with Tanas secretly playing both sides of the conflict. On one side, he openly supported Ash Addiel's work against the movement, but on the other side he was its anonymous leader, secretly spreading information, and sowing the seeds of hated against both the Hy-muns and Ash Addiel.

The final phase of Tanas's plan called for both the assassination of Ash Addiel, at the hands of a Hy-mun, and his own enthronement as leader. The Anti-Hy-mun Movement, which now included almost all the members from Tanas's advance force, would lead a raid on a former weapon hold that now acted as a lab and mass shelter for Hy-muns while Ash Addiel was visiting. Tanas would then kill Ash Addiel himself. Afterwards, he would force a Hy-mun to submit to him and take the blame for Ash Addiel's death. Then, once he was named leader, he would reverse the protection on the Hy-muns and completely wipe them out, "to protect ourselves from the same tragedy that befell our beloved Ash Addiel."

The plan almost worked. When Tanas met Ash Addiel he had a male Hy-mun with him. Ash Addiel embraced him when he arrived and looked straight into his eyes.

Does he know? Tanas wondered, quickly realizing Ash Addiel's face was filled with both joy and wonder.

"Tanas, I have incredible news. My friend Dema has just told me he is going to become a father." As Ash Addiel spoke the name Dema, he motioned to the Hy-mun next to him. "I've asked him to come with us on our tour and he agreed. When it's over and I get back to the Capital I am going to declare the Hy-muns sentient, they've even developed their own special language based on some of our older languages. Go ahead Dema, show him."

"Ad altiora tendo," Dema replied. "We call the language Platin, it means 'I strive toward higher things.'"

"And you and all the Hy-muns will 'strive toward higher things,'" Ash Addiel laughed joyfully. "Just wait until we get back."

Then the timing couldn't be better. Tanas thought to himself, as his men began their attack.

Tanas's forces quickly raided the lab, grabbing and destroying anything they could find, slowly making their way to the shelter. Meanwhile, Tanas ushered Ash Addiel and Dema into a different part of the shelter, leaving the three of them alone.

"The main army is nearby practicing maneuvers." Ash Addiel puffed, reaching into the pocket of his jacket and pulling out a communication device. "It will only take me a little while to call the army. Don't worry about your child Dema." But Dema wasn't looking at Ash Addiel, he was looking at Tanas, charging with a drawn knife.

Tanas expected to kill Ash Addiel and find him dead at his feet with a submissive Hy-mun next to them ready to take the blame. Instead, he found a Hy-mun shielding Ash Addiel, sacrificing his own life, and saving Ash Addiel, who stood shocked at both Dema's sacrifice and Tanas's betrayal. That single act of self-sacrifice bought all the time needed for Ash Addiel to attack and capture Tanas, and complete his call to the main army; who soon arrived, subdued, and captured the remaining members of the Anti-Hy-mun movement.

At Tanas's trial, it was discovered that he was the leader and inciter of the Anti-Hy-mun Movement, yet his motives for beginning the movement were never discovered. Ash Addiel decreed the sentence to be permanent genetic alteration and banishment.

***

In a laboratory opened to the sky, Tanas watched as his followers were injected with drugs to alter their genetic structure. The first alteration made them experience lethal pain when exposed to sunlight. Tanas stoically watched his followers wither in pain, some dying before the next phase of the procedure could be administered; but internally, he was haunted by the memories of when he and his legion first arrived on the planet.

Punishment that befits the crime, Tanas thought to himself dryly. Remembering how the planet's creatures burned to death from exposure to sunlight, a similar fate now visiting his legion.

The next phase of the alterations involved injecting each of Tanas's followers with a serum that kept them from having children. If any of Tanas's followers attempted to reproduce, a genetic tag on each reproductive cell would react with similar tags on the cells of the opposite sex, triggering a reaction, and causing all of the reproductive cells to self-destruct. The Nag-el did not want any of Tanas's followers to have a legacy.

As for Tanas himself, not only did he receive the same manipulations as his legions, but he was also injected with the Methuselah Drug—administered by Ash Addiel himself.

"So, not only will I have to suffer the cold existence, but you will condemn me to it *with your own hands*." Tanas spit, as Ash Addiel as he held the drug over Tanas.

"It may be my hand that administers this drug." Ash Addiel replied, tears in his eyes as he inserted the needle into Tanas's arm. "But the one who chose this fate and condemned yourself to it was you, Tanas."

The Methuselah Drug, part genetic drug and part nanotech, would allow him to live forever, but leave him permanently altered. He would become a being that lived off all forms of heat, constantly absorbing heat from sources around him. However, he would never feel it, remaining colder than space. No one would also be able to stay near him for a long period of time, Tanas was to be an exile among exiles.

The final drug added, a suppressant, kept the effects triggered by sunlight at bay for 48 hours. Ash Addiel allowed this because he wanted to give Tanas and his forces time to say good-bye, and take whatever bare essential they wanted into exile, before finally banishing them into the deepest caves they could find, caves later known as the Prison Caverns by the Hy-muns. Unknown to any of them however, was when Tanas's forces raided the lab, they stole a number of experimental Veils of Shadows—devices designed for infiltration, examination, and spreading misinformation—along with the data on how they were created and how to reproduce them, destroying everything else in the process. During their last 48 hours on the surface, Tanas and his followers retrieved those Veils, the data, and the material needed to reproduce them. Hiding them on their bodies and in their belonging as they took them underground into exile. Veils Tanas knew he would later use to gain both his freedom and revenge on both Ash Addiel and the Hy-muns.

P.J. Fenton

Chapter 30

First was Ash Addiel, Tanas mused, making his way through Decca-Ju Tower, remembering what became known as both the First and Second Great Attempts. *Despite all his talk about beginning again, it took only the right whispers to bring our people back to their glorious ways and incite the war that all but ended him.*

Soon after Tanas made contact with the Tribe of Shadows he began his attacks on the surface; whispering into the ears of the Nag-el and turning them from the new ways Ash Addiel tried instilling, back to the old ways that almost destroyed them. Tanas and the Tribe of Shadows incited gladiatorial combats, stimulated genetic research—regardless of the risk or cost, and encouraged aggression and combat almost too easily. The First Great Attempt culminated in a three-way civil war between the Nag-el, during which a series of chemical weapons were released—all encouraged by Tanas—that mixed together to create a plague lethal to the Nag-el, killing almost all of them.

However, during the war, Ash Addiel managed to discover the existence of the Veil of Shadows project, theorizing then that Tanas could be behind both the shift in the Nag-els' attitude following his banishment and the civil war. Unfortunately, by that point Ash Addiel could not gain the needed support from his people to go underground and find out. Finally, Ash Addiel took his few remaining followers who hadn't contracted the plague back into space, putting them into suspended animation until a computer on their ship revived them once the plague burned itself out. Yet a few Nag-el elected to remain on the surface, providing whatever guidance they could for the Hy-muns—who were immune to the plague—until they also succumbed and died.

However, prior to Ash Addiel's departure, he created the Ziggurat Security System. A system using seven Ziggurats scattered across the continent and a central station, one the Hy-muns would later call the Platinum Throne, to ensure sure that neither Tanas, nor any of his followers, would be able to leave the caverns. The eight structures, powered by sunlight and constantly searching for Tanas, would activate the moment he stepped foot on the surface. The system would detect the nanotech components of the Methuselah Drug he was injected with and attack him with light, leaving him in "a state worse than death," according to the Hy-muns' Tome.

Attempting to destroy the Ziggurats prior to and during the First Great Attempt was out of the question. Tanas simply didn't have the means to do it. Instead, Tanas started construction on the Great Tunnel he would use later for the Third Great Attempt to cut off the Ziggurats' power. However, since the Nag-els' departure, the Hy-muns created their own society and technology; basing it on what they could understand from the Ziggurats and the writings of the Nag-el driven crazy by the plague. The Hy-muns' religious devotion—a product of the submission programming—to those writings ended up making the Second Great Attempt almost a success.

On their own, without the Nag-el to submit to as their genetic programming demanded, the Hy-muns quickly found themselves in charge of their own destinies for the first time. With that freedom came all of the dangers that went with it. Having been created originally as gladiatorial beasts from the Nag-el's DNA, the Hy-muns were as prone to the same love of battle and glory that the Nag-el were. Only before, the submission programming kept those urges in check. The Hy-mun would instantly submit to the Nag-el before any conflicts could arise. Without the Nag-el, and with the help of Tanas and the Tribe of

Shadows, those urges flourished. Hy-muns challenged other Hy-muns in tests of strength, speed, endurance, and eventually in combat to the death.

The Hy-muns, however, still longed to submit to the Nag-el, eventually revering them as deities, and submitting themselves to anything supposedly written or touched by them. If a book was old enough that the memory of who wrote it was lost, the Hy-muns would say it was written by the Nag-el. And they would fight anyone who dared to contradict what one group, or what one text, said over another. This contradiction later gave Tanas the fuel to begin the Second Great Attempt.

The plans for the Second Great Attempt began when documents from the time Ash Addiel was preaching to "put the old ways behind us" and "live simply" were discovered. Tanas found that it was easy to convince the Hy-muns—who were already honoring those documents as a result of their submissiveness programming—to take those words and apply them as motivation to destroy all forms of technology, including the Ziggurats. Not only that, the land the documents was found on was declared sacred lands by the Hy-muns who lived there, creating more divisions among the different nations of Hy-muns. The end result, was the war the Hy-muns called the Great Rainbow War, a war that nearly destroyed all forms of technology through the widespread use of electromagnetic pulse weapons designed to destroy technology, followed by ground destroyers who would attack on land and physically destroy technology. The war was on the verge of destroying the Ziggurats, using an experimental uranium based weapon, when a Hy-mun freak appeared and was able to stop the war at the cost of his own life.

***

I still remembered that Hy-mun freak, Tanas mused, never forgetting the face of the Hy-mun who once stood before him. *Somehow, he was born without the submission programming so he could stand against me, something the Rodent's Hy-mun Horror obviously could not do. That Hy-mun actually looked like Dema, the Hy-mun who shielded Ash Addiel from my attack long ago. The Hy-mun, along with a few of the others who were captured and brought to Nis with him, escaped when one of my finest soldiers turned traitor. But not before that Hy-mun raided Decca-Ju Tower, taking with him an old copy of Ash Addiel's writings. Writings I kept to remind myself of who banished me. That Hy-*

mun took the documents, documents saying, "We must put the old ways behind us and live simply. The ways of our ancestors have betrayed us and we cannot let it happen again. We must put our warlike ways behind us and live in peace," and brought them to the surface.

That Hy-mun was later shot at a summit when he ran at the Virt Princes—the leaders of the Seven Dominions—to present the documents, but his last words, that "Ash Addiel wanted us to live in peace. He said it with his own voice, wrote it with his own hand, on this paper." Those words convinced them to stop the war and turn the documents into a sacred relic. Yet, while the war failed to destroy the Ziggurats, it did create the vaults of technology that the Tribe of Shadows were able to steal from and use to forward the tunnel.

Well, one step back, two steps forward, Tanas laughed out loud as he continued to reminisce. *The Great Rainbow War failed to destroy the Ziggurats but it did provide me with the technology needed to complete the tunnel. This time* nothing *will stop me from escaping this prison.*

Tanas began gathering the necessary supplies he needed once the explosion was triggered and the supervolcano began erupting, blackening the sky.

Once it starts, and the magma is on its way, I have to be as far away from Decca-Ju Tower and Nis as possible. The Methuselah Drug might keep me alive, but it doesn't mean I can't be killed, and the amount of magma that will be pouring into Nis is more than enough to kill me. I need to be in the right place, a place I've been preparing far from the city, so when the time is right I can finally break free of his prison and return to the surface.

Chapter 31

Stella threw up again, her third time. The first time was when Met-on fell asleep in her room, after she had decided that if she was going to escape it would soon be "*now or never.*" She thought that with all of the chaos going on in Nis, the "*reflection of her mind's chaos,*" it would be her best chance to make an escape, find the light, and "*wake up,*" while Met-on, "*her desires,*" slept.

Stella hoped she had acquired enough information from Met-on about the city she believed she had created to escape it. She knew that she was in the Third Circle of Nis, Lust Atrophied. She knew that near her cell was a passage called the Jac-ob Way that led to the city's main gate, she also knew which way to go in the Jac-ob Way, and that the traps in it were deactivated. What she didn't know was how to get to the Jac-ob Way from her room, but that was something she was willing to chance.

It's still my dream, Stella thought to herself, *I should be able to find my way through it.*

She was about to try to escape when the nausea swept through her. Stella barely made it to one of the magma vents before vomiting, allowing it to be quickly incinerated by the magma. Unfortunately, the noise woke Met-on up. When he asked her what she was doing, she quickly said that she was just cold and wanted to warm up, an excuse she used before when he found her near the door and gas rope, and one she hoped he would believe again—especially since she did warm herself on the vents. But instead of questioning her, he went over to sit at her side, trying to help warm her with his own body heat.

Tanas, Stella thought. *You are not going to make it easy for me to escape from this dream, are you?*

However, after the third vomiting fit, a new fear made Stella think that her "dream world" could be more than just a dream.

It can't be, she thought to herself frantically, *Am I pregnant? How could I be pregnant? This is just a dream, right?*

But doubts had been slowly eating away at belief, especially after what happened following her first vomiting fit.

***

Once Met-on went back to sleep—following Stella's first vomiting fit, Stella tried to escape again. She only cracked the door open a little when she heard voices on the other side of it.

"Did you hear, Lord Tanas defeated the Hy-mun Horror," a voice said. Stella froze, holding her breath, listening to the conversation.

"That's great," the other voice said. "Do you think that means the Warden will make someone else babysit the half-Rodent?"

"After we got caught calling the Warden a Rodent Lover, not a chance, you know what the Warden told the half-breed."

"Not really."

"Get this." The voice snickered as he talked. "The Warden told the half-Rodent if he could get the Hy-mun pregnant, or just make the Hy-mun fall for him and admit that she loved him, he would get his first branding."

"Ha! And I thought he really was falling for the Hy-mun. You know how first timers can get attached to someone."

I thought Met-on was constantly here for a reason, Stella thought to herself, looking back to Met-on's sleeping body. He had told her that each member of the Tribe of Shadows needed to complete certain assignments from different circles to gain brandings that granted them citizenship into the Tribe. Since he was half-

Rodent, Met-on knew he might never get a single branding but said that he, or any half-Rodent, would do anything to get even one.

You would do anything indeed, Stella thought—disgusted for "creating" Met-on the way she did—as she continued to listen.

"Personally, I think the half-Rodent *is* falling for the Hy-mun," the first voice said again. "Not that it matters one way or the other."

Well, maybe that's at least one redeeming trait I gave him, Stella thought to herself as the conversation continued.

"Yeah, the rumor is that all half-Rodents are going to be wiped out before the Third Great Attempt starts. Then there are our other orders," the second voice sneered.

"Yeah, if the Hy-mun is discovered to be pregnant, or if she confesses to having feeling for the half-Rodent, kill them all immediately. If not, then after the purge, kill the Hy-mun."

Stella silently closed the door without a sound, vomiting into the magma vents for the second time. Met-on told Stella that when women became pregnant, they were kept under lock and key, seeing no one until they came to term. After the baby was born, it would be immediately taken from her and placed into the care of others who would prepare it for the life that all members of the Tribe of Shadows faced, depending on the gender. If the child was female, it would be turned into another breeder. If it was a male, it became another soldier. The mother was then sent back to breed another child. But that was not going to happen to her.

It can't happen, Stella thought to herself. *This is still just a dream, one either Tanas or my mind must be trying hard to keep me in. Or is it?*

Stella looked to the sleeping form of Met-on and then back to the door of her room, which she now knew was guarded, her doubts and fears beginning to scream through her mind.

It can't be! Stella mentally exclaimed. *I created Met-on out of my physical and emotional desires, didn't I? But if I didn't, if he's real, if all of this; Met-on, the Tribe of Shadows, the city of Nis, Tanas, if everything that's been happening to me is real then...* Stella's mind blanked as the full implications of accepting the world around her as reality sank in. *It can't be, it has to be a DREAM!*

Stella still refused to accept anything that was happening to her as nothing more than a dream.

***

It has to be part of the dream. Stella thought frantically, trying to deny the truth that she was now realizing, that this was no dream world.

A result of my wants and desires. I've always wanted someone to have all to myself, someone who would only want me, someone whose children I could eventually raise.

Stella's mind was panicking now, coming up with whatever reasons she could to relate a pregnancy to her "dream world" belief.

I've read stories growing up about people who have had dreams that felt like years—living entire lifetimes—but turned out to be only a night long. This has to be one of those. Stella thought, laughing quietly as she continued to lie to herself.

Stella wouldn't say, or even dare think, that she already realized the truth about her "dream world." As Stella learned more about the history of her "dream world" from Met-on, she slowly became more certain that it had to be real and not a dream. Yet Stella still tried telling herself that it was a dream; that Met-on, the child of a member of the Tribe of Shadows and another group of subterranean people known as The Remnant, simply didn't exist.

All life on Prism was born from the Great Master Ash Addiel's light. Stella continuously told herself. *The only life underground should be Tanas.*

Met-on had told her about the prejudices he faced because of his mixed ancestry growing up in Nis. *The dream world's reflection of my own childhood's restrictions,* Stella manically rationalized. If a child could be born from the two of them, the life he/she would face was something she didn't even want to consider.

It's just a dream after all, right? Stella thought, but the truth was finally taking hold.

According to the guards, the moment a pregnancy was discovered, they were all going to be killed. Even if a pregnancy wasn't discovered, she knew now they were all going to be killed soon anyway.

It isn't a dream, it's real, Stella finally admitted to herself, placing her hands over her body as tears began running from her eyes. *You were never in any dream world. Everything that's happened since I first woke up here has really happened.* As Stella said the words to herself, a door opened in her mind. Stella remembered the attack on the camp, her first sight of the Tribe of Shadows warriors, Raymond's death, his last words, "Run, fight, live," and finally passing out from the shock of seeing him killed. Worse, she realized that if everything since the attack—including the pregnancy—was real, she knew what that meant.

If, no, when the pregnancy discovered, I'm dead. If I sit do nothing, they will still kill me anyway. If I escape the city, can I even go to the surface? If this child is born on the surface, will it die in the sunlight, will I die with it in the birthing process, will we both die just from me being pregnant with this child in the sunlight? Stella realized that returning to the surface was no longer possible, doing so would put both her own life and the child's life at risk. Looking back to gaze at Met-on, Stella thought about another option.

Could I go to The Remnant? Stella wondered, thinking about the other race of beings beneath the surface. *Would they accept a Hy-mun, even if it was just until the baby came to term? At least, I'm hoping, they are better than the Tribe of Shadows. But how do I get to them?*

Stella knew her first challenge would be Met-on.

My child's father, she whiffed. Met-on, a boy, barely a Hy-mun teenager, who first came upon her while she was drugged and captured in a section of an underground city reserved for women to do nothing but make babies for the Tribe of Shadows. An area where normally, according to Met-on, she would have been paired with other men from the Tribe of Shadows, men who might be a lot worse than Met-on ever was, but still managed to remain with Met-on because of a decision by someone called "the Warden."

Could Met-on really help me? Stella thought to herself. *Could I make him take me out of the city and to The Remnant?*

Not only that, just before the second case of vomiting, Stella discovered the Hy-mun Horror had been captured.

No matter what happens, we're all going to die soon, Stella thought to herself, realizing that she had only limited time to work with. *But can I convince Met-on of that?*

Stella knew she needed to find a way to get past the guards at her door and through the maze-like streets of the city. Because with the Hy-mun Horror captured, the Jac-ob Way would soon be booby trapped again, and the only one she knew who could possibly get her past the guards, and through the streets, was Met-on. Meaning she had to convince him take her out of the city, for all of their sakes.

Somehow, I have to get Met-on to help me, Stella reflected, understanding what she needed to do to escape. *Finding The Remnant—or any safe haven— after that is a problem I can face once I'm out of the city.*

Each problem appeared more difficult that the last, but for the sake their lives—the sake of her child's life, she had to figure them out, quickly.

Chapter 32

"Reye, Reye can you hear me," Ice said, as gently as he could.

Reye's only response was an occasional flutter of her eyelids.

Facing Lord Tanas has left her drowning in both her negative energy and cold feelings. Ice thought to himself, *Knowing* the result of Reye's encounter. It left her entire body cold to the touch, a fog of cold negative flaxen yellow energy surrounded her, while her mind kept dragging up her worst memories and feelings—constantly reflected in her eyes, keeping her in a submissive state.

Reye couldn't hear Ice even if she wanted too. She could only hear the screams. In her mind, she heard the screams of every warrior she killed, saw their faces, felt their breath, smelt their blood. Her entire rampage throughout Nis was constantly being replayed before her very eyes, but without any of the hot-blooded emotions she felt while charging through the city. All she felt was cold guilt and shame.

What have I done? Reye constantly asked herself. *What have I become?*

As Ice continued trying to rouse Reye, the guards carried both of them together in a cage to Maestri, the First Circle of the city of Nis.

Maestri, currently being resupplied with guards and soldiers from the inner circles, kept watch for invader from beyond the city, while crews worked outside it on the walls. But after learning they were getting to keep the Hy-mun Horror, every guard turned out to see what was left of her after challenging Lord Tanas.

Reye was a shaking, quivering, mass of flesh curled up into a ball. The warriors bringing her to Maestri referred to her as the Former Horror, because there was no sign of her horrible nature left. Reye was just a scared little Hy-mun, who couldn't even ask for death, and wasn't worth killing anymore. As for Ice, the Rodent who led her to Lord Tanas, he was desperately trying to revive her. Already branded a Light Bringer in the Grand Coliseum, which alone was enough to get him executed, Lord Tanas instead decreed that Ice feel his punishment, sentencing him to hard labor until death.

"Throw the Former Horror and the Rodent in with the other Rodents," the guard said. "The Former Horror can rot with the Rodents, she's not even worth killing or putting to work anymore, but the Rodent that helped her has orders to work in the stone fields outside the city. Start the Rodent after the next rest period."

The guards showed no gentleness, kindness, or respect, throwing both Reye and Ice unceremoniously into the cell holding all of the other "Remnant Rodents" captured when they protested the execution of the Third Great Attempt. However, for both of them, this mass cell was about to become a place of reunions, reflections, and reconciliations. Once the guards left, Ice tried again to rouse Reye from the shock of facing Lord Tanas.

"Reye, Reye come back to me." Ice pleaded into Reye's blank eyes, which felt colder than ever. "Can you hear me?"

Reye couldn't hear Ice, in her mind she was still facing the death and destruction she caused throughout the city.

Take it away, Reye screamed to herself. *I don't want to see it anymore, I don't want to see any part of it anymore.*

Reye was drowning further into her guilt, and Ice *Knew* it, the cold negative flaxen yellow energy around her was growing thicker. Her reactions went above and beyond anything that was ever talked about in stories regarding encounters with Lord Tanas. Ice also noticed that while he was agonizing about what to do with Reye, the other citizens of The Remnant started gathering near them. They were all part of the same group that originally came to Nis to argue against the Third Great Attempt. Two of them stood out from all of the others.

"Seat of Kindness," Ice exclaimed, keeping his voice low to avoid being overheard. He recognized the member of the Council of Rem who came with the group.

"Please, you have to help me. I'm Ice, I came with you and the others to protest the Third Great Attempt. I met this Hy-mun, she faced Lord Tanas and was left like this. Can you help her?"

The Seat of Kindness looked at Ice like he didn't *Know* him at all. However, he went to Reye's side and quickly realized how badly she had been hurt from the time when she first came underground, to her mad rush through Nis, to her paralyzing encounter against Lord Tanas.

"Stay clear, everyone make room," the Seat of Kindness ordered. Looking back to the crowd, he called to the other person Ice noticed, a Hy-mun woman about Reye's age.

"Ann, come over here. You need to talk to her."

Ann, Ice thought to himself. Ice was certain that he had heard that name before. It was during the first week Reye had laid unconscious, screaming in her sleep about her brother Raymond and her friends Stella and Ann. If this Hy-mun woman was Ann, then perhaps she would be the best, if not the only, person who might be able to get through to her.

"Reye, Reye, can you hear me? It's Ann from school." Ann took Reye's hand and held it in her own. "I'm alive and here. Can you hear me?"

Outwardly, Reye didn't seem to show any response to Ann's cries, but internally Reye heard her.

The call was extremely faint, but Ann's voice was the first new sound Reye could hear among the screams of dying warriors, and the only one she remembered from before the screaming began.

Who is calling me? Reye wondered. *Whose voice is that?*

Ice and the Seat of Kindness noticed the change in Reye as well. Her eyes showed slightly more life in them, and the fog of cold negative energy around her began dissipating in response to Ann's cries.

"Keep calling to her," the Seat of Kindness said. "I realize it doesn't seem like there is any response, but there is. Just keep calling to her."

"Reye," Ann repeated. "Reye, come back to us. You are not alone in the dark. I'm your friend. We went to Spectral Academy together. Come back, Reye!"

Friend... Reye said the word in her mind again. It felt like water in her mouth, refreshing and rejuvenating.

Spectral Academy... The other words also felt familiar to Reye. She said the words in her mind again.

Spectral Academy

A light appeared in Reye's mind. It was a dim light but it shone in a variety of colors that twisted into multiple forms. Fixing herself on the light, she constantly repeated "friend" and "Spectral Academy" in her mind until a Hy-mun began taking shape.

Reye's eyes started to shine brighter. She started speaking.

"My, f, fr, friend," Reye slowly stuttered. It was all she said, the word "friend," slowly over and over. Eventually, the word changed.

In Reye's mind, the Hy-mun in the kaleidoscope of light was becoming clearer. *I know you.* She thought to herself.

"Friend, friend, Stella!" Reye began repeating the name of her friend over and over. Ice also noticed that Reye's mood was changing, it was becoming cold, negative, and flaxen yellow again.

Stella! Reye screamed again, but with every scream Stella's image faded, and with it the kaleidoscope of light. Worse, the more Stella's image faded, the more Reye could hear the screams of the warriors she killed and see their faces again.

Go away! Reye yelled in her head, but the memories—and the guilt—just kept coming back even harder. *Give me back my light, give me back my friend, give me back Stella!*

The Seat of Kindness also knew that Reye was falling back into the same cold and flaxen yellow negative fog they were trying to pull her out of, and was quick to tell Ann.

"Ann, she's becoming lost in her own negative emotions of guilt, pain, and failure again. You need to do something to snap her out of it quick."

Ann was quick to follow the Seat of Kindness's orders by giving Reye a hard slap across her face, followed by a harsh reprimand.

"I am Ann! I am your friend Ann!" She slapped Reye again. "Get over the shock about how you couldn't beat Tanas and get vengeance for Raymond. Tanas is older than you, older than this *city*, what possibly made you think you could beat him. I'm sorry that Raymond is dead, but

I'm here and I am still alive. Stella might still be alive too. I heard some guards talk about a Hy-mun girl in Lust Atrophied, it might be her. But you can't do anything if you are going to sink into guilt and failure. You are alive and that means you haven't failed yet. You can try again. Raymond wouldn't want you to curl up like this, he would want you to live and come back to us!"

Reye felt the slaps across her face like an earthquake. A new figure appeared in the dimming light besides Stella, a figure that was repeating the same phrase, "I am Ann! I am your friend Ann!"

Ann, Reye thought. The name sounded just as familiar to Reye as "Stella" and "Spectral Academy." But the name "Ann" caused the kaleidoscopic light to grow brighter.

Ann, Reye thought again, the light growing brighter. Reye soon heard other words come from Ann's figure. She said, "I am still alive. Stella might still be alive too."

Those words caused the light to expand throughout her mind. The sights and screams of the warriors of Nis were still there, but they were quitter, not as consuming.

Ann is right, Reye thought to herself. *I am alive and that means I haven't failed yet.*

"Come back to us!" Ann screamed. Reye finally opened her eyes completely, looking up to Ann who held her like a newborn baby.

"Ann, Ann!" Reye cried, hugging Ann as if she were her mother back in the Orange Dominion. Reye felt like she had woken up from a nightmare. Her face stung from Ann's slaps, but she was grateful for it. It forced her to listen to Ann when she was falling back into guilt over not being able to kill Tanas.

I couldn't kill Tanas, Reye thought to herself. *But I can't feel sorry about it forever. Ann needs me now, and if Stella is still alive, she needs me more. I need to get out of here and find a way to get them back to the surface.*

Reye continued hugging Ann, crying all the time. Reye knew there was going to be a lot more for her to do, but for now, she just wanted to talk.

"Tell me everything that happened," Ann said, looking into Reye's eyes and completely understanding her desire. Reye took a deep breath and began telling her story.

Ice *Knew* Reye was restored to her original state, the way she was before came underground. There was no trace of the horrible red energy left on her, only her natural brown energy radiating softly. But at the same time, she was still tainted by all of the killing and acts of violence she committed since arriving. Reye carried a lingering acrid smell of blood from all the soldiers she killed, a smell that wouldn't go away. After awakening from her withdrawal, she was a mess of tears and words, relating everything that had happened to her from the time she had woken up, chained in the cell in the Fifth Circle of Wrath Eras, until the present moment, promising to fix every mistake she made.

Ice watched as Ann listen patiently and calmly, letting Reye speak every detail. Ice *Knew* Ann had seen her share of bloodshed as well in Nis, she also carried an acrid scent of blood on her—not as much as Reye though—and could feel her mental and physical energies becoming erratic as Reye recounted her story.

For a Hy-mun to be stuck in Maestri for a week and still be alive; she must have been placed in one of the lower level gladiator arenas in this circle and managed to just stay alive. Reye's rampage through Nis might have even helped her, because it would have pulled warriors who could have fought her out of Maestri to chase after us, Ice figured, thinking about how Ann managed to survive here.

Ice gave Reye some room, deciding to let her stay with Ann. However, as soon as he was a short distance away from them, the Seat of Kindness beckoned him over to talk to him privately.

"Now, who are you?" the Seat of Kindness asked firmly.

"What?" Ice was genuinely surprised. He knew the Seat of Kindness was looking at him as if he were a stranger. Ice realized he must have changed a little himself after his own ordeal, but he had studied with the Seat of Kindness long before he and Dan-te even came to Nis. If anyone would be able to recognize him—regardless what might happen to him, it would be the Seat of Kindness.

"Seat of Kindness," Ice began. "I am Ice, your student. I studied with you since I was a child. I came with you and my sister, Dan-te, to Nis. How could you not recognize me?"

"There is no way you could be Ice, young member of The Remnant, and I ask that you do not use his name." The Seat of Kindness's tone was firm, but there was remorse in it too.

"Seat of Kindness, how could you speak that way? You must *Know* I speak the truth." Ice was starting to worry. He remembered that when the Beings of Light first appeared in "The Coming," seven members of the Council were changed so much by it they eventually suffered the Tribe's Second Death, the Death of the Self, causing the split that led to the forming of The Remnant of the Tribe and the Tribe of Shadows. Listening to the Seat of Kindness, he began to fear he might have suffered the Second Death without realizing it.

"I *Know* that you are not lying, and that is precisely the problem. I *Knew* Ice, as did every other member of The Remnant here, and we *Know* you are not him. That is why I ask you to please not use his name again, out of kindness and respect for he who has passed."

Ice couldn't believe what he was hearing, but he *Knew* that the Seat of Kindness's words were the truth. The Seat of Kindness and the other members of The Remnant of the Tribe all looked at him with cold expressions. Regardless of what he said, he *Knew* they would never see or acknowledge him as Ice.

Ice's mind started turning over again and again inside his head like a wheel.

No...it didn't happen to Reye. If it didn't happen to her, how could it happen to me? How could I have suffered the Second Death? I didn't do anything.

Just then, a couple of guards holding plates came to the cells.

"Hey, Rodents!" one of the guards called. "We got some nice Rodent grub for you. We even found some of those nice and shiny Hy-mun plates for you to eat off of. We figure that one of you," the guard said "one" with a sneer targeted toward Ice, "could at least get a nice looking meal before we put him to work. Enjoy."

The guard dropped the plate of meat stew in front of Ice.

Ice knew that the food was made from dead members of The Remnant, but this time made a quick attempt to grab it. It wasn't the food that he was concerned with, even though he was ravenously hungry, but the plate itself. Dumping the food off it, he used the plate to look at his reflection. In Rem, everyone knew everyone, and mirrors, the devices Hy-muns used to see their own reflections, were a rarity—found once in a long while among Nis's garbage. So, the only way to *Know* one's own self was by looking at one's own eyes through reflections in water, another set of eyes, and by the observations of others. The eyes held someone's true nature, and as long as they didn't change, the Second Death hadn't happened. Throughout her rampage, Ice knew that Reye eyes—while clouded—never changed. But after looking at his own eyes, he felt if he had any food left in his system, he would have thrown it up at the eyes he saw mirrored in the plate before him.

The Seat of Kindness was right. The eyes and being that Ice saw in the reflection were not his own. He realized with a broken heart that he had died, not the physical death but the Second Death, the Death of the Self. The very death that he was afraid would happen to Reye as she became more of the Hy-mun Horror and less of her old self had happened to him. The being reflected in the plate he *Knew* to be apathetic, not acting unless forced to. His eyes radiated pale umber contentment, the energy of someone who used other people to "do the hard work for him" while staying in a relatively safe position to reap the rewards from their successes. The being was also easily enchanted by power. His eyes emitted a gluttonous dark green energy. He was a tribesman who, instead of trusting his own strength, gravitated to the strength of others and hovered around them in happy contentment.

Ice has died. He realized with a heavy heart.

The Tribesman—realizing he had no right to call himself Ice—saw and Knew his new self. He wondered how he could have become this, and as he heard the cries from Reye as she continued to tell her story to Ann, he got his answer. The reason his old self died wasn't because of something he did, but because of what he hadn't done. He became so enchanted at Reye's fury and capacity for death and destruction that he handed over the burden of making a frontal assault on Lord Tanas, and every warrior they could come across, to her while he just led her on, simply doing the bare minimal amount of work and protecting her at the safest place—behind her back. He *Knew* his old self would have stood up to her, even if it meant his death, and tried to stop her; or change her back to the way she was, instead of leading her on further down the road of death and destruction, telling himself that it was "for the greater good." If he couldn't, and still lived, he would also have fought beside her as an equal, not as her backup. The Tribesman was completely disheartened. He *Knew* that the one known as Ice was dead to his people in the worst way, replaced by a new kind of being that they would now have to live with. Even worse was the fact that he referred to himself as Ice, because now everyone knew that Ice suffered the Death of the Self, and that he had essentially killed and replaced him.

"Rodent, it's time to go!" a guard said as he came up to the cells, looking directly at the Tribesman.

Short rest, the Tribesman thought as they took him out of the cell and led him away to work outside of the city. The other members of the Remnant watched him go, feeling their mournful energy rolling off of them. They were mournful for two reasons, their companion Ice was dead, and that he, who killed him, was being taken away—to what accounted as a death sentence—without getting the chance to atone for his actions.

Everyone might Know *that the old me is gone now, including myself,* the Tribesman thought as they took him away. *But I will start over. I'm being taken to the Great Tunnel after all. I will make it to the Keyblast Point where Lord Tanas plans to start the Third Great Attempt and do something. It's the only thing I can do now, for the memory of the person I was, and for the memory of my former sister. I'm just glad she never ended up* Knowing *what became of her brother, and I hope she's at peace now, wherever she is.*

Unknown to the Tribesman, his former sister was at peace, at peace asleep, until a hand pushed her shoulder.

***

"Dan-te, wake up, that's your second nap. We're almost at Wanton City, we have work to do."

Dan-te climbed out of the hammock and looked at Virgil, in costume and preparing for their imminent arrival in Wanton City. Over the last day they have slept, eaten, practiced, trained, and slept some more. Now it was time for practice. They were approaching Wanton City and with it the continuation of Dan-te and Virgil's journey back to the city of Nis.

The story continues in "Reunions, Reflections and Reconciliations"

As Tanas and the Tribe of Shadows move closer to triggering the Third Great Attempt, Virgil and Dan-te continue to travel across the surface of Prism toward the Tri-Dominion Caverns and a route back to Nis. Along the way, Dan-te's exposure to the Hy-mun way of life leave both of them much to reflect on, especially after a ghost from Virgil's past begins casting its own shadow on their journey. Meanwhile, the Tribesman slowly makes his way toward the Keyblast point to stop the Third Great Attempt, reflecting on his past life's actions along the way. Elsewhere, back in Maestri, Reye undertakes a Remnant Reconciliation Ritual at the recommendation of her friend Ann, reuniting her with the ghosts of her own past, and presenting her a choice she needs to make for the future.

46935007R00149

Made in the USA
Middletown, DE
12 August 2017